The Fourth Horseman

The Gareth and Gwen Medieval Mysteries

The Bard's Daughter

The Good Knight

The Uninvited Guest

The Fourth Horseman

The After Cilmeri Series:

Daughter of Time

Footsteps in Time

Winds of Time

Prince of Time

Crossroads in Time

Children of Time

Exiles in Time

The Last Pendragon Saga

The Last Pendragon

The Pendragon's Quest

Other Books by Sarah Woodbury

Cold My Heart: A Novel of King Arthur

A Gareth and Gwen Medieval Mystery

THE FOURTH

HORSEMAN

by

SARAH WOODBURY

The Fourth Horseman
Copyright © 2013 by Sarah Woodbury

This is a work of fiction.

www.sarahwoodbury.com

Cover image by Christine DeMaio-Rice at Flip City Books
http://flipcitybooks.com

For my mom

A Brief Guide to Welsh Pronunciation

c   a hard 'c' sound (Cadfael)

ch a non-English sound as in Scottish "ch" in "loch" (Fychan)

dd a buzzy 'th' sound, as in "there" (Ddu; Gwynedd)

f   as in "of" (Cadfael)

ff as in "off" (Gruffydd)

g   a hard 'g' sound, as in "gas" (Goronwy)

l   as in "lamp" (Llywelyn)

ll a breathy "th" sound that does not occur in English (Llywelyn)

rh a breathy mix between 'r' and 'rh' that does not occur in English (Rhys)

th a softer sound than for 'dd,' as in "thick" (Arthur)

u   a short 'ih' sound (Gruffydd), or a long 'ee' sound (Cymru—pronounced "kumree")

w as a consonant, it's an English 'w' (Llywelyn); as a vowel, an 'oo' sound (Bwlch)

y   the only letter in which Welsh is not phonetic. It can be an 'ih' sound, as in "Gwyn," is often an "uh" sound (Cymru), and at the end of the word is an "ee" sound (thus, both Cymru—the modern word for Wales—and Cymry—the word for Wales in the Dark Ages—are pronounced "kumree")

Cast of Characters

Owain Gwynedd – *King of Gwynedd (North Wales)*
Rhun – *Prince of Gwynedd*
Hywel – *Prince of Gwynedd*
Gwen – *spy for Hywel, Gareth's wife*
Gareth – *Gwen's husband, Captain of Hywel's guard*
Mari – *Gwen's friend*
Rhys – *Prior of St. Kentigern's Abbey (St. Asaph)*
Evan – *Gareth's friend*
Gruffydd – *Prince Rhun's captain*

Empress Maud – *daughter of King Henry (deceased), claimant to the throne of England*
King Stephen – *nephew of King Henry (deceased), King of England*
Robert – *Earl of Gloucester, illegitimate half-brother to Empress Maud*
Prince Henry – *Maud's son*
William of Ypres – *King Stephen's right-hand-man*
Ranulf – *Earl of Chester*
Amaury – *Norman knight*

Stephen de Blois came to London,
and the people received him
and hallowed him to king on midwinter day.
But in this king's time was all dissension,
and evil, and rapine;
for against him rose soon the rich men who were traitors.

Then was England very much divided.
Some held with the king and some with the empress;
for when the king was in prison,
the earls and the rich men supposed that he would never
more come out,
and they settled with the empress,
and when the king was out,
he heard of this, and took his force,
and beset her in the tower.

By such things, and more than we can say,
we suffered nineteen winters for our sins.
To till the ground was to plough the sea:
the earth bore no corn,
for the land was all laid waste by such deeds;
they said openly that Christ and his saints slept ...

–The Anglo-Saxon Chronicle

And this time shall be known to history as ... the Anarchy.

1

May 1144

Gwen

"You two keep your ears and eyes open," Hywel said. "Earl Robert may be courting friendship with Wales, but I want everyone to remain on their guard nonetheless. I don't trust these Normans."

Gwen glanced at Gareth, who laughed. "Of course," they said together.

Gareth's eyes glinted, and if Gwen hadn't been married to him for five months already, she would have blushed. It wasn't the first time they'd spoken in unison.

Hywel mumbled something Gwen didn't catch—half-laughing too—and led the way into the bailey of the enormous Norman castle at Newcastle-under-Lyme. In its shadow lay a prosperous village which, according to Hywel, had grown in recent years. What had once been a few huts planted in the lower bailey of the original timber castle was now a thriving market town beyond the new castle's stone walls.

The castle bailey teemed with soldiers, and Gwen knew why: the war between King Stephen and Empress Maud was in its ninth year. The man they had come to see, Robert, Earl of Gloucester, was Maud's brother and led her armies. Although most men agreed that Robert would have made a better king than either Stephen or Maud, he was a bastard, so he could never claim the English throne for himself.

The steps up to the stone keep, which had replaced the original motte and bailey castle, lay two hundred feet in front of them, on low lying ground to the north of the Lyme Brook. Hywel and his brother, Prince Rhun, urged their horses through the crowd. Gareth and Gwen followed, along with their other companions: Evan, Gareth's second-in-command; Gruffydd, Rhun's captain; and Rhys, the prior of St. Kentigern's monastery in St. Asaph, whom Gareth had befriended last winter.

Three Normans waited for them on the flagstone pathway that ran from the gatehouse to the keep. The men stood with their hands behind their backs and bowed at the princes' approach. Then one stepped forward and spoke in French. "Welcome to Newcastle. Earl Robert sends his greetings. Please dismount, my lords." He caught sight of Gwen. "Madam."

Gwen waited for Gareth to get down first so he could help her. He always wanted her to wait for him, even when she didn't need his help. When he held her a moment longer than was strictly necessary, once she was on the ground, she smiled up at him. She would have kissed him, too, but for the large audience around them.

After a long look, he let her go, and Gwen swished her skirt into place. She was wearing finery today, as were they all. They had dressed well and deliberately that morning in their camp, located less than a mile from Newcastle, in order to present the Welsh cause to Robert in the best light possible.

Hywel, with his deep blue eyes, broad shoulders, and handsome face, would do well wherever he went. Rhun, with his shock of blonde hair and thick shoulders, looked more like a Dublin Dane than a Welsh prince. As the Normans were themselves descended from the same Viking ancestors as the Danes, his visage was one the Normans could respect. King Owain of Gwynedd, the princes' father, knew what he was doing when he sent his sons to foster diplomacy between the two kingdoms.

The stable boys led the horses away, and the companions turned towards the keep. Built into the curtain wall of the castle, it had towers on every corner and loomed above them. "Here comes Earl Ranulf himself," Hywel said, leaning in to speak to Gareth and Gwen.

"Sir Amaury de Granville walks with him, my lord," Gareth said. "I told you about him. He is Ranulf's man at Chester Castle."

"I remember," Hywel said.

3

It was good news that Ranulf had come to greet the Welsh princes. He wasn't Earl Robert himself, of course, but he was Robert's son-in-law and the Earl of Chester. Maybe Earl Robert truly had invited the princes to visit Newcastle out of goodwill and a genuine interest in an alliance with Wales, not as a ploy to put the Welsh at a disadvantage and intimidate them with Norman power.

Gwen tried to watch Ranulf without staring at him. He appeared slightly unkempt. The brooch holding his cloak closed at the neck had drifted towards his left shoulder, he had mud on his boots, and a dark stain marred his brown breeches. Then a ray of sunlight shot over the castle wall, forcing Gwen to blink and turn her head away.

She put up one hand to block the light and nudged Gareth. "I can't see. Let's move over here." She tugged him to the right of the steps that flared out from the keep and into the long shadow cast by the castle's old motte, which rose up on the east side of the bailey.

Several men who'd been milling about in the courtyard pressed forward, eagerly filling the space which Gwen and Gareth had vacated. These onlookers seemed to want to hear the princes' exchange with Ranulf, or maybe they were Ranulf's men and had been waiting for him to appear from the keep.

"Thank you." Gwen squeezed Gareth's hand, glad she was with him, even if visiting a Norman castle had never been something she'd wanted to do.

4

A dozen yards away, Rhun and Hywel bowed slightly, as did Ranulf in return. "Welcome," Ranulf said, in French.

From where she stood with Gareth, Gwen couldn't hear Hywel's response, though she could see his lips move. She stepped closer, trying to make out what the men were saying, but then a movement on the tower at the top of the keep distracted her. She glanced up and saw two men, their faces clearly visible in the sunlight.

They looked down on the Welsh party for a heartbeat, one man clutching the other's shoulders. Then they separated: one to disappear from view, and the other to fall head first over the battlement and land flat on his back at Gwen's feet.

2

Gareth

When Gwen had squeezed Gareth's arm, drawing his attention away from the princes and up to the battlement, he'd seen two men, one with hair blonder even than Rhun's and a beak for a nose, and the other with dark hair, a pale face, and blank eyes. While he watched, the first man reached down and flipped his companion over the battlement.

Time didn't stand still and Gareth, choking on his own breath, had been helpless to stop the headlong plunge or the nauseating *thud!* that followed. The man's body hit the hard-packed earth of the bailey like a cabbage thrown against a stone wall. *Sickening.*

Last winter, Gareth had saved King Owain from a murderer's knife. He'd seen the danger and *moved*. But Gareth hadn't the power to stop this murder. Gareth stared at the body and then looked to Prince Hywel. The princes had been exchanging pleasantries with Ranulf. Now, all three men looked Gareth's way, disbelief and horror on their faces. Gareth brought his gaze back to the dead man at his feet.

Gwen stood with her hand to her mouth, not saying anything. Gareth had killed men and seen them killed, but he'd never seen a man murdered right in front of him. Gareth's immobility lasted long enough for him to breathe in and out three times, and then he wrapped his arms around Gwen and pulled her to him.

She pressed her face into his neck for an instant before collecting herself. "Did you see the man who pushed him?"

Gareth nodded. The murderer's cold blue eyes were burned into his memory. "Someone needs to stop him," he said.

Gwen clenched Gareth's arms. "Look around. Nobody is moving. We may be the only ones who saw what the man looked like or what he did. It's you who needs to go!"

This wasn't Gareth's castle. This wasn't *his* fight, but he had no difficulty following his wife's direction. As usual, she made immediate sense. He thrust past the other onlookers and took the steps up to the keep two at a time. Two men guarded the door. A Welshman racing into a Norman keep was something they were trained to prevent, but neither responded quickly enough to stop Gareth nor asked what he was doing. Likely, they were as stunned as the other bystanders by what they'd just seen.

Gareth skidded to a halt in the anteroom to the great hall, though the room was bigger than the main hall at Aber Castle. Two dozen people who clustered on the margins of the room stared at him. Gareth took in their expressions, ranging from stunned surprise to haughty condescension. His plain cloak, tunic, loose breeches, and low boots marked him as Welsh. At the same time, the men waiting to attend to Earl Robert looked foppish to Gareth, with their floppy hats and high, fringed boots into which they'd tucked the ends of their too-tight breeches.

"Which way?" Rhun's voice rang around the room. The prince bumped into Gareth as he, too, tried to stop his headlong rush.

"One way or the other, the man has to come down from the tower," Gareth said. "We should split up, my lord. If you could go that way." He pointed to a stairwell to the right. "You're looking for a man with a shock of hair so blonde it's nearly white. And tall."

"Right!"

Rhun and Gareth took off in opposite directions. Gareth raced up the left stairwell, keeping his hand on the hilt of his sword so it wouldn't slap against his thigh. Gareth judged that the murderer would be looking for a less obvious exit than the front door to the keep: if Gareth had just thrown a man over the battlement, he wouldn't have walked down a main stairwell afterwards. Then again, it puzzled Gareth as to what the man could have been thinking, killing in broad daylight in front of so many potential witnesses. While Gareth had never murdered anyone, he had more experience with it than was probably good for him, and in his estimation, murder was best accomplished in the dark.

He came out of the stairwell into a corridor, empty but for two maidservants gossiping at the far end. They leaned against opposite walls, their buckets of water on the floor and their washing cloths forgotten. Gareth fumbled for a moment with his English and then managed, "Did a man come through here? One with light hair?"

They gaped at him. One girl put her hand over her mouth and giggled. Gareth got a grip on his impatience and tried again, this time in French. The second girl—woman, really, as she was older than Gwen—shook her head and added a very French, *"Non!"*

"Thank you!" Gareth continued up two more flights of stairs and came out at the top of a tower. A weathered roof protected the thirty feet of wall walk between his tower and the one opposite, from which the dead man had fallen. That was the stairwell he'd just sent Rhun up, but perhaps Rhun had found either more luck or more trouble, because Gareth saw no sign of the prince.

Gareth took a moment to peer over the battlement into the bailey of the castle. So many people were clustered around the body, Gareth couldn't see it. He could see Gwen, however, standing with Prince Hywel and Ranulf, and nodded to himself. He could leave the dead to his wife and Hywel. Gareth had a living man to catch.

He pushed off the embrasure and raced along the wall walk of the castle, dodging past two guards who paced it, pikes resting on their shoulders. Gareth couldn't guess where this pair had been when the murderer had dropped the dead man from the tower. He wouldn't like to be in their boots when their captain got wind of their negligence.

As Gareth neared the southeast tower ahead of him, still without seeing the culprit, what little hope he'd had that he might catch him faded. If he hadn't met the murderer yet, the man had already descended to a lower level and Gareth was too late. The murderer could lose himself in the castle, and nobody would be the wiser. Newcastle was so huge, it might have thirty rooms in which a man could hide until such a time as he felt it was safe to depart.

At least Gareth knew what the man looked like, which should help Earl Robert identify him and track him down. Gareth reached the southeastern tower that overlooked the Lyme Brook, intending to find stairs that would take him down again, but then skidded to a halt at the sight of a rope looped around one of the merlons that formed the battlement. Gareth touched the knot, noting how tightly it had been tied, and then peered through the crenel (the gap between two merlons). Thirty feet below him, a man hung above the river.

Gareth looked around for the guards he'd passed, but when he didn't see them, he waved a hand to a man who stepped from the southwestern tower. And then he realized that the man was Prince Rhun. "My lord!"

As Rhun crossed the wall walk that separated them, Gareth looked down at the murderer again. He was almost at the water. Even with Rhun's help, Gareth wouldn't be able to haul him back over the battlement. Gareth pulled out his knife and began to saw at the rope.

Rhun reached Gareth and peered over the wall. "Don't bother. You're out of time."

Gareth followed Rhun's gaze just as the murderer tipped back his head to look up at them. The man lifted a hand in salute, unexpectedly grinning, and released the rope. He landed in the brook with a splash.

"I'll tell Ranulf to search the river for him," Rhun said.

"He'll be long gone by then," Gareth said. "That man knows what he's doing."

Rhun leaned out to haul the rope back up the wall. "He was prepared; I can say that for him."

Gareth's brow furrowed. "Surely he was, if he had the foresight to leave himself a way out of the castle, but none of this makes sense."

"How so?" Rhun allowed the rope to coil onto the walkway at their feet.

"I could accept that the murderer prepared his escape route in advance," Gareth said, "if I could say the same about the murder itself. Who plans to murder a man at mid-morning, in front of two hundred people? And what are the chances that the murderer would drop the body at our feet?"

Rhun had been fingering his lip, gazing south across the English landscape, but then he came out of his reverie. With a laugh, he clapped Gareth on the shoulder. "Very high, I would think, given that you and Gwen seem to find evil-doers everywhere you go. Another murder for you, Gareth. I'm sure Earl Robert will be delighted that we brought you with us to help catch him."

3

Gwen

As Gareth and Prince Rhun raced up the stairs and into the keep after the assassin, other men surged towards Gwen and the dead man at her feet.

"Isn't that just our luck?" Hywel reached Gwen's side and studied the body, a finger to his chin. "Or rather, yours."

Gwen glanced at the prince, a knot forming in her stomach. Other men appeared on her right, jostling her. The prince nodded at Evan, who stepped between the onlookers and the body and began setting up a perimeter around it.

"Sweet Mary." Ranulf appeared on the other side of Hywel. "I've never seen the like."

Hywel met Gwen's eyes, his own flashing with impatience. Her lord had already assessed Ranulf and found him wanting. Gwen pressed her lips together, hiding amusement and stifling her irritation that Hywel had the capacity to make her laugh, even under these circumstances. Then Hywel canted his head toward the body, a hint of a smile hovering around his lips. Gwen knew what that meant. Prince

13

Hywel didn't care if she was wearing her finest dress and newly polished boots. *Here was a dead man! Let's have a look at him!*

A growl of disgust rose in Gwen's throat, but she obeyed Hywel, lifting her skirts to step to the far side of the body and moving in unison with him. A cluster of spring flowers grew against the wall of the keep, and Gwen was careful not to crush them beneath her boots. Hywel crouched on the near side and put a hand to the man's throat, feeling for his pulse.

"What are you doing?" Ranulf said.

"Checking to see if he's dead," Hywel said in French, not looking at the Norman lord. "It was a long fall but not impossible that he might have survived it."

Ranulf cleared his throat and grunted something in French that Gwen didn't catch. Unsurprisingly, the fallen man had no pulse. Hywel shot Gwen a look of resignation. Ranulf's teeth snapped together. His hands, which had been on his hips, dropped to his sides. Then he raised his head and faced the men who'd gathered behind him. Those in the back were clustered six deep, craning their necks to see over the heads and shoulders of their neighbors.

"This is no place for lay-abouts! See to your duties." Ranulf said the words first in French and then in English for the benefit of the few craft workers and servants who might not understand the language of their masters. He didn't speak in Welsh, not that there was any reason for him to know how. All of the Welsh folk Hywel had brought with him understood

French, though Gwen probably spoke it the least well of anyone, despite her father's many attempts to teach her better. Hywel, of course, was fluent.

The onlookers murmured their dismay at having to leave the scene, but after some hesitation, most of them dispersed. Meanwhile, Hywel and Gwen briefly examined the body. As Ranulf turned back to them and came to stand at the dead man's head, Hywel rose to his feet and brushed his fingers off on his cloak. "You know him, don't you?"

"What makes you say that?" Ranulf said.

"He fell from the tower of a Norman keep, one that just happens to belong to your father-in-law." Hywel raised his eyebrows. "Besides, I saw recognition in your eyes."

"Surely—surely, you aren't accusing me of anything!" Ranulf said.

Gwen glanced up, startled at Ranulf's defensiveness. Hywel hadn't been accusing him of anything, but Ranulf's reaction made her want to ask him what he *had* done. Hywel, for his part, watched Ranulf steadily.

Ranulf puffed out his cheeks. "But, yes, he was one of my men."

"And now he's dead," Hywel said.

Gwen looked away, too uncomfortable to watch Hywel antagonize a Norman lord in a Norman castle. It was *dangerous* to speak to such a powerful man in that way. But her head jerked back involuntarily at Hywel's next words: "One of your men, did you say? That surprises me, since he is a Welshman, one David ap Ianto, who has served my father well for many years. Or so my father has always thought."

Ranulf cleared his throat. "Is that so?" His face suffused with blood, turning his cheeks a color approaching purple.

Hywel's gaze didn't move from Ranulf's face. He didn't actually accuse Ranulf of using David to spy on King Owain, but if David had served both lords, he couldn't have been anything but a spy. And not for Hywel's father. Both men knew it.

Ranulf didn't seem to know what to say to Hywel. Instead, he craned his neck to look up at the battlement and changed the subject. "How could he have fallen from there? Only a fool would lean that far over the edge."

Gwen blinked. Even if Ranulf hadn't seen the assassin push the dead man, he had to know that no man could mistakenly fall over a chest-high wall. She glanced at Hywel, who didn't correct the Norman lord, and then decided she could do it herself. "He didn't fall on purpose, my lord."

Ranulf's eyes narrowed. "What do you mean?"

Gwen almost wavered under the earl's stare. *Almost.* "Another man pushed him."

"*Pushed him.*" Ranulf had gone from angry and defensive to disturbingly calm.

She gestured towards the body. "Furthermore, he didn't die from the fall. When he went over the wall, he was already dead—or dying."

Ranulf's eyes narrowed. "How do you know that?"

Gwen glanced at Hywel, who lifted his chin, indicating that it was his turn to speak. Gwen was happy to let the prince tell Ranulf the rest of the bad news. "Before he fell, David was stabbed in the back," Hywel said.

As they'd been talking, Gwen had been edging away from the body. A pool of blood had formed in the dirt under David's back and begun trickling towards the flowers that grew against the stones.

Looking where Gwen pointed, Ranulf snorted his disgust. Then he went down on one knee, reached under the body, and pushed up on David's left shoulder blade to reveal the entry wound.

Hywel knelt with him and traced it with one finger. "A slit only, made by a very narrow blade, sharpened to a fine point so it could penetrate his armor."

"Fool." Ranulf jerked away, leaving Hywel to lower the body back to the ground.

Gwen hadn't often heard a dead man called a fool, but Ranulf seemed more irritated than saddened by David's death. "The killer tried to choke him first," she said.

Ranulf glanced at the body out of the corner of his eye, nodding when Gwen tugged on David's collar to reveal the purpling at his neck. He looked away again. Perhaps his thoughts, like Gwen's, were moving beyond the dead body to its living consequences. Now that he knew the worst, Ranulf seemed anxious to have this ordeal over. He turned to Amaury, who'd been standing on the steps observing the crowd while Ranulf talked to Hywel and Gwen. "We can't leave him here," Ranulf said.

Hywel made a choking sound, disguising laughter with a cough and narrowly avoiding open mockery of Ranulf. *No … not a good idea to leave a dead man in the bailey.*

"I'll see to it." Amaury waved a hand at two men who stood together on the bottom step to the keep. "Find a board on which to carry him."

"Yes, sir," one of them said. Both bowed and departed at a quick walk, heading towards the gatehouse and the barracks.

If Gareth hadn't already described to Gwen his previous meeting with Amaury, she would hardly have noticed him. He was of average height, slender, and a generally inconspicuous sort of person, except that now that she looked at him more closely, he appeared to hold himself as tightly as a strung bow. She was a little surprised that Amaury hadn't followed Gareth into the keep as Rhun had, but perhaps Gareth was already by him before he realized what was needed.

While Ranulf and Amaury were distracted by their preparations to move David's body, Hywel focused on Gwen. "Did you see the second man clearly?"

Gwen shook her head, regretting her failure. "I only saw him for an instant. Truthfully, it was David who caught my attention. His eyes were so flat; I knew something was wrong with him before he fell."

"I think we're looking at more than a simple murder."

Gareth had come up silently behind Gwen, accompanied by Prince Rhun. Gwen spun around and sighed, relieved that Gareth had returned. She took the hand he offered her, and some of the tension of the moment eased just because he was beside her.

"I saw the killer before he threw the body over the wall," Gareth continued. "I looked in his eyes a second time just now as he hung from a rope over the brook."

"We could do nothing to stop him," Prince Rhun said.

"What did he say? Did your man lose him?" Ranulf stepped closer, his brow furrowed. They'd been talking in Welsh and now switched to French out of courtesy to Ranulf and Amaury.

"He did," Prince Rhun said.

"Would you recognize him again?" Ranulf said, this time speaking directly to Gareth.

"Of course," Gareth said.

"Perhaps you could draw an image of him, Sir Gareth?" Amaury said, coming to stand beside Ranulf. "You have a fine hand."

Ranulf stared at Gareth as if he had suddenly grown three heads. "Is that so?"

"It is, my lord," Gareth said.

Ranulf gave a stiff nod. "That would be very helpful."

"Sir Gareth is one of my most trusted captains," Hywel said, stepping into the conversation. "He has other skills that might be useful to you in finding the killer."

Ranulf eyed Gareth suspiciously, but Gwen's heart warmed at the respect Prince Hywel was showing her husband. Without further ado, Gareth sat down on one of the steps and pulled out a scrap a paper from inside his coat to sketch his drawing in charcoal.

"My lord, if I may interject?" Prior Rhys said, speaking for the first time. Rhys had aided Gareth last winter in the pursuit of the man who'd tried to murder King Owain. Like Amaury, Gareth thought well of Rhys and was on the way to trusting him.

"Please." Ranulf gestured that Prior Rhys should come closer.

"There was a third man at the top of the tower, along with the two so far mentioned," Prior Rhys said, "but all I saw was the back of his head, not his face."

Gareth looked up at Prior Rhys's words. "You are sure, Prior? I didn't notice."

Gwen hadn't noticed him either, but then, the dead man's expression was still all she could see behind her eyes.

"Even as the body fell, I saw a shadow against the battlement and a flash of dark hair. I'm sorry that I can't tell you more. But he was there."

Hywel turned to look at David's body again, muttering under his breath in Welsh and only for Gwen's ears, "A third man. Just what we need."

Ranulf's mouth worked as if he wanted to spit on the ground but was too polite to do so. "I must speak to Earl Robert immediately to tell him what has transpired. Amaury, stay with our guests until I call for you."

"Yes, my lord." Amaury bowed to Ranulf, though the earl had already turned his back. He stalked up the steps to the great hall, leaving Amaury as the lone Norman left among the Welsh visitors. He stood with them in a semi-circle near David's body: the two princes, Hywel and Rhun; Gareth and Gwen; Gruffydd; Prior Rhys; and Evan.

Amaury bowed slightly at the waist. "My lords, I don't know what to say." He stopped.

"Unless you killed David, which would have meant being in two places at once, no apology is necessary," Prince Hywel said.

Gwen shifted uncomfortably. Hywel was very forthright sometimes. Amaury didn't seem to know how to respond. *Had Hywel just accused him of murder?* It was hard to say. His mouth worked, but then he managed a thin smile. "Thank you, my lord. I appreciate your understanding."

If they had been home at Aber, Gwen knew what would have happened next: Hywel would have turned to Gareth, and by extension, to Gwen herself, and told them to get on with it.

21

But here, Rhun and Hywel had no authority and hadn't even spoken to Earl Robert yet. Except for the fact that David had been King Owain's man, or so Hywel had assumed, the next step might be to return to their tents outside the walls and await events.

But not yet. The two guardsmen arrived with a board, distracting Amaury and breaking the awkward silence. The men placed the board on the ground and loaded David's body onto it. "Take him to the chapel," Amaury said. "He can lie in a room off the vestibule."

"My lord, may I attend to him?" Prior Rhys's eyes flicked from Hywel to Amaury. Hywel nodded, and Amaury said, "Of course."

Gareth rose to his feet as Rhys passed him, and the two men nodded at each other. Then Gareth handed his drawing to Amaury. The Norman lord scrutinized it, sucking on his teeth. His expression was noncommittal, but Hywel must have read something in it, because he stepped closer to Amaury and looked at the image over his shoulder.

"What's wrong?" Hywel said. "Do you recognize the assassin?"

"I do." Amaury puffed out a breath of air. "His name is Alard. And he is my friend."

4

Gareth

"You're telling me that the dead man, this—" Earl Robert snapped his fingers at Ranulf. "What was his name?"

Ranulf stepped forward and replied, without informing his father-in-law that he wasn't a dog, "David, my lord."

"Yes. David. You say he was your man?" Robert stood near the dais in the great hall with his legs spread and his hands behind his back. At fifty, he was tall and still slender, without even a slight paunch. His full head of hair was turning grey at the temples, and he wore it swept back from his face.

"Yes, my lord," Ranulf said.

"But you didn't know he had returned to Newcastle?" Robert said.

"No, my lord." Ranulf clenched his hands tightly behind his back. He was not enjoying being questioned by his wife's father. The set of his shoulders spoke of a man within inches of storming from the room. Then he took in a deep breath and let it out. "I gave him a certain degree of independence in order to complete his tasks. I had not seen him in some time."

Ranulf's red hair stood straight up; he'd worked his hands through it too many times in the past hour since David's body had fallen at Gwen's feet. Gareth had heard that Ranulf's temperament was more volatile than King Owain's, which was saying something. King Owain was quick to anger and equally quick to cool. But while Owain might forget his ire within moments of the offense, Ranulf was one to bear a grudge.

"Define 'some time'," Hywel said.

If Ranulf didn't like being questioned by Robert, he liked it even less from Hywel. Still, he answered civilly enough. "Since the winter."

Earl Robert turned to Hywel and Rhun. "Meanwhile, your father believed David to be his servant."

Rhun dipped his head. "That is so."

Earl Robert sighed and smoothed the hair back from his face. He turned towards the dais, paced back and forth along it once, and then halted, his hands on his hips, contemplating each of the men before him in turn. Robert of Gloucester had a reputation as a measured thinker and a steady leader, providing a strong counterpoint to his half-sister, Empress Maud. She was known for her arrogance, mercurial temperament, and capriciousness. Rumor had it that men stayed true to the empress less because of a direct allegiance to her than out of loyalty to her brother, who was her strongest supporter. "And you accuse Alard of murdering him?"

"Sir Gareth saw him," Ranulf said. "Alard is a traitor to the empress, of that we can be sure."

Earl Robert raised his eyebrows. "Alard has served my sister for many years. How is it that I am only hearing of his treachery now?"

"His defection to King Stephen's side is very recent," Ranulf said.

Gareth shifted, wishing Gwen was beside him. She could have helped him read the undercurrents in the room. As it was, Gwen, Evan, and Gruffydd had found seats at a table near the front door to the hall. While the anteroom beyond remained full of retainers, Earl Robert had requested that only his Welsh visitors and a few of his own men witness this conversation.

Up until this moment, Gareth had thought he was primarily interested in bringing David's murderer to justice for King Owain's sake. Yes, Alard had murdered a man in broad daylight; yes, David was working for Ranulf and spying on King Owain at the same time, but that meant it was only a matter of time before *someone* killed him. Now, however, the questions began to pile up in his mind. Chief among them was the nature of Alard's relationship to David. He'd killed him, after all. One would presume he had a reason.

Gareth also wondered if it was significant that Alard had murdered a Welshman in front of a party of Welshmen. If his intent was to get the attention of the two princes, he'd surely succeeded. Gareth didn't sniff the air to find the source of the

25

bad smell wafting from the stories everyone was telling, but they stunk nonetheless.

"If you knew Alard was a traitor, how was it that he entered my castle unmolested?" Earl Robert said, still talking to Ranulf.

"I do not know," Ranulf said. "He escaped by rope into the Lyme Brook. Perhaps he entered the castle the same way."

Amaury made a derisive snort that he quickly turned into a cough. Prince Rhun had suggested the same thing to Gareth as they'd left the wall walk, and Gareth hadn't contradicted him, but Ranulf was clutching at straws. That Alard would climb up the rope into the castle made no sense at all. It was hard to imagine an entrance that was more likely to get him noticed. The most logical course of action would have had him coming through the main gate unremarked, as just another visitor to the castle, one that some men in the garrison recognized and still believed to be an ally. Alard could have left the rope tied around the merlon as a precaution, an escape route of last resort that he would use if he had to and leave behind if he didn't.

Ranulf seemed not to have heard Amaury's understated disapproval. Perhaps to make amends anyway, Amaury cleared his throat and stepped forward, deflecting Earl Robert's attention away from Ranulf to himself. "I have men scouring the banks of the brook for any sign of the man, my lord." He paused and didn't say what Gareth expected to hear, which was *it is only a matter of time before we find him.*

It seemed that Earl Robert had expected to hear those words too. When they didn't come, he said, "But you believe him to be long gone."

"Not necessarily gone," Amaury said, "but certainly untraceable unless Alard wishes to be found. He had a significant head start, and he knows the area well."

"And why would he want to be found?" Earl Robert remained focused on Amaury, who stood steadily before him.

"Alard may have murdered David, but that doesn't make him less intelligent than he was yesterday. He has a plan. He would return to Newcastle if he believed his work unfinished," Amaury said.

Earl Robert raised his eyebrows as Amaury hurried on.

"As you may be aware, Alard's skills as a knight and a purveyor of information have always been considerable. If he killed David, as it appears he did, he did it for a reason he believes in. I find it unlikely that the matter will end with the death of one Welshman."

Earl Robert transferred his attention to the two princes of Gwynedd, both of whom had been listening with great interest to the Normans' conversation. "I suppose you have a man whom you would like me to include in this investigation? I will allow him to participate as a courtesy to your father, since it appears that he has been wronged in this matter."

"We do, sir," Prince Rhun said, speaking for both himself and Hywel.

Robert turned on his heel and canted his head at Gareth. "It's you, is it?"

"Yes, my lord." Gareth stepped forward.

"Ranulf!" Robert waved a hand at his son-in-law in much the same way Ranulf had waved at Amaury earlier. "See to this matter but keep me informed."

Ranulf bowed. "Yes, my lord."

"Now." Earl Robert nodded towards the two princes. "If you would come with me to my receiving room, I would like to welcome you properly, without this troublesome event hanging between us."

"Certainly, sir." Rhun bowed, though the act came off a bit stiff. Strictly speaking, as a prince of Gwynedd, Rhun outranked the earl, but not if rank depended on men at his command or wealth. The question of status had been making their conversation awkward from the moment Earl Robert greeted the two princes, *especially* in front of so many observers. It was better for the three of them to meet in private.

"Good." Earl Robert led the way out of the room.

Prince Hywel clapped Gareth on the shoulder as he passed him. It was a sign of confidence that Gareth knew what to do and would do it. At least that's what Gareth hoped it meant.

When Gareth had ridden into Chester last winter, from the moment he entered underneath the gatehouse, he'd felt the eyes of every Saxon in the city on him. Here at Newcastle, the feeling was similar, if not worse, and Gareth had to acknowledge that he was more out of his depth in this Norman castle than he'd ever been, even when he'd sailed to Dublin to find Gwen after she'd been abducted by King Owain's brother, Cadwaladr. Gareth glanced at Gwen, who noticed his attention and lifted her hand to him. Seeing her there settled him and started him thinking more coherently about the investigation that faced him.

"I would have you see to this matter, Amaury," Ranulf said, passing off the responsibility.

Amaury tipped his head in assent.

"You can work with this Welshman?" Ranulf spoke as if Gareth wasn't in the room.

"Yes, my lord," Amaury said.

"Good. I expect you to come to me before speaking to Earl Robert," Ranulf said.

Amaury bowed from the waist. Ranulf left the hall through a back entrance, following the path his father-in-law and the princes of Gwynedd had taken.

Left alone with Gareth, Amaury rubbed his temple with two fingers. "I hope you did not take offense, Sir Gareth. My lord can be a bit ... abrupt at times. With this murder, everyone's machinations and strategies will come under unwanted scrutiny from Earl Robert."

Last winter, Ranulf had negotiated a deal with Prince Cadwaladr. They'd discussed deposing King Owain and putting Cadwaladr on the throne of Gwynedd. Gareth wondered if Amaury was subtly telling him that other such dealings were in the works and that David might have played a role in implementing some of them. And would have still, had he not been killed.

"I am not offended, my lord," Gareth said. "An earl does as he pleases."

Amaury coughed a laugh. "That he does." Then he gestured to where Gwen and the others waited. "You brought a woman with you?"

"She is my wife and is here at the request of Prince Hywel," Gareth said.

Amaury eyed him. "I gather she is not one to be underestimated either, if one were so inclined? I am to forget that she is a woman?"

Gareth grinned. "As you say." Gwen may have been intimidated at first by all the Normans around them, but she knew her own mind, and Gareth thanked God every day for it.

"Empress Maud is such a woman, though I would hope that your wife speaks more gently than the empress." Amaury pursed his lips. "It would be better to clear this up quickly before she arrives."

Gareth glanced at him, his gaze sharpening. "I noted that Empress Maud's banner flies above the tower, but we were told she wasn't in residence. She is coming to Newcastle?"

The corners of Amaury's mouth turned down. "Her flag flies wherever the Earl of Gloucester resides as a sign of his allegiance. The empress, however, arrives tomorrow." From Amaury's expression, encountering the empress didn't delight him any more than it did Gareth. "Rather than at the castle, she will stay at the friary of Dominicans down the road to the east."

Gareth nodded, accepting that information with equanimity. It didn't matter to him where the empress chose to lay her head. "What is it about this incident in particular that would disturb Empress Maud?"

Amaury chewed on his lower lip and looked down at his feet, not answering at first. Then he cleared his throat. "Alard has always been one of her favorites."

5

Gwen

While the noblemen discussed the murder, Gwen sat. She was glad that Gareth had been included in whatever they were deciding, but she felt restless staying with Evan and Gruffydd and not knowing what was going on. Gareth would tell her all about the conversation later, but that knowledge wasn't helping her right now. Gwen had seen enough of this Norman castle already. She wanted to go home to their cottage on Anglesey.

Gareth and Gwen had married before Christmas the previous year and immediately traveled to the lands Prince Hywel had bestowed upon Gareth as part of his knighthood. As a captain in the prince's *teulu*, it was no less than he deserved.

The estate was near St. Eilian's, a little church on the northeast coast of Anglesey. Their home didn't look like much— no more than a small cottage, byre, barn, and stockade, with fields around, farmed by the common folk who tithed to Gareth, who in turn would tithe to Prince Hywel. Still, it was home, and Gwen could walk out her door every morning and watch the sun rise over the Irish Sea. In the years of wandering with her father since they'd left Gwynedd, she'd forgotten what it was like to stay in one place and to have a home.

Gareth, of course, couldn't really stay in one place if he was to continue in Prince Hywel's service. Gareth and Gwen had spent the winter and spring at their new home but, even so, had ridden the twenty miles to Aber each month so Gareth could confer with Prince Hywel. Soon, most likely after this trip to England, Hywel would want to go south, to his own lands in Ceredigion. He would want Gareth to ride with him as the captain of his *teulu*, and Gwen might not be allowed to go with them.

Abruptly, she stood, stomach churning and no longer able to sit still. "I'm going to see how Prior Rhys is getting on with the body."

Evan gaped up at her but then snapped his mouth shut. "I don't know that any other woman could get away with saying those particular words, but coming from you, they make sense."

Gwen smiled. "Few women have my particular history."

Evan smirked. "I don't object to you going, and I don't think Gareth would either. But I will come with you."

"There's no need—"

"Gareth would have my head if I let you wander this castle by yourself without an escort. You are among strangers," Evan said. "Best you remember it. I'll take you there and then return to the hall, provided your presence is acceptable to Prior Rhys."

Gwen nodded. It would do no good to argue, and she could believe that Evan wanted an excuse to leave the hall too. He'd been jittering his leg underneath the table since they sat down, and if she hadn't decided to leave, she would have had to speak to him about it.

She and Evan left the hall, passed through the anteroom in which two dozen people still clustered—though what exactly they were doing other than gossiping, Gwen couldn't determine—and left the building. Once in the bailey, Gwen had to acknowledge that Evan had been right to escort her. This wasn't Aber, her home on Anglesey, or even Wales. She shouldn't go about on her own.

"Did you ever meet David when he came to Aber Castle?" Gwen said.

"I saw him a few times, but we never had a conversation," Evan said. "He would arrive late at night and leave early the next morning." Evan glanced down at her. "We all knew that he spied for King Owain, so we kept our distance."

"Hywel knew him," Gwen said.

"He did indeed," Evan said.

"I will ask him about David later," Gwen said.

"You do that—and then let me know what he tells you," Evan said. "Far too many secrets are being kept here for my comfort and—strangely—only a few of them by our lord."

"When did you last see David at Aber?" Gwen said.

Evan shook his head as he thought. "Oddly, not since the winter, just as Ranulf said. It would have been nice to know what he was doing."

"And where he was doing it," Gwen said.

"David should have known better than to choose a *Norman* over King Owain."

Gwen couldn't help smiling at the derogatory way Evan said *Norman*. She was sure he meant it exactly the way it sounded.

"I wonder how that came about," Gwen said.

"We may never know now," Evan said. "King Owain will need to think twice from now on about the men he trusts."

Now Gwen shook her head. "It isn't that easy to know who might be a traitor. Prince Hywel is usually very wary, and *he* didn't suspect David was dealing falsely with his father."

Evan took Gwen's elbow, leading her around the horses and men—and manure. King Owain kept the offal under control at Aber, but it seemed impossible to keep up with here. Gwen would have held her nose as she picked her way around the piles, but holding up the hem of her dress meant she didn't have an extra hand.

When she and Evan had appeared at the top of the steps to the keep, two dozen heads had turned towards them, and many still hadn't turned away. Gwen didn't know how to interpret their expressions, whether it was scorn or dismay—or even admiration in the eyes of some of the men. It was the kind of admiration that made Gwen uncomfortable. She was glad that it was Evan who walked with her and not Gareth, for the looks would have made him angry.

"How many soldiers do you think Earl Robert houses here today?" Gwen said.

"Soldiers haven't made the castle so full," Evan said. "Earl Robert's barons have brought hangers-on with them. Only a hundred of us rode with Hywel and Rhun, and few will ever enter Newcastle. Think about how many men of rank *Ranulf* has at his command, not to mention Earl Robert. They will expect to enter the castle and be well received."

"At Winchester, when Ranulf and Cadwaladr barely escaped with their lives and Queen Matilda captured Earl Robert, how many men did the earl have with him?" Gwen said.

"Well over a thousand," Evan said. "He wasn't outnumbered. He got caught while defending his sister's retreat."

"That's what I'd heard," Gwen said. "What's strange is that he lost so many and yet still has enough men at his command to fill this castle. I don't know that King Owain has more than a few thousand men in all of Gwynedd upon whom he can call."

"He has that many," Evan said, "but you are right in principle. The English outnumber the Welsh tenfold. It's why we are here in the first place: King Owain must tread carefully so as to not offend either Earl Robert or King Stephen. The day an English king decides to direct the full weight of his armies towards conquering Wales might be our last day of freedom."

Gwen shuddered at the thought. The Normans held the Welsh in disdain and always had.

"My greatest concern is not the men here, nor these Norman barons. It's the undercurrents," Evan said.

"What do you mean?" Gwen said.

"Even without the matter of this dead man, which is sure to sour relations between Earl Ranulf and King Owain, I sense defensiveness in Ranulf's manner. He is not as solid in his allegiance to Earl Robert as his attendance here implies."

"How can you be sure?" Gwen said. "He's married to Earl Robert's daughter, after all."

"And how often has kinship stopped our own people from betraying those to whom they claim allegiance?" Evan said.

Gwen had to admit Evan was right. "Disloyalty does seem to be in our blood; you only have to look to Prince Cadwaladr."

King Owain had contained his brother for now. Cadwaladr was living on his estates in Merionnydd. Gwen didn't doubt, however, that King Owain would be hearing from him again, and when he did, the news of him would not be good. After Cadwaladr had been caught conspiring with Ranulf against King Owain, Ranulf had made amends, sending messages and gifts to King Owain, who wanted to have peace with his brother—if not with Ranulf—but the tension between the brothers remained. Cadwaladr could never be trusted again. As Gareth had said more than once, putting trust in Cadwaladr would surely lead to disappointment later.

"You there! What's your business?" A young soldier who'd been talking to some of his fellows near the armory ran over and accosted Gwen and Evan in French as they arrived at the chapel.

Gwen and Evan eyed him instead of answering.

He glared back and added, "Who are you?"

Evan dug into Gwen's ribs with his elbow. "Say something. My French is poor and my English worse."

Gwen lifted her chin. She didn't know why she needed to tell this soldier anything. At the same time, she saw no need to offend him unnecessarily. "We are companions of the Princes of Gwynedd. I intend to join Prior Rhys in watching over the body of the Welshman who died."

The man's brow furrowed. "That is acceptable. You will find Prior Rhys through the first door on the right."

"Thank you," Gwen said.

The guard turned away, and Gwen and Evan made to enter the building. Before they reached the door, however, a shout came from behind them. "Evan!"

They turned together to see Gruffydd waving at them from the steps to the keep. Gwen patted Evan's arm. "It looks like something's happened. You've done your duty."

Evan held his hand high above his head so Gruffydd could see it. Then he poked his head into the chapel to look at the interior with Gwen. A deserted vestibule with a single table beside the doorway into the nave faced them. "Go on, then. I'll watch until I know you're safe."

"I'll be fine. Thank you for escorting me." Gwen hurried along the corridor to the door the soldier had indicated, knocked, and then smiled when Prior Rhys's voice rasped back at her, "Come in!"

She waved at Evan, who held up a hand in acknowledgement before he disappeared back into the bailey. Gwen pushed through the door and into the room.

The body lay on a waist-high table in a room that was entirely plain except for a wooden cross hanging on the wall above David's head. If this was the usual place for dead bodies to be kept before burial, it seemed optimistic for the room to hold only one table. Still, Gwen immediately felt a peacefulness in the room and slowed her steps.

Prior Rhys sat on a stool near David's head, his prayer beads loose in his hand. He looked up as Gwen shut the door behind her. "My dear."

"Prior Rhys." Gwen curtseyed.

"What brings you here?"

Gwen wrinkled her nose, at a loss for words. She had assumed that Gareth would have told the prior about her role in his investigations. Although Gwen and Prior Rhys had chatted during their journey to Newcastle, Gwen hadn't discussed anything substantive with him either. But then she decided it was best to say what she wanted straight out. "I thought I would examine the body while Gareth and Prince Hywel are otherwise occupied."

Prior Rhys regarded her, his face impassive, allowing a silence to fall between them that Gwen hesitated to fill. Then a smile twitched at the corner of his mouth. "A host of questions passed through my mind just now, chief among them being 'why?'—which, after consideration, should have been obvious. I might ask, however, 'why you?'"

"Because this is what I do," Gwen said, and then hastened to add, "What Gareth and I do, I mean."

"You examine dead bodies?" Prior Rhys said, and now he was almost laughing in his incredulity. "I did wonder what prompted the prince to include you among his delegation to Newcastle."

"Believe me, I wondered it myself," Gwen said. "Gareth might have prodded him a bit."

"And this has been going on for how long?" Prior Rhys said.

Gwen lifted one shoulder. "A while. As a younger son, Prince Hywel has often been called upon to ..." Her voice trailed off as she reconsidered what she'd been about to say. The role that Prince Hywel played in his father's rule was perhaps not something that she should share with someone she barely knew, even if Gareth trusted him.

"Ah." Prior Rhys nodded. "His tasks include some of the less savory, shall we say?"

Gwen sighed in relief. Prior Rhys had understood without her having to articulate it. No wonder Gareth thought so highly of him. She gave the prior a quick nod. "It has always been that way, ever since Prince Hywel became a man."

"And you assist him?" The amusement was back.

"Prince Hywel and I grew up together," Gwen said. "Intrigue is ever-present in a royal court. One day, Prince Hywel asked me to help him, and it seemed like the right thing to do at the time."

"And then once you started, it seemed impossible to stop, even as a married woman."

"Especially as a married woman." Gwen laughed. "You do remember I'm married to Sir Gareth, do you not?"

Prior Rhys laughed too and bowed his head. "Your logic is impeccable, my dear. Surely, though, you didn't start out examining dead bodies?"

"I am a bard's daughter and traveled the length of Wales for much of my life, following the music. At first, all I did was keep my eyes and ears open and report to Prince Hywel what I learned."

"At first ..." Prior Rhys continued to suppress laughter. "And when did Gareth become a part of this?"

"He's been a member of Prince Hywel's *teulu* for nearly five years," Gwen said. "He and I were married this last December."

"Gareth is a lucky man," Prior Rhys said.

Gwen grinned. "I think so!" She stepped towards David's body. "Has anyone touched him beyond what was necessary to move him?"

"No," Prior Rhys said.

Gwen studied the dead man's face. She hadn't really looked at him when he'd been on the ground. He was older than she'd thought at first, with lines around his eyes and on his forehead from a lifetime spent outdoors. She picked up one of his hands, noting the age spots and the loose skin. She revised her estimation of his age even higher, past forty at least, maybe even to an age equal with the prior.

She glanced up at Prior Rhys. He was gazing at her with a bemused expression. Gwen gave him a quick smile back and returned to her task, moving to the bottom of the table and tugging at one of David's boots. She struggled a bit as she tried to get it off; the dead man couldn't flex his ankles to help her. She was just opening her mouth to ask for Prior Rhys's help when he cleared his throat and said, "Would you mind if I stepped out for a moment?"

Gwen suppressed her surprise. "Not at all."

As Prior Rhys exited the room, Gwen wondered if he was squeamish but decided this was unlikely, given that the man had been a warrior before he became a monk.

Gwen finally wrestled David's boots off of him. He'd hidden nothing inside them, nor did he have a knife strapped to either calf. Gwen ran her hands along his tunic and cloak, looking for a purse or a pocket in which he might have hidden something out of the ordinary. She found nothing there either, and nothing in his scrip beyond two coins. Many men kept their most precious possessions with them at all times, but it didn't seem that David had.

Time was passing, and still Prior Rhys didn't return. Gwen resigned herself to attempting to remove what of the man's clothing she could, though she would leave his complete denuding to Gareth. Most of the time, she didn't concern herself with what was proper, but she had her limits, even as a married woman. At a minimum, she wasn't strong enough to flip the body over, and Gareth would want to get a closer look at that knife wound. Alard had taken the murder weapon with him, but if there was anything unusual about the cut, Gareth might be able to match the blade when they found it.

She unpinned the brooch that held David's cloak closed at his neck and tugged at the fabric, trying to pull it out from under him. It was then that she noticed a ragged interior seam running down one side of the cloak. Someone had picked it out and then sewn it back together unevenly. Something hard and round had caught—or been placed—within it. Taking out her belt knife, Gwen picked at the threads that held the seam together. It was a matter of a few moments' work, and when the ends came loose, a single polished green stone dropped into her hand.

Gwen looked at it, stunned. She'd been looking for something unusual within David's clothing, but this went far beyond her wildest notion of what she might have found. She put away her belt knife and poked at the stone with one finger, turning it around in her palm. She was having trouble comprehending the fact that she was looking at an emerald. To possess such a gem, even a small chip like this, put David far above his normal station. It defied all rational belief that he could have owned it legitimately.

Her heart began to beat faster, and she clenched her fist around the stone. It was so precious, she felt she was holding a flaming piece of charcoal in her hand. She fumbled with the strings on her purse, finally got them untied, and dropped the gem inside.

Before she could cinch the strings tight and tie them, however, the door latch rattled. In dealing with the stone, Gwen had forgotten about Prior Rhys. Her first instinct was to hide the bag, but as she gazed down at David's body, hesitating, she acknowledged that deception had never been her strong point. At the same time, telling Prior Rhys the truth wasn't an option, not before she talked to Gareth and Prince Hywel. She swallowed hard. At any moment, Rhys would ask her if she'd found anything interesting, and she needed to have an answer that he would believe.

But then a man who wasn't Prior Rhys flung his arm around her neck and pulled her to him. She was so surprised, she didn't even shriek—and then she couldn't shriek.

"I'm not going to hurt you." His was a voice she didn't recognize, low, almost guttural, speaking French as one who'd been born to it. The man held her while she struggled to breathe, keeping a pressure on her neck that was almost gentle—and all the more terrifying for all that.

Gwen knew she should do something—say something. At the very least, she should try to scream, but when she opened her mouth, no sound came out. Her feet had frozen to the floor, and it felt as if her head was no longer attached to her body. Blackness swam before her eyes, and then—

6

Gareth

As Gwen left the hall with Evan, a messenger arrived for Amaury with the news that his men had found indications of Alard's presence along the Lyme Brook. Relieved, Amaury took his leave to see to his men, with the promise that if Gareth would just wait for him, they could investigate together as soon as he returned. Amaury asked politely, but it wasn't as if Gareth had a choice in the matter. He was in a foreign land, in a foreign castle. He couldn't question the residents of Newcastle on his own.

Gareth was glad, nonetheless, to finally have something constructive to do. He collected Gruffydd, who'd waited for him on the steps to the keep, and then both men met Evan as he hastened towards them across the bailey from the chapel.

"Where's Gwen?" Gareth said at Evan's approach.

"With the prior," Evan said.

"Good."

Evan eyed him. "You're not finding it difficult to control your new wife, are you?"

46

Gareth laughed, not at all offended. That Evan felt comfortable jesting on such an issue was testament to their friendship. "The man who tries to control Gwen is a man destined for frustration. No ... if she's with the prior, that means she can have a look at David's body. We need that to happen before any more time passes. I want to have a better idea of what we're dealing with."

"And before one of these Normans gets to him first. They would think nothing of stripping him down and hiding anything of interest from us." Evan paused. "Did you tell Amaury what she was doing?"

"He noticed that she'd gone, and Gruffydd told him that she'd decided to sit with Prior Rhys," Gareth said. "If I neglected to mention that she planned to examine the body while she was at it, you can hardly blame me."

"He wouldn't understand," Evan said.

"Who would?" Gareth said. "It's better to ask forgiveness from Earl Robert if she finds something useful, than permission from Amaury to inspect him, which he might well deny."

They reached the spot where they'd left the horses. Gareth ruffled the hair of the boy who'd watched over them. "Much obliged, Ifor."

The boy ducked his head and relinquished the reins of Gareth's horse. The stables here were full, so they'd arranged for Ifor, a stable boy from Aber, to stay with their mounts. Little had they known that murder had been in the offing and how long their initial visit to the castle would take.

"This way, my lord." One of Amaury's men gestured that Gareth should follow him.

Amaury and the soldier who'd brought the message met Gareth, Evan, and Gruffydd at the gatehouse. At Amaury's nod, the messenger urged his horse into a trot and led them through the open gate. Once on the road that passed in front of the castle, the man turned east. Gareth glanced west, in the direction of the Welsh encampment. If Gwen had been with him, he might even have turned that way to ensure her safety before he continued on with Amaury. But he knew Gwen wouldn't have liked it, and he supposed she was safe enough with Prior Rhys.

A quarter of a mile from the castle, the gatehouse to the friary appeared on Gareth's left. Both the Lyme Brook and the road to London bisected the Friary grounds, which encompassed lands to the north and south of the road. Amaury rode by the entrance without a glance. Another half-mile on, the small company left the road for the woods that lined the Lyme Brook. Another hundred yards and the scout pulled up in a small clearing.

Gareth swallowed down a grunt of disgust. A man lay face-up on the ground, blood pooling beneath him, though he'd been killed long enough ago for much of the blood to have soaked into the ground. A horse cropped the grass nearby. They all dismounted, careful to step lightly as they approached the body.

"At least one other horse was tethered in the clearing." The scout pointed to hoof prints set deep in the soft earth under a nearby tree. "It's gone now."

"I can see that." Amaury said.

The man looked down at his feet. Woe to the underling who wasted Sir Amaury's time with obvious truths. Gareth caught Evan's eye and nodded. Evan elbowed Gruffydd, and the two Welshmen headed towards the river. The man who'd spoken followed, along with three more of Amaury's men who'd been waiting by the body for further orders.

Gareth and Amaury contemplated the dead man. Like David, the deceased was twenty years older than Gareth, though from a distance, his blonde hair would have hidden the gray at his temples. He'd pulled back his hair and tied it at the nape of his neck with a leather thong, which had since come loose, the ends trailing in the dirt on which he lay.

Gareth crouched beside the body and turned the man's head towards the sky with one finger at his bearded jaw. The man's eyes were closed in death, and Gareth wondered who had closed them—the killer or one of Amaury's soldiers, unable to bear his stare. The killer had stabbed the man's heart, indicating that they'd fought face-to-face.

"Just what we need. Another dead man." Amaury ran his hand through his hair and then dropped his arm in a gesture of frustration.

"A dead body is one thing. Murder another." Gareth felt Amaury's concentration and glanced up at the Norman knight. "You know him, too, of course."

"His name was John," Amaury said.

Gareth licked his lips, debating whether to ask straightforwardly for more information or if it would be better to draw Amaury out gradually. Gareth decided to take the long way around, to see if Amaury would volunteer what Gareth wanted to know. "He knew his attacker."

"For him to get that close, he had to," Amaury said.

Gareth waited through five heartbeats and then said, "The killer took the knife."

"Perhaps it could identify him," Amaury said.

That Amaury wouldn't say outright that John was dead because Alard killed him presented Gareth with a dilemma. Amaury appeared reluctant to admit the possibility. It would be an assumption at this point, and assumptions were nothing without proof. Still, Gareth decided it needed to be said. "This looks like Alard's work."

Amaury sighed. "My men will comb the countryside for him."

Gareth straightened, studying his surroundings. The trees were fully leafed, and here in the shade beside the river, the ground remained damp even when the sun was out.

"Over here, Sir Gareth!" Evan didn't leave off Gareth's title as he might have done had they been alone.

Gareth turned to Amaury. "He's found something." Without waiting to see if Amaury would come with him, Gareth crossed the clearing to where Evan and Gruffydd had entered the woods. Thirty feet on, he reached the two men. Evan crouched near some footprints on the bank, while Gruffydd hovered near a cluster of reeds growing at the water's edge.

"What have you found?" Gareth said.

"Two sets of footprints." Evan pointed to the thick mud that bordered the brook.

The print of a boot was sunk deep into the soil, indicating that a man had come out of the water there. Then Gruffydd showed Gareth several damaged reeds, as if something—or someone—large and heavy had passed through them.

The second pair of prints faced the brook, indicating that the man coming out of the water had been greeted by a second man, who'd perhaps grasped his arm to help him from the brook. Following Evan's pointing finger, Gareth traced the path of the departing sets of footprints as they headed back to the clearing. They followed a different path through the undergrowth than the one Gareth had just taken.

"We've got more, Sir Gareth," Gruffydd said. "Look at this."

Amaury had followed Gareth from the clearing, and now he peered over Gareth's shoulder as they looked at the spot on the ground that Gruffydd indicated. "I would say that's blood." Amaury waggled a finger at the dark patches speckling the leaves of several plants beside the trail.

"Indeed. Someone is wounded. If it's Alard, it indicates that David may have fought back." Gareth turned his head to look at the riverbank. "If I read the signs right, Alard left the brook here. A man greeted him—"

Gareth broke off his sentence without finishing it and ran back to the clearing. John lay as they'd left him, with a lone guard standing over the body. Gareth crouched and ran a finger along the bottom of John's boot. His finger didn't come away clean, but it wasn't coated in mud either.

Just to be sure, he tugged off John's boot and brought it back to the riverside. Crouching, he placed it in the first print Evan had found, the one belonging to the man who'd gone for a swim. Unsurprisingly, his boot didn't fit the print.

Then Gareth placed the boot into the second print, fully expecting it to fit, only to find that John's boot was two fingers' width larger.

Amaury had watched Gareth's antics with interest and now leaned in. "Could the print have shrunk?"

"The sun doesn't shine in here. The mud should have preserved the boot's shape perfectly. If anything, the print should be wider than the wearer's actual boot and deceive us into thinking it's John's." Gareth straightened and surveyed the water's edge. "So Alard met a third man, who was not John; I don't have enough information yet to say how John fits into this story, other than to say that it is likely that either Alard, or the one who met him, killed him."

The four men moved back to the clearing. Unfortunately, the boot prints around John's body had been smeared and jumbled by all the activity, and it was impossible to link a particular print to the man who had killed him. "My bet is on the third man from the wall walk," Amaury said.

"Provided the one who came out of the water was actually Alard," Gareth said.

Amaury shot Gareth a puzzled look.

"I'm not rejecting my earlier supposition that the Alard killed John," Gareth explained, "but the additional boot prints and the overall complexity of this investigation have given me renewed resolve not to assume anything."

Amaury's expression cleared. "Oh, I see. We have prints and blood, but nothing suggests that either is tied to Alard, except that he went into the water at Newcastle, and someone came out of the brook here." He pursed his lips. "It is well not to assume. Thank you."

"We all have assumptions, and sometimes those assumptions prove true, but with two murders now, I think it might be best if we take it one step at a time and focus on what we know," Gareth said. "The more we learn, the more we can explain, until the murderer reveals himself without us having had to *assume* anything."

Amaury gazed towards the river, though Gareth didn't think he was really seeing it. He was silent through a dozen heartbeats and then said, "May I have a moment of your time, Sir Gareth?"

"Of course." Gareth turned to Evan and Gruffydd and spoke in Welsh. "Would you excuse Sir Amaury and me? Perhaps if we are alone, he will tell me something of the truth. So far, I don't know that we've heard much of it from anyone."

Evan and Gruffydd nodded, and Amaury and Gareth returned to the bank so they could be alone by the river. Amaury jerked his head towards a tree that hung over a small waterfall. When Gareth followed him to where he indicated, the rush of the water grew even louder than on the trail. Amaury was right in thinking that the sound would drown out their voices to all but them.

Amaury leaned his shoulder against the trunk of the tree, and Gareth stepped close, such that they stood only two hand-spans apart. Gareth didn't find it comfortable being so close to the Norman, but if it was the only way to get him to

54

talk, he was willing to endure it. This had the makings of a secret worth hearing.

Amaury thought for another count of ten, his eyes on Gareth's face, and then said, "What I have to tell you must not go beyond you and your lords."

Gareth nodded, grateful that Amaury understood that Gareth was honor-bound to report everything he learned to Prince Hywel.

"And if someone asks how you came by this knowledge, it didn't come from me."

Again, Gareth agreed. He clasped his hands behind his back, patient and attentive. Finally, Amaury found it within himself to speak, though he didn't look at Gareth and stood as he had when he'd delivered the bad news about Alard to Gareth earlier in the great hall: "Once there were four men. The empress called them her 'four horsemen', and to her they represented everything you think of when you hear that phrase."

If Amaury's expression had been less anxious, Gareth would have whistled through his teeth. He knew his Bible, of course. At the ending of the world, the four horsemen of the apocalypse would be visited on mankind: conquest, war, famine, and death. That Empress Maud would refer to her men in such a fashion made Gareth's stomach clench. At the same time, maybe he shouldn't have been surprised. Unlike King Stephen, who had such a fine sense of honor it was costing him the war, Maud was known less for her piety than for her vindictiveness.

"In what way did they work for her?" Gareth said, more to say something than because he feared Amaury wouldn't tell him.

Amaury took in a deep breath through his nose. "Remember the rebellion in the southwest of England in the early days of Stephen's reign? It forced Stephen's focus away from fighting Maud to fighting his own barons, when he wasn't at odds with the Scots or the Welsh."

"I remember," Gareth said. "I was fighting Normans in Ceredigion around that time."

Amaury gave him a wry smile. "Who do you suppose were instrumental in helping Earl Robert foster that rebellion? Who infiltrated castles, made promises Maud might never keep, and put steel in those half-Saxon spines?"

"The horsemen, clearly, or you wouldn't be telling me this," Gareth said.

"I don't know where she found them, exactly, or in what fashion she gathered them together, but they were her spies, and by that I mean they were trained to a degree few men have attained. Two were Welshmen, another was a Saxon, and the fourth was a Frenchman."

"I'd wager that David was one of the Welshmen," Gareth said, and at Amaury's nod added, "though Ranulf said he was his man, not Maud's."

"Ranulf thought David belonged to him; he was meant to think so," Amaury said.

"But you know differently?" Gareth said.

Amaury gave him a long look, and when Gareth didn't add to his question, he said, "You need me to lay it out?"

Gareth chewed on his lower lip, studying Amaury's face. "Your liege lord is Ranulf as well. Are you implying that your allegiance is also broader, to the empress, just as David's was? Are you a spy for her too?"

Amaury coughed a laugh. "Hardly. I am a knight, as you see." He spread his hands wide. "But that does not mean I am not party to certain information."

Gareth hated such obliqueness, but he didn't want to throw Amaury off his stride. "I accept that. We were talking about the four horsemen."

Amaury nodded. "To continue, that man there—" Amaury tipped his head towards the clearing where John's body lay, "—the Saxon, John, along with the second Welshman who died years ago, were under Earl Robert's authority."

"And the fourth, the Frenchman, was ... Alard?" Gareth said, seeing where this was going.

"He was a favorite of the empress, a man she'd known for twenty years, ever since he was a boy. He was the most trusted of the four," Amaury said.

"And Alard has now killed both David and John," Gareth said, "two of the four horsemen."

57

"So it seems," Amaury said

Gareth eyes narrowed. "We know Alard killed David. How can you think otherwise?"

Amaury sighed and did not answer.

Gareth reminded himself, not for the first time, that Alard had been Amaury's friend. "At the very least, you have to grant that he is involved in his death."

"Yes. I grant that," Amaury said.

Gareth glanced away, thinking. "Could these four men— or rather, the remaining three—have had some kind of falling out?"

"They were never natural friends," Amaury said, "and if they had a falling out, it was years ago. What people will assume now, if we cannot prove otherwise, is that Alard has betrayed the empress for Stephen, just as Earl Ranulf said."

Gareth wished his French came as naturally to him as his Welsh. Amaury seemed to feel the need to assume the best of his former friend, despite all evidence that condemned him. Gareth decided to allow his skepticism and ignorance to show. "You don't believe Alard is a traitor either? Ranulf seemed sure. All of this would make more sense and be quite straightforward if he was."

"When one is dealing with spies, things are rarely straightforward," Amaury said. "I don't believe it. For all that he is a spy, Alard is not a coward. If he had defected to

Stephen, he would have told the empress himself. He would have told me."

In Gareth's experience, one of the most predictable aspects of intelligent men was how unpredictable they could be. But again, Alard had been Amaury's friend. "Yet now we have John," Gareth said. "He could have been the third man on the tower."

"Of course he could have. I assumed it, right up until his boot didn't fit the print, which means that we are looking for a *fourth* man." Amaury shook his head. "I am as much in the dark as you."

"The fourth horseman?" Gareth said.

"He's dead," Amaury said.

"What was his name?"

"Why does it matter?"

Gareth shrugged. "I'm just gathering information. I don't know what might become important later."

Amaury picked at his lower lip. "Peter."

"Right," Gareth said. "Well ... if Alard is as intelligent as you say, he had a reason for coming to Newcastle."

"Ranulf would say it was to murder David," Amaury said.

"But you still don't think so?"

Amaury sighed. "I admit that dropping David's body at your wife's feet implies that he killed him. But again, Alard is very intelligent. If he were planning to kill David, do you think he would have done it in broad daylight? He's a spy. He lives in the dark."

Gareth had thought much the same thing earlier and couldn't disagree. "It does appear to be an absurd act, and yet I saw his eyes. He knew what he was doing."

"Perhaps he merely meant to speak to David and their conversation turned to violence," Amaury said.

Gareth swallowed down a mocking laugh. "David was strangled *and* stabbed. And then thrown over a battlement. Alard wanted him dead."

As he spoke, however, Gareth suddenly doubted his surety. Now that he had the chance to think more about it, the determination in Alard's face might have reflected a decision to drop David at their feet once he was dead, rather than leave him on the wall walk to be found after Alard escaped. There was still something about that act that nagged at Gareth. It was so public and obvious. Alard had to know that someone would recognize him. And yet, he'd done it anyway.

"Ranulf will say that when David and John refused Alard's invitation to join him in his service to King Stephen, Alard killed them," Amaury said.

"Earl Ranulf is your lord, in name if not in fact," Gareth said. "And yet you—"

Amaury cut Gareth off. "You presume too much, Sir Gareth."

Gareth blinked, surprised at Amaury's sharp tone and unsure of what he'd done to deserve it. "Excuse me?"

The tenseness in Amaury's expression eased. "I apologize for my abruptness, but I have told you all I can, and we shouldn't linger here any longer. Alard was my friend. I must discover the truth of what happened, for good or ill."

Gareth nodded. "I will help you, if I can."

"Thank you for that." Amaury made his hands into fists. "I have a task I must see to alone, but when I am finished, I will find you."

Gareth nodded. "In the scriptures, the fourth horseman is death. Whatever happens, we cannot allow Alard to kill again."

7

Gwen

Gwen pushed up onto her hands and knees, moaning. The wood floor beneath her was worn smooth from many years of treading feet and felt good beneath her fingers. It gave her something to think about besides the pain in her head.

"Shush, Gwen. You're safe now."

Gwen managed to separate her eyelids enough to find the face of the woman crouching in front of her.

"Mari? What are you doing here?" Gwen stared at her beautiful friend, thinking she must still be dreaming. Mari wore a gown of deep green, and her long, dark hair was wound elaborately around her head in a manner Gwen couldn't have begun to emulate. The style was similar to those Gwen had seen on a few of the women who'd passed through the hall while she'd been waiting for Gareth.

"Looking for you." Mari smiled and put a gentle hand on Gwen's temple. "Are you all right?"

"I don't know." Gwen couldn't think straight. She touched her throat, feeling for marks, but she felt nothing but smooth skin where the man had pressed on her.

Mari spoke to someone behind Gwen. "Find Sir Gareth. Now."

Gwen turned her head to see a young man hovering in the doorway of the room. "My lady—"

He looked from Gwen to Mari, who waved a hand. "Go, Edmund!"

Mari's sternness made Gwen smile. She was glad for it. Gwen wanted her husband to come here too.

Mari brushed back a loose strand of hair from Gwen's face and said, "Let's get you up." She put an arm around Gwen's waist and helped her to the stool on which Prior Rhys had been sitting when Gwen had entered the room earlier. "I won't ask if you're all right, but are you feeling a bit better than you did?"

Gwen sagged against the wall at her back, still finding it hard to take full breaths and focus her thoughts. She touched her throat again, remembering the man and the fear, and looked into Mari's eyes. "By what chance did you find me?"

"I've come to Newcastle with Lord Goronwy. His wife was Norman, if you remember, and he still holds lands that tithe to England—specifically, to the Earl of Gloucester."

Gwen rubbed at her temples, struggling to remember what she knew about Mari's complicated family relations.

Goronwy had become Mari's foster father when her parents died, but he was her uncle too.

"Can you tell me what happened to you?" Mari said. "I've never been so scared in my life as when I entered the room and saw you on the floor."

"I remember ... everything." Gwen straightened on the stool as she realized that she did—or thought she did. "I was examining the body of the dead man, David—" Gwen glanced to the table where David's body lay. Except that nothing lay there now, not even the cloth that the guards had used to cover his face.

"What body?" Mari said. "What dead man?"

Gwen's head hurt more than ever. "That's exactly it, isn't it? *What has happened to the body?*"

"Have you involved yourself in another murder?" Mari's voice held disapproval and concern, but then her eyes lit. "Can I help you solve the mystery this time?"

Gwen choked back a laugh. "I don't think you really want to do that. I wouldn't want you to get hurt. Besides, you helped last time, you know."

"I did?"

"Very much so. It was you who realized that the purpose of the murders at Aber was to prevent King Owain from marrying Christina, and everything else that happened was in service to that." Then Gwen leaned forward, her head in her hands, forcing down the bile that had risen suddenly in her throat.

"What's wrong?" Mari put an arm around Gwen's shoulders. "Is it your head?"

"My stomach is queasy—"

The door, which Edmund had left half-closed, flew open and slammed into the wall behind it. Gareth bounded into the room. He took in the scene with a single glance, and then his eyes fastened on Gwen. He reached her in two strides. Mari moved out of the way so Gareth could kneel in front of Gwen and put his arms around her.

"Cariad!"

Gwen pressed her face into Gareth's neck, holding on to him with all her strength. She'd been struggling with control before he came, but now, just by his presence, he'd brought her to tears. He pulled back briefly to study her face and then kissed her forehead and both eyes.

"What happened here?" he said. "Where's David's body?"

"She hasn't yet told me," Mari said, her voice matter-of-fact. "I felt at her head and there's no lump—"

Gareth had been looking Gwen up and down, and now he put his fingers under her hair at the back of her head.

"There's nothing there." Gwen patted Gareth's chest to get him to stop feeling at her head. "Shortly after I arrived in the chapel, when I was still removing David's boots, Prior Rhys

65

stepped out of the room for a moment. I thought he'd returned. Instead, someone else entered the room. I never even saw him. He came up behind me and pressed on my neck." Gwen gestured to her throat to show him where.

Gareth nodded. "I know what he did. Put pressure there, and it renders a person unconscious after a few heartbeats. It's a way to silence a man without killing him."

Gareth's knowledgeable tone suggested that he might have done it himself a time or two, but now wasn't the moment to ask him about it. "He spoke to me softly," Gwen said. "The experience was almost more terrifying because he was so sure of himself—and treated me gently."

Gareth held Gwen's face in his hands and looked into her eyes. "Can you see me fine? How do you feel?"

"I found her unconscious on the floor," Mari said. "How do you think she feels?"

Mari's tone was one that Gwen had heard her use a few times, usually in conversation with Prince Hywel. It spoke of no-nonsense thinking and impatience with anything but the facts. Gwen found Mari's lack of drama soothing. "I have a headache, though it's already beginning to fade," Gwen said. "I will be fine in a moment if I can sit here a bit longer."

"Gaah." Gareth slapped his hand on his thigh and got to his feet. "This gets worse by the hour. First David, then John, and now this ..."

Gwen looked up at her husband. "Who's John?"

Gareth shot her a worried look. "Amaury's men found another body outside the castle, near the place where it looks like Alard came out of the water." He leaned in close to her and lowered his voice. "He told me some things that I shouldn't repeat here. David's murder seems to be a piece of a larger puzzle, one which we haven't even begun to find the edges of."

"I still don't understand why someone would take a dead body," Mari said.

Gwen glanced at her friend and then back to Gareth. "Do you think Alard could be responsible for the removal of David's body?"

"I don't want to presume that he was or wasn't," Gareth said. "My instincts argue against it. Why flee the castle only to return an hour later? And with everyone on the lookout for him, he would have found it nearly impossible to get inside, much less out again with a dead body."

"He might have taken it if he was worried about us examining it," Gwen said. Hywel himself had removed a body from Aber Castle the previous summer, rather than risk Gareth uncovering his role in the murder of King Anarawd.

"Then why dump it at our feet in the first place?" Gareth said. "No, we are missing too much of our puzzle. To suggest that Alard harmed you is like adding two and two and reaching five. I am thankful, however, that whoever this man was, he had the grace not to kill you or Prior Rhys."

"Prior Rhys!" Gwen had forgotten about the prior's absence in thinking about herself. "What has happened to him?"

"Moments ago, one of Ranulf's men found him unconscious near the postern gate," Gareth said.

"Oh no! I would never have wanted him involved in something like this—" Gwen made to push to her feet, but Gareth crouched down again, rubbing at her arms to settle her and keep her on her stool.

"What happened to Prior Rhys is not your fault," Gareth said.

Gwen swallowed. "You give me too much credit if you were worried I was thinking that. I don't believe it was my fault, but you and I both know that wherever we go, murder follows. I don't like seeing him caught up in it."

"He wasn't always a monk," Gareth said.

"I know that," Gwen said, "but he is older now and used to a quiet life in the monastery."

Gareth smirked. "I won't tell him you said that. I suspect he takes pride in remaining as fit as he ever was."

"Where is he now?" Gwen said.

"He has been given a room in the keep." Gareth turned to Mari. "Thank you for caring for Gwen. We had just returned to the castle when I learned of the attack on Prior Rhys. My first thought was of Gwen, of course. I'm so glad you were here to find   her.”

"What is the hour?" Gwen said.

"It is not yet noon," Gareth said.

Gwen's brow furrowed as she thought. "I spent some time examining David before the man came. It felt like Prior Rhys was gone a long time. Perhaps I wasn't unconscious for more than a quarter of an hour."

"It was too long for you to lie on the floor," Mari said.

"Prior Rhys may have lain unattended at least that long," Gwen said.

Mari's brow furrowed. "You would think that in a castle this crowded, someone would have noticed him sooner."

"Our culprit had hauled his body behind a stack of wood." Gareth focused on Mari. "How is it that you found Gwen?" he said, and then added before she could answer, "Why are you even at Newcastle?"

"I came with Uncle Goronwy," Mari said, answering Gareth's second question first. "I found Gwen because I asked—" Mari stopped, and her face suffused with color. Gwen had never seen her look so embarrassed before.

Mari tried again. "While my father saw to our accommodations, I spoke with Prince Hywel. He was in the hall, having recently completed an audience with Earl Robert. He didn't know where any of you were, but the guard at the door had seen Gwen enter the chapel with Evan." Mari smiled and touched Gwen's cheek. "You can't go anywhere unremarked, you know."

Gwen didn't know what to make of that, but Gareth's jaw clenched, and he hugged her closer. "Do you think you can walk, Gwen?"

"I'm fine, really." Gwen allowed Gareth to help her to stand and then took a step. In so doing, she realized that she really was fine. She didn't even weave on her feet. "You survived worse last winter and walked home to Aber after."

Gareth's eyes narrowed. "I swore to your father that this trip would not be dangerous."

Suddenly, Gwen found herself smiling. "Did you forget whom we serve, husband?"

Gareth gave a snort of laughter but then immediately sobered. "You would have told me if you'd seen anything that might help us, right? Even if you didn't see the face of the man who took David's body."

"I can't think of anything that would help." Gwen gave a short laugh too. "I assumed Prior Rhys had returned to the room, and I was trying to figure out how to tell him—"

Gwen broke off as the rest of her memory came flooding back.

"What? What is it?" Gareth said.

At that moment, Mari bent to the floor. "What's this?" She held out her hand. The emerald lay nestled in her palm.

Gwen fumbled for the purse at her waist. The strings hung loose, and she remembered that she'd never closed them around the stone.

"How came this here?" Mari said, awe in her voice.

"I dropped it," Gwen said. "I had just put it in my purse when the man grabbed me. David had sewn it into the hem of his cloak. It must have fallen out of my purse when the man sent me to the floor."

The three friends stood together, looking down at the stone.

"Do you think the person who took the body knew about the gem and wanted it—or wanted it back because he had given it to David in the first place?" Mari said.

"If that is true, when he examines David's body and doesn't find it, he may come looking for you, Gwen," Gareth said.

Gwen didn't like the sound of that. "No. No, he won't. Prior Rhys was shocked to learn that I planned to examine David's body. He left the room because the very idea of it made him uncomfortable."

"Really?" Gareth said.

Gwen shrugged. "Or so it seemed at the time. Regardless, if the man who took David's body was worried that I'd found the emerald, don't you think he would have harmed me more?"

Gareth made a growling sound deep in his throat. "I like Newcastle less and less with every hour that passes."

"You'd better take this." Mari dumped the emerald into Gareth's hand.

Gareth clenched his fist around the stone. "I must speak to Prince Hywel. We have two bodies now and a gem so valuable I'm afraid to keep it with me."

"How would David have come by an emerald?" Gwen said. "He didn't appear to me to be a rich man."

"This would make him rich, but—" Mari tapped Gareth's fist so he would open it, and she peered at the gem again, "—not that rich. It's very small."

"You mean it isn't worth as much as I thought?" Gwen said.

"I don't know what you thought it was worth," Mari said. "Certainly, it could buy David some land. It has a value of more than most villages."

"So does my sword," Gareth said.

"Was David a thief, do you think?" Gwen said. "Or could the gem have been meant as payment for a task?"

"If the latter is the case, it would be nice to know if he still had to complete it," Mari said, "or if it was for services already rendered."

"I can't answer that, but I know more about David than I did when I saw you last." Gareth stowed the gem in his scrip. "According to Amaury, David was a spy, and not just for Earl

Ranulf." He pointed at Mari, a sternness in his demeanor that he usually reserved for the men under his command. "And that knowledge does not leave this room, do you understand?"

Mari's eyes widened, but she nodded.

Gareth turned to Gwen. "That goes for you, too. I don't want you involved in this anymore."

Gwen thought about getting angry, but then she decided to take Gareth's attitude for what it was: concern for the welfare of his wife. She put a hand on his arm. "I'm already involved, as you well know, and short of sending me home—which isn't necessarily the safest proposition either—your only choice is to leave me at our camp. It's full of men, but a lone intruder could reach me easily if you're not there with me." She gestured to the room around her. "Certainly, I wasn't safe today in a chapel in a guarded castle. Whoever removed David's body did so without calling attention to himself. How easy would he find it to enter our encampment if he chose?"

Gareth looked as if he was going to argue with her as a matter of principle but swallowed down any response beyond, "I don't like it." And at Gwen's shrug, he added, "We'll see."

8

Gareth

Gwen's logic was sound, but the fact that a man had touched her—even if his intent had been only to subdue her—burned in Gareth. He had sworn that he would keep her safe, and here she was, in danger on their first day at Newcastle. He was having a hard time controlling his anger, and he clenched and unclenched his fists, breathing deeply to rein in his temper.

That Gwen had involved herself in the investigation, and that he'd allowed her to do so made him even angrier. What kind of husband put his wife in harm's way? And yet, she was her own person. He'd known that when he married her, and it was one of the many things he loved about her. She would still love him if he sent her back to the camp—she might even forgive him. At the same time, he was afraid that she was correct in thinking that their encampment would prove no safer for her than the castle. If the man who took David's body guessed that she had the emerald, she wouldn't be safe anywhere.

Gareth had almost ripped off Evan's head a moment ago as they'd left the chapel. His friend had been waiting anxiously for them near the entrance to the great hall. But Evan's expression had made Gareth swallow down his ire. It wasn't Evan's fault that Gwen was hurt, any more than it was Prior Rhys's, who had already paid for his mistake in leaving her alone. Together they would find the man who harmed her. Gareth resolved to be more diligent about keeping Gwen with him at all times, or to ensure that another could protect her during those times when they had to be apart.

In truth, he blamed himself more than anyone for what had happened. Gwen was his wife, and her welfare was his responsibility.

The emerald, tiny as it was, lay heavy in Gareth's scrip as he escorted Mari and Gwen into the great hall, Evan and Gruffydd trailing behind them. Their hands rested on their sword hilts somewhat more conspicuously than usual. Gareth looked right and left, feeling as if everyone was watching him and could see through his scrip to the gem. Even King Owain had few gems in his treasury. How had David come by his?

They passed through the anteroom and into the great hall. Prince Hywel stood near the dais, and at their approach, his expression filled with concern. He gave a quick nod and said, "I can see you have more news than just the harm to Prior Rhys. We shouldn't speak here."

Then the prince's eyes drifted to Mari. It was only a brief glance, but it sent a tingling sensation down Gareth's spine. The look spoke of interest and was one Gareth hadn't seen in his lord's eyes in a long while.

"Come this way." Hywel held out his arm to Mari, who took it. The pair stepped off the dais, heading for a side door that led to a stairway and other parts of the castle.

Watching them go, Gwen tightened her grip on Gareth's arm. "Gareth—"

"I see it," he said.

Gareth counted Gwen among the few women Hywel had not been able to charm into his bed. Mari should have known better than to look for companionship there, but sometimes a woman's heart overrode her common sense. And sometimes a girl might need reminding when faced with the reality of this handsome Prince of Gwynedd. Even Gwen had admitted to Gareth once—when pressed and given assurance that nothing she could say would make him take offense—that God had given Hywel more gifts than any man had a right to.

"How is Prior Rhys?" Gwen said to Hywel's back.

"Ill." Hywel turned his head to look at Gwen and Gareth. "He has a rising lump on his head from a hard blow. It might have killed him, and the wound continues to bleed. I'm worried that he might never regain his right mind. We won't know until he wakes. If he wakes."

"I'm glad he's alive," Gwen said.

"But he's not conscious?" Gareth said.

Hywel shook his head. "He hasn't spoken, or at least he hasn't said anything that makes sense. Why someone would attack a prior—"

"I'm afraid I can help with that," Gareth said. They halted in a corridor before a half open door, one floor above where Gareth had seen the two maids talking when he'd gone looking for Alard that morning. "David's body is gone, my lord."

Hywel's teeth snapped together. "Explain."

"Mari found Gwen collapsed on the floor of the room which had housed David's body," Gareth said.

"Sweet Mari!" Hywel said. And then his eyes went to Mari beside him. He flashed a grin and reached for her hand to clasp it. "Thank you for looking out for Gwen." Still holding Mari's hand, Hywel pushed at the door and made to enter the room with her.

Gareth put out a hand to stop him. "There's more I must relate to you, my lord, before we speak to any Norman."

"I guessed that," Hywel said from the doorway. "Rhun and I have been assigned to this room. We can speak privately in here."

Rhun sat on a bench at the end of the bed, polishing his sword with a fine cloth. He stood up as they entered. The room was larger than Hywel's room back at Aber Castle—twice as large, truth be told—with a wide bed large enough for the brothers to share, even if Hywel would have preferred female company. The room was well-appointed with a trunk, a rack upon which to store weapons, a tapestry on the wall depicting a boar hunt, and a fireplace (unlit, as it was May).

"Earl Robert has honored you with this room, my lord," Mari said.

Hywel snorted a laugh. "Has he? I'm not so sure."

"What do you mean?" Mari said.

"What Prince Hywel is saying is that the honor might not be as great as it first appears," Gareth said. "It's too easy for these Normans to decide that a Welsh prince might make a useful prisoner."

Mari's eyes widened. "Earl Robert wouldn't do that!"

"There is very little my father wouldn't agree to if it meant freeing Rhun and me from captivity," Hywel said, with a nod towards his brother. "Earl Robert may not wish to alienate his Welsh allies to that extent, but not all Normans have been so restrained."

Then Prince Hywel canted his head towards Evan and Gruffydd, who'd remained in the doorway. "Keep a watch."

They nodded and stepped back into the corridor. Gareth made to ease the door closed, but Evan stopped him before he could. "Wait—"

Gareth hesitated, looking at his friend.

"I know I don't deserve your forgiveness," Evan said, "but I wanted to say that I am so very sorry for what happened to Gwen. She was in my charge and I—"

Gareth cut him off. "I know you care for her and would never want to see her hurt. Blame lies at the feet of the man who harmed her, not at yours."

"But if I—"

"Or if I had taken proper precautions, or not underestimated what we faced here, she would not have been hurt," Gareth said. "As I said, blame lies on the man who stole David's body and on me. She is my wife."

The two men regarded each other for a heartbeat, and then Evan nodded. "Gruffydd and I will be here. Call if you need us."

Gareth closed the door and turned to face the room. "Did Earl Robert speak to you about David's murder, my lords? About any of this?"

"No," Hywel said.

"He talked only of alliances and good will," Rhun said. "*You are most welcome*, and so on. It wasn't anything we didn't expect to hear, though his choice to house us inside the castle surprised me."

"As it concerns me," Gareth said.

Hywel chewed on his lower lip. "I think an excursion back to camp is in order at the first possible opportunity, just to see if Earl Robert will allow us to leave."

Rhun glanced at Hywel. "You have worse news than this, brother. I can see it in your face." Then he gestured to Mari that she should rest on the bench where he'd been sitting.

Gareth escorted Gwen to sit beside her. Gareth still wasn't sure that Gwen should be here at all, but other than sending her home to Wales—a logistically challenging proposition—he didn't see what choice he had just now. "Tell them what happened, Gwen," he said.

Gwen gave Hywel and Rhun a detailed account of the events in which she'd played a part, and then Gareth brought out the emerald for inspection.

Rhun couldn't see it from his position by the window and approached with three quick steps. "St. Simeon protect us." He fingered the gem and then glanced around at the circle of companions. "I take it as a given that we think he acquired this through nefarious means?"

"It was hidden in the seam of David's cloak," Gwen said. "More than that, I cannot say."

"With the appearance of the gem and the removal of the body, already this is not a simple tale of murder," Rhun said.

Hywel pursed his lips and turned to Gareth. "I have not heard from you yet. You left the castle with Sir Amaury, which is why you weren't with Gwen when she examined David's body."

Gareth nodded. "At the time, following a lead with Sir Amaury made the most sense to me. In that regard, I'm happy to report that he seems to have some confidence in me and my discretion."

"As he should," Hywel said. "What did you discover?"

80

Gareth related what had transpired beside the river: the finding of John's body, the footprints, Amaury's tale of Empress Maud's four horsemen, and all that they didn't know, including the identity of the man helping Alard.

"Who do we think took David's body?" Rhun said.

"I have no idea," Gareth said, "not even a good guess."

"Alard?" Hywel said, and then shook his head, answering his own question in the same way Gareth had. "He wouldn't have dropped David's body at our feet if he knew about the gem."

"More likely, our culprit is the one for whom the gem was intended," Rhun said. "It might have made sense for Alard to have killed David for the emerald, but since he didn't take it, clearly that's not the case. His motive is something else entirely." Just because Rhun had never been much involved in the less savory aspects of ruling Gwynedd didn't mean he didn't understand them.

"I agree with you, as far as it goes," Hywel said, "and provided the intended owner wasn't David himself—" He glanced around the room and smiled at the skeptical looks on his companions' faces, "—but what we know so far is obviously a very small part of a much larger conspiracy."

"Or could it be more than one conspiracy?" Gwen said. "That's happened before."

"Whatever is going on, it isn't good," Gareth said.

"At least, I find it unlikely it has anything to do with *us*," Rhun said.

"Perhaps, my lord," Gareth said. "Alard did put the body at our feet, and David did work for your father, or so we thought."

"What about John's body?" Mari said, speaking for the first time.

"What about it?" Gareth said.

"Do we think he might have an emerald hidden on him too?" Mari said.

Hywel drew in a breath. "What did Amaury do with John's body, Gareth?"

"He told me he'd have it taken to the friary, since it's closer than Newcastle," Gareth said.

"If he finds an emerald on John, he might wonder if we found one on David," Gwen said. "What if he asks about it? Are you going to tell him I found it?"

Hywel's fingers closed around the emerald. "My instinct is to tell no one, to keep it to give to my father."

"We probably don't have that luxury," Rhun said, prying open his brother's fingers and taking the gem. "At the very least, we should show it to Earl Robert."

Hywel made a grunting sound that might have meant agreement.

"Worse, what if Amaury doesn't ask about it?" Gareth said. "I can't inquire of him without giving away the existence of the one we have, but to know that John had a gem too would mean that John and David *were* paid to do a task."

"Such a task would have had to be both important and dangerous to cost so much," Mari said.

"Amaury could be correct that Alard isn't a traitor," Gwen said. "What if it is David who was the traitor, and he was paid to kill Alard?"

"That would make his death a very expensive one," Gareth said.

"We will assume nothing without evidence," Hywel said, looking hard at each of his companions in turn. "Let's begin with what we know."

Rhun focused on his brother. "We have four horsemen: Alard, John, David, and Peter, who is dead."

"And we have four men involved in this plot," Hywel said, "Alard, John, David, and a fourth man whose identity we don't know."

"What if Amaury isn't telling you the truth? What if the fourth horseman isn't really dead?" Mari said.

"Now you're thinking like a true conspirator, Mari," Hywel said, grinning.

Gareth's brow furrowed. "Amaury wasn't lying about Peter's death, of that I am sure. Why would he?"

Mari deflated, her shoulders sagging. Gareth hadn't intended that, and he made a gesture with his hand in silent apology. Gwen put an arm around her shoulders. "Don't be sad.

You were thinking out loud with us. This is what we do." Gwen glared at her husband. "Besides, she's not wrong. We're looking for at least one more man besides Alard and the mystery man beside the river."

"How so?" Gareth said.

"If John, David, Alard, and his companion beside the river are all dead or accounted for outside the castle, who hurt Prior Rhys and me and took David's body? How many culprits are we really looking for?"

Gareth grimaced. His wife was right, and he was about to say so when a knock came at the door, followed by Evan's voice. "My lords?"

At a gesture from Rhun, Gareth opened the door.

Sir Amaury stood on the threshold. "I apologize for interrupting." He peered past Gareth into the room, and when he saw Rhun and Hywel, he bowed. "May I speak with you, my lords?"

Prince Hywel nodded, and Gareth stepped aside to let Amaury pass through the doorway. Then Gareth closed the door again and leaned against it, his arms folded across his chest.

"How may we assist you, Sir Amaury?" Prince Rhun said.

"I have been asked to escort Sir Gareth to see—" Amaury cleared his throat and gave the impression that he was struggling to get the next words out. He was a knight, a chief servant of Earl Ranulf of Chester, and yet he shifted from one foot to the other, uncomfortable with everyone's gaze on him, "—the empress."

Gareth gaped at him, dropping his arms and taking a step towards Amaury. "What? I thought she wasn't supposed to arrive until tomorrow?"

Amaury glanced behind him at Gareth, and while his back was turned, Hywel made a silencing motion with his hand. Gareth subsided, and Hywel drew Amaury's attention back to him. "Why would she want to see Sir Gareth?"

Amaury swung around to face Prince Hywel. "I am only the messenger, my lords."

"No blame to you, Amaury." Hywel grinned, though Gareth couldn't see what was funny. If they'd been alone, he might have made a comment along the lines of *just you wait*, but to do so wouldn't have been appropriate in front of Amaury.

Prince Rhun clasped his hands behind his back, playing the more serious older brother. "Empress Maud is here? And she's not happy, I imagine."

Amaury hands were clenched behind his back too. "No, my lord."

Gareth met Hywel's eyes, asking for permission to join the conversation. Hywel nodded.

"Why me?" Gareth left the door and moved so that Amaury could speak to him and the princes at the same time.

"I don't know," Amaury said.

"Surely this isn't usual?" Gareth said.

"Not usual at all, but not without reason." Amaury canted his head towards Hywel and Rhun. "She will meet the Princes of Gwynedd formally in the hall of the castle, but she hates to be kept in the dark about anything. Earl Robert must have sent her word that you were part of this investigation, and since both Gwen and Prior Rhys were injured when David's body was stolen ..." Amaury's voice trailed off, leaving (to Gareth's mind) a great deal unsaid.

Hywel filled in one of the gaps. "She wants to hear what happened from the horse's mouth. She can question Gareth without thought of protocol or how it will affect the relations between her and my father."

"My lord, speaking to an empress puts me out of my depth," Gareth said.

Amaury's eyes grew bright with the same amusement Gareth saw in Hywel's face. "She has been known to reduce even grown men to gibbering fools," Amaury said.

"Tell her what you deem wise," Hywel said to Gareth. "We don't even know what questions she is going to ask. I trust you." He didn't need to tell Gareth not to mention the emerald, and they both knew it.

"Yes, my lord." Gareth swallowed hard. "Though I don't find this nearly as amusing as you do."

Hywel clapped Gareth on the shoulder. "She'll take to you, far more than she will to either Rhun or me. Consider yourself an emissary from us."

Gareth bowed, though his insides were churning. He turned to Amaury. "We might as well get this over with."

"While you are about royal business, Mari and I will call upon Prior Rhys." Gwen rose to her feet.

"That's a good idea," Gareth said.

If he hadn't caught her hand and pulled her close, he would have missed Gwen's next words, which were said just about as sourly as any he'd ever heard from her: "It seems to be all I'm good for."

Gareth looked down at her, concerned. "Gwen—"

She reached up and patted his cheek. "Not to worry. I'm just out-of-sorts."

"Do *not* get yourself into any more trouble," he said.

Gwen laughed. "I'm not the one going to visit an empress."

9

Gwen

“**D**on’t you find that strange?” Gwen said after Gareth and Amaury had left the room and Evan had closed the door again.

“If Empress Maud thinks speaking to one of our knights is going to gain her information she wouldn’t have discovered otherwise, she is very much mistaken,” Hywel said. “Gareth will give away nothing of substance—nothing that we do not want to share.”

“And he no longer has the emerald,” Rhun said, holding out his hand. “What do we do with it?”

Hywel pursed his lips. “We keep it quiet. When Gareth returns, depending on what he tells the empress, we can decide what role in the continuing investigation we choose to have.”

“Father would not want us to leave yet,” Rhun said, “not with so much unsettled.”

“He would want us to leave if staying meant risking our lives and those of our companions. When Gareth returns, we will ask to speak again with Earl Robert.” Hywel shook his head. "I wish I understood more about what is happening here."

Rhun scoffed under his breath. "I don't think I will ever understand Normans."

"Since I told Gareth I would, it's probably best if Mari and I visit Prior Rhys," Gwen said. "Perhaps he is well enough to talk. Regardless, he shouldn't be left alone."

"He's not alone," Hywel said. "One of the ladies of Earl Robert's court is sitting with him."

"Even so, my lord, I think you know what she means." Mari had a way of speaking to Hywel that skirted the edge of disrespect.

Hywel bowed. "You are correct, of course. I give way to your better sense."

Gwen looked down at her feet to hide her expression. It had her worried that Hywel didn't seem to mind how Mari talked to him as long as she did and in fact seemed to enjoy sparring with her. Gwen took her friend's hand, and they left the room, though not before Mari threw yet another admiring look over her shoulder at Prince Hywel.

"He is a very handsome man," Gwen said.

"Who?" Mari said.

Gwen glanced at her friend. "Prince Hywel."

Mari blushed. Gwen shouldn't have had to clarify who *he* was, and Mari knew it. "Yes. Very handsome."

They'd reached the lower landing in the west wing of the castle and came to a halt when a guard, who'd been leaning against the wall with his arms folded across his chest, straightened at their approach.

Gwen nodded to him. "We're looking for Prior Rhys," she said in her halting French.

The man pointed to a door. "At the end of the corridor."

Gwen thanked him, but Mari swept past him like he wasn't there. Such behavior was expected of high-born Norman women, and here at Newcastle, Mari was Norman, not Welsh. With that thought, Gwen's brow furrowed, suddenly unsure as to how it was that Mari was accepted as a Norman. Gwen had never asked her friend what exactly her relationship was to Lord Goronwy. It had never been important to know before.

They reached the door. Mari hadn't looked at Gwen since the mention of Hywel, and her color remained high. She lifted her hand to knock, but before she could, Gwen asked, "Did you grow up in England, Mari?"

Mari's hand stayed suspended before the door, and Gwen wished she could take back her words. Mari's face had crumpled. She looked down at her shoes and took a breath, smoothing out her features and returning to her usual composed self. "I am as Welsh as you, Gwen."

Gwen put a hand on Mari's arm. "I know that." Her voice was as gentle as she could make it. "I didn't mean to ask you so abruptly. I would never mean to imply that we did not share a love for Wales."

Mari blinked twice, and the tears that had threatened to spill out of her eyes receded. "My mother was a Welshwoman. She died before I was ten."

Gwen ducked her head. "I asked because I was admiring your poise. You look as if you belong at Newcastle far more than I do. And then for the first time it occurred to me that as a cousin to Cristina, whose mother was Norman, that you might have Norman blood too."

Mari looked away. "I do." She cleared her throat. "My mother was Uncle Goronwy's sister, but my father's family came from Normandy. Although they lost their lands there several generations ago, my father served in King Henry's retinue, and later in his son's."

"You mean he served Henry's son, Prince Edward? The one who died when the White Ship was lost at sea?"

"No." Mari pursed her lips. "I thought you knew all this. My father was one of Robert of Gloucester's men."

Laughter bubbled in Gwen's throat at getting such an unexpected answer, and yet one which so perfectly explained what she hadn't understood before. "No wonder you feel so comfortable here."

"It is only because of my father's introduction that Lord Goronwy married my aunt in the first place." Mari gave Gwen a sheepish smile. "I'm not sure that this was my father's intent.

He was very proud of his Norman ancestry, and in introducing his wife's brother to his Norman friends, he sullied their bloodline."

"And yet he married a Welshwoman himself," Gwen said.

"He did." Mari shrugged. "He loved my mother. I know he did."

"I believe you." Gwen bent her head close to Mari's. "If he hadn't married her, he wouldn't have had you for a daughter."

Mari's tears threatened to undo her again. "My father died as the war between Empress Maud and King Stephen was getting started."

"I am so sorry," Gwen said. "May I ask how he died?"

"Drowned. They never found the body," Mari said.

Gwen wanted to hug her friend, but the stiffness in Mari's shoulders told her to keep her distance. "You must have been just a girl."

Mari nodded. "I came to live with Lord Goronwy immediately thereafter."

Gwen could picture Mari, small and shy, not yet grown into womanhood, faced with her outgoing cousin, who was two years older and already attracting—and inviting—male attention.

"This is all so much more recent than I'd supposed. For some reason, I thought you never knew your father," Gwen said.

"I don't talk about him," Mari said. "And since he left me nothing, Lord Goronwy doesn't talk about him either."

"But you are here because Lord Goronwy is landed, didn't you say?" Gwen said. "Lands he acquired when he married?"

"Yes. Uncle Goronwy and his wife lived on the English estates she inherited. They have friends among Earl Robert's court, and Lord Goronwy takes pleasure in remembering those times. Because his estates come through his wife, it's important that he stay on good terms with the earl."

"If your father introduced your uncle to his wife, he must have been more than a knight, too. Was he a nobleman in his own right?" Gwen said.

"Yes."

"So ... if your father was one of Earl Robert's men and your mother Lord Goronwy's sister, I don't understand why you were left with nothing. Why don't you have a dowry—"

Mari pushed open the door to Prior Rhys's room before Gwen could finish her sentence. Left out in the corridor, Gwen took in a deep breath. Even as close as she felt to Mari, she had skirted, and then overstepped, the boundary between them. Although Gwen thought of herself as Mari's friend and believed that Mari viewed her in the same way, Mari was of the superior social class. She'd terminated their conversation, as was her right. Gwen was glad she knew more about Mari's past, but she wished she'd asked her questions more delicately.

By the time Gwen had collected her thoughts and entered the room, Mari had slipped onto a stool beside Prior Rhys and was holding his hand. A woman Gwen didn't recognize sat in a chair in the far corner of the room, working silently on a needlepoint square.

Gwen tipped her head towards the door. "Madam, could you excuse us? We'll sit with him a while."

The woman curtseyed and left the room without Gwen ever getting her name, which she supposed was her own fault for not asking. Gwen hesitated for a moment, mustering her courage to risk more conversation with Mari, and put a hand on her friend's shoulder. "I'm sorry. I overstepped."

Mari patted Gwen's hand. "Don't be sorry. I'm too sensitive, but I would rather not talk about my father."

The cramp that had formed in Gwen's stomach at the tension between them eased. She squeezed Mari's hand before walking to the other side of the bed so she could put her hand to Prior Rhys's forehead. It was cool.

"I am awake."

Gwen jumped. Hywel had implied that Prior Rhys was at death's door. "I'm glad!" Gwen was so relieved, she was tempted throw her arms around the prior and hug him. His austere expression restrained her, however. "How do you feel?"

"My head hurts."

He said it with such an injured tone that even Mari smiled. "Someone hit you very hard," Mari said. "Did you see him?"

"I've been lying here going over what I remember," Prior Rhys said. "I recall praying beside David's body in the little room off the chapel. Then Gwen entered the room, hoping to examine the body." His eyes flicked to Gwen and then away again, back to Mari. "I admit that surprised me."

"I'm sorry," Gwen said. "I didn't mean to disconcert you."

Prior Rhys turned his head, very carefully, to look fully into Gwen's face. "You were very matter-of-fact about it. I didn't know what to make of such behavior in a woman, and I confess that I didn't like the idea of you undressing the body in front of me. I chose to take a walk while you worked."

Gwen, for her part, didn't know how to answer him. She could have used his help, and as before in the chapel, his squeamishness surprised her. Still, the fewer people who knew about the emerald, the better.

Prior Rhys didn't seem to need a response from Gwen. He continued, "By the time I had strolled some distance from the chapel, I had come to terms with what you were doing. In fact, I made a list in my head of a dozen other women whom I had known in my days as a soldier who might have had the capacity to behave as you were. I was wounded fighting in

France and left to heal among a community of nuns. You reminded me of them."

"Gwen is not a nun," Mari said.

Now it was Prior Rhys's turn to smile, canting his head in acknowledgement of the truth of Mari's statement. "Still, she has some of the same qualities I admired in them. Did you find anything important on his body? Anything that might tell us why he was killed?"

"A man subdued me too," Gwen said, taking Hywel at his word that the emerald was not a topic for discussion. "When I awoke, the body was gone."

"What?" Prior Rhys struggled to push himself more upright on the soft bed. "Gwen! I am so sorry! I should have been there to protect you."

Gwen knew that Gareth thought much the same thing and might even speak to the prior about it eventually. She, however, wasn't going to admonish him. "It isn't your fault."

"Are you all right?" He looked her up and down. "You look well."

"I am well. He didn't hurt me. I'm still not entirely sure what caused me to faint, but he put his arm around my neck—" Gwen broke off, stroking her throat and remembering what it had felt like. She was afraid that the memory, and the feeling of helplessness the man's action had engendered in her was going to haunt her for a long time to come. At the very least, she needed to be more careful about leaving her back to doors in strange castles.

Prior Rhys reached for Gwen's hand. "My dear."

"We have been assuming that Gwen and you were both harmed for the same reason—because you were watching over David's body," Mari said.

Prior Rhys shook his head. "But what is it about David that would make someone do that? It's nonsensical."

"Not to the man who did it," Mari said.

Prior Rhys lifted his eyes to look into Gwen's. "If I could stand, I would take you home to Wales before the sun sets. Why hasn't Gareth sent you home already?"

"Because he's afraid she wouldn't reach the border safely." Hywel pushed through the door and entered the room. "I thought I heard your voice, Prior. It's good to see you awake."

10

Hywel

"I am glad to be awake," Prior Rhys said. "It is my understanding that whether or not I would ever wake was an open question."

"So it was." Hywel closed the door behind him. "You were speaking of what happened to you?"

Prior Rhys nodded. "Do you have an idea as to why someone would want to steal David's body from the chapel?"

"We don't yet know." Hywel caught Gwen's eye for a moment but then quickly looked away. He was glad to know she'd stayed silent on the topic of the emerald.

"Can you think of anyone who might want to hurt you in particular, Prior Rhys?" Gwen said. "The man didn't cause me any lasting harm, but he almost killed you."

"If it was even the same man," Mari said.

"I'm not sure it matters," Hywel said. "If two men were responsible, then they were working in concert. To steal the body, our culprit needed the prior out of the way long enough for him to get inside the chapel and get out with the body, which come to think of it, would have been quite a feat in and of itself. There's no reason to think he targeted Prior Rhys specifically, other than that he had taken on the task of watching over David."

While Hywel was speaking, Gwen had moved closer to Prior Rhys, going so far as to sit on the bed. Something about the way she was looking at the prior made Hywel stop talking. He'd been showing off in front of Mari, making a logical argument because he could. But Hywel trusted Gwen's instincts, and he realized that he and Mari had jumped into the conversation before Prior Rhys could answer Gwen's question. Prior Rhys still hadn't answered it.

"Prior." Gwen kept her voice soft. "May I ask you something?"

The churchman turned his head to look at her and as his gaze sharpened, a wariness came into his face. "Of course, my dear. Anything."

"When did you join the monastery in St. Asaph?"

"Gwen—" Mari leaned forward as if to shush her friend, but Hywel stepped closer and caught her hand.

"Let her be," he said, his voice low.

"It was a long time ago, Gwen," Prior Rhys said.

"I'm thinking it wasn't so long ago as all that. You were a soldier, weren't you?" Gwen said. "Whom did you serve?"

Prior Rhys scoffed under his breath and looked down at his hands as they rested on the bedcovers. "Gareth spoke to me of your intelligence. I should have listened." He took in a breath and let it out. "You have asked the right question, my dear. Empress Maud was my mistress."

Mari's hand gripped Hywel's, and Hywel found that his feet were fixed to the floor. The silence stretched out for a long count of ten, and then Gwen spoke again. "You're part of this somehow, aren't you? You were involved even before we rode through the gates of the castle."

"Did you join my retinue because you still work for the empress?" Hywel found himself struggling to push down a rising anger that the prior had kept this from him. He swallowed hard, acknowledging that his anger had less to do with the secrets Prior Rhys had kept than his own hurt pride at not knowing them already.

"No." Prior Rhys eased back into the pillows. "As you may recall, it was you who asked me to join your company."

"But you said 'yes,'" Hywel said.

Prior Rhys's eyes flashed. "Because you asked."

"You weren't worried that you might meet some of your old compatriots?" Gwen shifted on the bed, easing back from Prior Rhys to give him more space.

"Years have passed," Prior Rhys said. "Men die, they move on, and I have changed in appearance and vocation. Besides, even if I did encounter someone I knew before, why would it matter? I swear to you that my involvement with what is happening at Newcastle is as a bystander only."

"Someone apparently doesn't think so," Hywel said.

Prior Rhys lifted one shoulder. "I cannot account for that. I have had no contact with any of the empress's men since I left."

"Why did you leave royal service?" Gwen said.

A flash of a smile. "Leave it to you to wonder that, Gwen. In all these years, the only man who ever asked me why I left was the former prior of the monastery. I put him off with a piece of the truth—that I was aging, that I was tired of war. I didn't tell him all, not even the man to whom I owe so much." He contemplated her face. "I wonder that I am considering telling you."

Hywel could feel Mari holding her breath beside him. None of them moved or said anything. Prior Rhys looked past Gwen to Hywel, but he didn't focus on his face. Hywel thought Prior Rhys wasn't seeing him as much as the ghost of what had driven him to the Church.

"For many years, I was a warrior," Rhys said. "I fought in battles. I killed more men than I can count. Their faces hover before my eyes each night when I pray. But even I could not stomach the conflict that I saw coming between Stephen and Maud. From the moment Prince Edward's ship went down, war was inevitable."

"You didn't leave then, though," Mari said.

"My dear," Prior Rhys said. "It wasn't that simple."

In response, Mari released Hywel's hand so she could lean forward and take Prior Rhys's. Hywel flexed his fingers, missing the warmth of her hand in his.

"I acted only when my loss of honor weighed on me more heavily than I could bear." Then Prior Rhys blinked and hitched himself straighter on the bed.

"Empress Maud must have been none too pleased at your departure," Hywel said. "I confess I'm having trouble believing that your current circumstance has nothing to do with your past."

"Or the way you left," Gwen said.

"I thought we agreed that the man disabled me because he wanted to steal David's body?" Prior Rhys said.

"Maybe what we should be asking is why you wanted to watch over David." Hywel's anger had receded, which meant he was starting to think.

"Wasn't it my duty as a servant of God?" Prior Rhys said.

A second question. If Gareth were here, he would have said that Prior Rhys was trying to deflect Hywel. Hywel leaned forward, a hand on the bedpost. "Then tell me the truth, as a man of God, Rhys."

"I have told more truth to you today than I have ever told anybody."

"And yet you now evade," Hywel said. "Was David one of the men you used to know, before you left the empress's service?"

"My lord, surely—" Prior Rhys put his fist to his mouth and coughed.

"Please don't prevaricate," Hywel said. "You know what I am asking."

Hywel thought he wasn't going to answer, but then Prior Rhys dropped his hand to the bedcovers in a gesture of resignation. "Yes, I knew him."

"You knew him when you served the empress?" Hywel said.

"Yes."

The truth came to Hywel in a flash of understanding, in the time it took for each of them to breathe in and out once. "You were one of them, weren't you? You were one of the four horsemen."

Prior Rhys's brow furrowed. "The what?"

Gwen's hand had gone to her mouth. "Were you? Is Prince Hywel right?"

Prior Rhys turned his gaze on Gwen. "You know nothing of what you speak."

"But you do. You were more than a warrior. You spied for Empress Maud. Tell me I'm wrong." Hywel had allowed a hint of admiration to creep into his voice, and he glared at Prior Rhys to compensate for it. "We already know some of the story from another source, more than you might think."

Prior Rhys looked away, towards the door, as if wishing he could get up and walk through it. Then he nodded. "I would have preferred never to speak of this again because it was never my intent to be a spy or to be involved in the doings of the royal court at all. This legend that Empress Maud has cultivated is … abhorrent. " Rhys's regret seemed genuine. "I wish the subterfuge and enmity she fostered had ended with my departure. I tried to make it so, but I failed."

"Your three fellow horsemen continued in her service up until this very day," Gwen said. "You should know, however, that David and John died today, and Alard is accused of murdering them both."

Prior Rhys shook his head. "I don't see—" He stopped, lifting his chin and looking straight at Hywel. "I told you the truth when I said that I have had no involvement—no contact—with any of them since I joined the monastery. I knew when I left that it would be hard on all of us, and it would be better to cut all ties. They were my brothers, and I abandoned them when they needed me the most."

"You were following your heart," Mari said.

"I was a warrior," Prior Rhys said. "I left my brothers to fend for themselves, and I cannot forgive myself for that." He pointed at Hywel. "You've fought battles; you know what it's like to depend on other men and trust them."

"I do know," Hywel said, "but it would be a cruel day when I chose to fake my own death rather than serve my liege lord, as you faked yours … Peter."

"Ah." Prior Rhys gave a low, mocking laugh. "You already know about that."

"We do," Hywel said.

"How could you?" Gwen said.

Prior Rhys held her gaze. "All I can tell you is that I did what I felt was necessary."

"All the more reason to wonder who injured you today and why," Hywel said.

"Are you suggesting that one of my former colleagues recognized me in the few minutes we were in the bailey, before David fell, and bore a serious enough grudge against me all this time that he felt it necessary to nearly murder me?" Prior Rhys said.

"You tell me," Hywel said.

"Perhaps someone did," Rhys said, "but whatever I did was done a long time ago, and you said yourself that John and David are dead. Alard left the castle by rope. My assailant can be none of them."

"Would another have a grievance?" Hywel said. "As a spy, you must have made enemies."

"Of course," Rhys said, "but none that I know of who are here today and who would steal David's body. I swear to you, the reason behind David's death is a mystery to me."

"What if you were to encounter Empress Maud?" Gwen said.

"She is here?" For the first time in their conversation, Prior Rhys looked genuinely concerned.

"Gareth has gone off to speak with her, at her request," Gwen said.

"Empress Maud is—"Rhys ran a hand through his hair, not finishing the thought.

"She never forgets or forgives, or so I hear," Hywel said.

Prior Rhys waved a hand dismissively. "Even if she learns of my existence, it shouldn't concern her. Alard was always her favorite. She used me but cared for my well-being only in that I was willing to do her bidding. She sent me to serve Earl Robert in England almost immediately upon my joining her retinue."

"If you were associated with Earl Robert, have you been to Newcastle before?" Mari had been silent a long time, but her question was one Hywel himself hadn't thought to ask. Another reason to be glad she was in the room.

"Oddly, yes," Rhys said. "We—the four horsemen, if you must call us that—established our base at a farmhouse on the other side of the Lyme Brook."

Hywel's attention sharpened. "A farmhouse? Is it still there?"

"I wouldn't know."

"That should have been the first place we looked for Alard." Hywel turned to Gwen. "Why didn't Amaury mention it?"

"Perhaps he doesn't know of its existence," Prior Rhys said. "It was ours—we chose it and stocked it for our benefit. Perhaps my former companions continued to keep it a secret to all but a few confidants, of whom Amaury wasn't one."

"You didn't even tell Earl Robert?" Gwen said.

"Not specifically." Prior Rhys glanced at her. "You think that's odd, don't you? But he made it clear that he didn't want to know the details of our activities, and I rarely saw him anyway. It was his spymaster who held my reins, though he drowned before I left, and you would be right to think that I chose to make my departure on the heels of his death."

Mari had been picking at the ends of Prior Rhys's blanket while she listened. She'd appeared less overtly focused on the conversation than Gwen and Hywel, but her head came up at Rhys's last words. "Say that again? Your spymaster drowned—?"

"Yes, my dear," Rhys said.

"What was his name?" Mari said.

Prior Rhys's brow furrowed, but he answered civilly enough. "The man I served, before his untimely death, was Ralph de Lacy."

"But how can that be?" Mari swallowed hard. "Ralph de Lacy, if we are speaking of the same man, was my father."

11

Gareth

Gareth again rode from the gate with Amaury and his men. This time, instead of continuing down the road to the Lyme Brook, they dismounted before the friary door.

"Tell me again why the empress isn't staying at the castle?" Gareth said. "Surely it's much better fortified against attack."

Amaury shot him a wary look. "She has her reasons."

"She isn't concerned that Earl Robert might be wavering in his loyalty, is she?" Gareth said.

"Not that I am aware," Amaury said.

"Then why isn't she staying at the castle?" Gareth said, pressing him a little. He'd felt from the start that nobody, including Amaury, was telling him the whole truth and was determined to find out what was really going on. If that meant asking a few direct questions and offending a few Normans, so be it.

"She is a pious woman," Amaury said. "She likes having a church near."

Gareth stared at Amaury, who colored and looked away. He was openly lying now, and they both knew it. What Gareth couldn't figure out was *why*. For the first time since he'd arrived at Newcastle, he felt a trickle of fear. Dismounting among the men who had escorted him and Amaury to the friary, he wondered if he'd chosen to ride a different way—back to the Welsh camp, for example—they would have stopped him.

Amaury gestured Gareth into the friary without saying anything more. The Dominican friary occupied higher ground to the southeast of the castle but was a less elaborate construction. A head-high wall separated the road from the main buildings of the friary.

They led their horses through the gate and into a cobbled, square courtyard. The chapel, cloister, monks' dormitory, and meeting hall filled the northern and western side of the square. The stables were to their east, abutting the road, and to the northeast, the courtyard opened onto gardens, a cemetery, and green fields with scattered outbuildings beyond.

A boy in sandals and a worn robe ran to take their horses, and then Amaury led Gareth through a narrow door into a central dining hall.

"I must leave you for a short while," Amaury said. "Please wait for me here."

Given the awkwardness of their previous exchange, Gareth didn't ask for more information and halted in the middle of the floor. Amaury left the room through a far door and closed it behind him. Left alone, Gareth gazed after him, wondering what might come next and feeling slightly better about whether or not he might end the day in chains. The fear had abated, replaced by curiosity and a sense of righteousness. These Normans thought they could intimidate him; he was going to prove him wrong.

He clasped his hands behind his back, settling into position to wait. Gareth had only stood silent for a single count of twenty, however, when the door behind him opened. He turned to see two young boys dash into the room. The first pulled up short at the sight of Gareth, causing the second to stumble into him.

The boys recovered quickly, and the first boy said in heavily accented French, "Who are you?"

Gareth peered at him. If he wasn't mistaken, the accent came from Gwynedd. "You're Welsh, aren't you?" he said in that language. "What are your names?"

"You first." The second boy folded his arms across his chest and stuck out his chin.

Gareth managed to hide his amusement at the boy's defiant stance and saw no reason to hide his identity. "I am Gareth ap Rhys, a knight in the company of Prince Hywel of Gwynedd."

The boys hesitated, and Gareth wondered if he'd misjudged their origins. Then they both began to speak at once in Welsh.

"We heard that you—"

"Our father was a merchant from—"

Gareth held up his hands to stop the barrage and signaled the boys to come closer. He bent at the waist, his hands resting on his knees, to look into the younger boy's face. "One at a time. Tell me your name."

"I'm Dai, and this is my brother, Llelo," the first boy said, while his brother nodded. "Our father was a merchant; he traveled through England and Wales, even to London, selling our wool. This was my first trip with him." Dai stopped, looking all of a sudden like he might cry.

With a glance at his brother and a gentle hand on his shoulder, Llelo took up the story. "We'd stopped here at the friary for the night. My father and I had stayed with the monks in the past because they bought our wool. We didn't have wool to sell yet, you understand? We were just collecting orders."

Gareth nodded. Sheep outnumbered people in Wales by a large margin, and a good merchant maintained his ties with his customers from year to year. Most shearing occurred in the spring, culminating in festivals in June throughout Wales. "Where is your father?"

"He died, that first night here, in his sleep." Llelo imparted this information without emotion or expression.

Gareth looked at him closely. "I'm sorry to hear that. When was this?"

"St. Dafydd's Day," Dai said.

"That was over two months ago!" Gareth said. "And your mother?"

"Run off years ago." Llelo shrugged, masking his anxiety by renewing his tough façade. Given his height, Gareth guessed him to be a year or two older than his brother. Gareth had acted the same at that age when he'd spoken of his losses.

He studied the boys. They were dressed in the plain undyed robes of the Dominican order, but they were too young to have taken vows. "Are you pledged as novices?"

"Not yet," Llelo said. "I will be twelve next week, and the monks say that I will be old enough then to choose this life and stay here forever."

"Is that what you want?" Gareth said.

Both boys shook their heads vigorously. "No," Dai said. "We have an uncle who runs sheep near Dolbadarn. He would take us in."

Dolbadarn Castle was in Gwynedd, not far from Aber Castle, the seat of King Owain. Gareth rubbed his chin and eyed the boys. Llelo shifted from foot to foot. "Are you sure, Llelo?" Gareth said. "I sense you're keeping something back. Do you want to become a monk?"

"No, sir!" Llelo said.

Gareth nodded, convinced of that at least. "Will the friary be sorry to see you go?"

The boys glanced at each other, both with the same sheepish expression on their faces. "I'd guess not," Dai said.

Gareth clapped a hand on each boy's shoulder. "If you warn the master of novices that I am here, I will meet with him later. With his permission, I will take you with me when I leave the friary in an hour or so. You will be safe at Prince Hywel's encampment until we can return to Wales."

The light in both boys' eyes warmed Gareth's heart, though he wondered what he was getting himself into, taking on two boys in the midst of an investigation. Yet he couldn't turn them away.

Then Llelo stepped closer, his expression more serious. "I don't like the man you're going to see. He leaves his quarters in the middle of the night and meets with strangers in the gardens."

Gareth's brow furrowed. "What man—?"

"Sir Gareth!" Amaury had returned.

Gareth ruffled the hair on their heads, intending to imply comfort and discretion at the same time. "Off with you."

"Yes, my lord!" the boys said together.

Gareth coughed a laugh and turned to face Amaury, who looked past him to the boys' retreating backs. "An unexpected meeting with fellow countrymen," Gareth said, by way of explanation.

Amaury gestured towards the open doorway behind him and the passage beyond. "Please come."

Despite Llelo's warning, Gareth still expected to find himself in the presence of the empress herself. Instead, Amaury ushered him into a room at the end of the corridor with a lone man sitting behind a table strewn with papers. Although the day was warm, a blazing fire burned in the grate behind him. Smoke curled around the ceiling instead of out the chimney, and Gareth wished the window shutters were open so he could breathe. The air was dense, humid, and smoky.

While Amaury closed the door and stood at attention against the wall to the right of the doorway, Gareth stepped closer to the table. The man's face was gaunt and drawn, too white for someone who was experiencing good health. Gareth's attitude of defiance faded, though he remained no less determined to find the truth.

"My lord," Gareth said in French. "It was my understanding that the empress asked to speak with me?"

"I asked to speak with you." The man made a fist to show Gareth the broad ruby ring he wore. "This means I speak for the empress."

Gareth glanced at the ring and then into the man's face. "Yes, my lord."

The man leaned back, gripping both arms of his chair tightly. "Do you know who I am?"

"No, my lord." Gareth silently cursed Amaury for not giving him more information before he invited him to the friary. At the same time, if Amaury was following this man's orders, Gareth could understand better why he'd lied. If Amaury hadn't, Gareth might have balked long before he reached this room.

"I am Philippe de Nantes." The man said this as if it should mean something to Gareth. Gareth bowed his head, and Philippe smiled. "You have never heard of me?"

"No, my lord." Gareth felt more foolish with every moment that he stood before Philippe.

"Excellent. That is the way I prefer it," Philippe said. "Suffice it to say that I wear the empress's ring, and thus, I assure you that I have her ear."

"Yes, my lord." Gareth was willing to grant him that, for now.

"Amaury tells me that Earl Robert has included you in the inquiries regarding the death of this Welshman, David, tossed over the battlement by the empress's man, Alard."

Gareth nodded. "Yes, my lord."

Philippe poured wine into a cup and took a long sip. From the way he held the carafe, Gareth judged it to be almost empty. "Alard is a dangerous man," Philippe said.

Gareth felt like saying that under the right circumstances, any man was dangerous, but he held his tongue.

Philippe's illness meant that he spoke slowly, forming each sentence carefully. Gareth didn't want to interrupt.

"Alard has been a friend—to all of us," Philippe said. Out of the corner of his eye, Gareth could see Amaury nod his agreement.

"So I understand, my lord," Gareth said.

Philippe kept his eyes fixed on Gareth's face. "I know that Amaury has told you of the empress's name for her most loyal servants."

"The four horsemen," Gareth said.

Philippe licked his lips. They were cracked and looked painful. "What he has not told you is that they served the empress under my direction."

Finally, Gareth was getting somewhere. "You are the empress's spymaster."

Philippe allowed himself a snort of laughter. "So, you do understand." Without waiting for an answer, he added, "Then you should also understand that it would be better for you to return to your encampment and leave this investigation to me and my men."

So that's what this was all about. "I don't know that I can. Earl Robert himself spoke to me about seeking the truth."

Philippe's jaw clenched once and then relaxed. He reached out for his goblet of wine and drank again.

Gareth couldn't tell if he was stalling because he didn't want to answer Gareth or if he merely was thirsty.

"He doesn't know that I have arrived."

"Surely he has spies, too," Gareth said. "He will know soon."

"Will you tell him?" Philippe said.

"My lord, please understand that I must answer whatever questions he asks." Gareth didn't want to anger the empress's chief spy, but he couldn't lie to Earl Robert.

"You cannot be bought, is that it?" Philippe said. "You are above such things?"

Gareth's eyes narrowed. The conversation had strayed far from David's murder, and Gareth was getting lost. "I fear I cannot help you, my lord. I ask that you allow me to return to Newcastle."

"Alard is a traitor!" Philippe's sudden passion brought him half out of his chair, but then he calmed and slowly settled down into it again. "He murdered David, did he not?"

"Perhaps it was David who had switched sides," Gareth said.

Philippe scoffed. "You are naïve."

Gareth flushed. "So I have been told more than once. Still, Alard is a traitor to whom? The empress?" Ranulf had said the same as Philippe, but as far as Gareth knew, Alard was only accused of killing two of his fellow horsemen. That was a crime, certainly, but it wasn't treason.

"I tell you this so you will understand my position," Philippe said. "It has been discovered that Alard has plotted against the life of the empress's son, Prince Henry."

Amaury took one step forward, tension in every limb. "I didn't believe it when the messenger said that. I don't believe it now."

Phillipe ignored Amaury, still speaking to Gareth. "Last week, we intercepted a messenger sent to Alard from William of Ypres, King Stephen's most trusted confidant. The messenger had been instructed to tell Alard that payment for the murder of Prince Henry was on its way."

"Why would you believe anyone sent by William of Ypres?" Amaury said.

"You were the one who interrogated him," Philippe said, "and yet you don't trust your own results?"

Gareth looked from Amaury to Phillipe. Amaury's duties for Empress Maud were clearly more extensive than Amaury had led Gareth to believe. "Even if this is so, isn't Prince Henry in France with his father?" Gareth said. "Surely Alard is no threat as long as Henry remains in France and Alard stays here."

Philippe's right shoulder hitched up and dropped in a half-shrug. "You are quite wrong. Prince Henry has been living at Robert of Gloucester's stronghold in Bristol since the Christmas feast and is journeying to Newcastle even now. He should arrive in three days' time."

Gareth leaned forward, going so far as to put both fists on the edge of Philippe's table. "The empress allowed Henry to come to England? Why? Surely he can learn the art of war just as well in Normandy as here. What is he ... all of twelve years old?"

"He's ten," Philippe said, "but England is his birthright, for he will rule it after his mother; he had never seen it. The English will accept him better if they know him to be one of them."

The revelations just kept coming. Gareth felt like leaping across the table and shaking the man; he might have if Philippe hadn't already been half in his grave—and if Gareth hadn't been afraid that Philippe might direct his wrath towards him. Philippe could prove to be a dangerous enemy under the best of circumstances.

"This is because the Londoners turned the empress away, isn't it?" Gareth said. "She has realized too late that she cannot rule England without the goodwill of those she governs."

Phillip sniffed. "Prince Henry will make a great king."

Gareth shook his head at Maud's arrogance. To have allowed the boy to sail for England in the middle of a war was madness.

Amaury moved closer to Philippe's table, his face pale. "How can you believe that Alard, the empress's most faithful spy, has turned against her so completely that he seeks to murder her son? All reason argues against it."

Philippe glared at Amaury, who didn't subside. Gareth, for his part, admired Amaury's fortitude in standing up to Philippe and his continued loyalty to Alard.

"You imply that King Stephen condones this plot," Gareth said.

"He does," said Philippe.

"I'm sorry, my lord, but I cannot believe that." Gareth was reeling inside but was trying to keep his tone reasonable. "Stephen would never condone such a plan. He's honorable to a fault, which is one reason he hasn't yet won this war. In addition, to allow a plot against Maud's son to continue, Stephen would be asking for retribution against his own son, Eustace."

Philippe pursed his lips. "The loss of Prince Henry would establish Eustace's claim to the throne upon his father's death. There is nothing King Stephen wouldn't do to accomplish that."

Gareth bit his lip and didn't reply, even though he still thought Philippe was wrong. Philippe was either lying about King Stephen's involvement or had been seriously misinformed.

Amaury's jaw remained clenched, and his back was poker straight. "My lord—"

"Enough, Amaury. It is not your place to believe or disbelieve." Philippe turned back to Gareth. "Alard has switched sides and is supporting Stephen. This truth is not open to further discussion."

Gareth took in a long breath, deciding to obey Philippe and ask a question of his own: "Tell me, my lord, did you send David to kill Alard?"

Philippe's taut expression didn't change except for a further tightening around the eyes. "No."

Gareth blinked several times. He had genuinely expected Philippe to say 'yes'.

Philippe straightened in his chair. "You should understand now why David's death is not within your purview, Sir Gareth. Leave it alone."

Gareth understood no such thing. After this conversation, he was more determined than ever to get to the bottom of David's death. "I can do nothing without the approval of my lord."

Philippe snorted his disgust. "You hide behind your prince?"

Gareth wasn't going to be taken in by that gambit. "We are both here out of loyalty to our masters."

Gareth knew the Normans didn't want a Welsh knight poking around Newcastle, but he had absolutely no intention of leaving this to Empress Maud's spymaster. He eyed Philippe carefully. Gareth had seen Alard throw David over the battlement, but since that moment, all of his information had come from Norman mouths. When dealing with a murderer, he'd learned to trust only what he saw with his own eyes.

Hywel could lie so well that Gareth would never have known the truth about King Anarawd's murder if Hywel hadn't told Gwen of it. How much more easily could Philippe, who lived and breathed lies, deceive Gareth with a composed face? With each superior sniff, Philippe confirmed Gareth's feeling that all was not well in Newcastle. This went far beyond Alard.

"I have a great deal of experience in investigating murder," Gareth said. "Surely you would do better to have my help."

Philippe's eyes narrowed. "I have my own men who are skilled in dealing with circumstances such as this."

"Excuse me, my lord, but where are they?" Gareth said. "You haven't had any success in containing your former man. He has murdered two men today, by my count, and so far you have no leads and have made no progress in finding him."

Gareth held his breath, thinking that he'd gone too far in challenging the old spy. It was Gwen who was better at asking questions of men that they didn't want to answer.

Philippe didn't seem to have enough blood left in him to darken his face, but his already pale lips pinched whiter. He'd opened his mouth to speak when a knock came at the door. Philippe tipped his head to Amaury, who went to it. "Yes?" Amaury said.

A man spoke in French from the other side of the door. "I have news that Lord Philippe should hear."

Amaury glanced to Philippe, who nodded. Gareth moved aside, and the messenger came to a halt in front of Philippe's table, put his heels together, and bowed.

"What is it?" Philippe waved a hand.

Gareth recognized the motion as the kind of expression Prince Hywel would use at times: *yes, yes, thank you for your obeisance, but don't waste my time.* In Philippe's case, he truly didn't have any time to spare.

"Earl Robert's men have found another body, my lord."

Philippe didn't respond at first, not even to straighten in his chair. He studied the messenger, who wilted under his gaze, and then moved his eyes to meet Gareth's. "Another, did you say?"

"Yes, sir," the man said, not realizing he was being mocked. "That of a woman."

"Her name?" Amaury said.

Although the Philippe hadn't moved, Gareth had the sense that he was dangerously close to ordering the messenger throttled for not spilling all of his information at once. Gareth would have thought that Philippe's associates and servants should know better than to drag out the telling of anything of importance. Speed and efficiency were vital to a man who hadn't long to live.

"One named Rosalind, an older woman and a known companion to the renegade, Alard."

From Gareth's right, Amaury made a disgusted noise in his throat, and Philippe nodded. "You will lead Sir Amaury to the scene."

"Yes, my lord," the man bowed and beat a very fast retreat.

Philippe gestured with one hand towards Amaury. "Go. See to it." His words came out as an order but in a tone that was resigned. At the same time, Philippe didn't reiterate that Gareth shouldn't continue with the investigation at Amaury's side. It was just as well, since Gareth had no intention of stopping.

Gareth headed towards the door and had reached it when Philippe's hacking cough stopped him. The old man tried to sip his wine, but his cough wouldn't let him. Finally, he took a rasping breath, and Gareth said, "May I send the friary's healer to assist you, my lord?"

Philippe's eyes went blank; then he shook his head and gave a cynical laugh. "Tell Earl Robert that I have seen you."

"Yes, my lord," Gareth said.

Philippe lifted his chin. "Amaury, one moment."

Gareth and Amaury exchanged a glance, and then Amaury moved around the table so Philippe could speak to him without having to raise his voice above a low whisper. From the doorway, Gareth strained to hear what they were saying, but he couldn't make out anything more than a murmur, especially because they spoke in rapid French and Gareth wasn't as fluent in the language as he would have liked. Gareth was quite sure, however, that Philippe's exhortations included an order to keep an eye on Gareth.

Then Amaury joined Gareth at the door, and they left the room together, heading back to the main courtyard. Before Gareth could excuse himself to retrieve the two boys, Amaury put a hand on his arm to stop him. "I assume you will ignore Philippe's suggestion to return to your camp and cease your investigations."

"Yes."

Amaury nodded. "I am not sorry; I need your help, and I don't trust Philippe."

"That makes two of us," Gareth said.

12

Gwen

Gareth stood at the feet of the dead woman, his head bent, one arm folded across his chest and his hand to his chin. Gwen came up behind him, slipped an arm around his waist, and squeezed. Gareth started, but when he saw who it was, he smiled. "How did you know where to find me?"

"The great hall is abuzz with rumor and gossip," Gwen said. "Someone reported that a dead woman had been found in one of the pantries, stuffed inside an empty beer cask, and thus I knew where you'd be."

"How is Prior Rhys?" Gareth said.

"Awake and talking," Gwen said. "I will tell you later."

"Is someone with him?"

"Mari said she'd stay with him for a while," Gwen said. "Prince Hywel says he will see that they are both well protected."

Gareth nodded, back to studying the body. "Good."

Gwen half turned away, not wanting to look at the dead woman, who'd been strangled; the bruising was evident on her neck even from a few feet away. "Who is she?"

"A lesser noblewoman," Gareth said. "Her name was Rosalind, a widow."

"What was her role here?" Gwen said.

Gareth gestured to Amaury, who was rubbing at his forehead as if he had a headache. "Her husband had been Earl Robert's man, with a manor near Bristol. She came here with the earl's court," Amaury said.

"And why is she dead?" Gwen said.

Amaury shrugged. "I have no idea, except that she was a friend of Alard."

"You mean his lover?" Gwen said.

Amaury tsked through his teeth. "That was the rumor."

"So we don't think that Alard would have been the one to kill her?" Gwen said.

"Not unless he returned to the castle since his escape," Gareth said. "We'd already decided that he didn't return to take David's body or attack Prior Rhys. Are we ready to reevaluate that assumption now?"

Amaury looked over at him, interest in his eyes. "Her death is that recent?"

"She's been dead an hour, maybe two," Gareth said.

"You're sure about the time?" Amaury said. "How can you possibly tell?"

"Even now, the body is warm and not stiff," Gareth said.

"It would have been warm inside the cask," Amaury said. "Could it have prevented the body from cooling?"

Gwen sniffed the air in the pantry. It wasn't a nice smell, but the air wasn't putrid either, such as a decomposing body in late spring might cause. "If anything, the temperature in the pantry might have made the body cool more quickly." Gwen was surprised that Amaury didn't know more about this, but then again, he probably hadn't seen as many murdered people as Gareth had.

"The last I saw of Alard, he was falling from a rope into the river," Gareth said. "Unless his friend found him dry clothes immediately and he was able to wander unremarked enough through the castle to meet with Rosalind and kill her, this death is not his fault."

"I need to be sure of that before I speak to Earl Ranulf or Philippe," Amaury said.

"I made copies of Alard's image to pass among the servants. They should have been on the lookout for his face," Gareth said. "One should never say 'never' I suppose, but I am confident enough in my supposition to tell this to my prince."

Gwen glanced at the body, remembering another pantry in a different castle, before she and Gareth had found each other again. That time it had been her father who was accused of a crime he didn't commit. "I don't think that's a reassuring thought. It means at the very least we have two killers: Alard and a second man."

Amaury picked at his lower lip with his fingers. "Two killers."

"Perhaps he left us something on the body that will identify him," Gareth said. "I won't know until I examine her more thoroughly. For now, I can tell you that it is very likely that she was put in the barrel shortly after her death."

"How do you know that?" Amaury said.

"The blood has pooled in her feet and in her lower torso from how she was folded into the barrel," Gareth said.

"We should begin by questioning the kitchen staff," Gwen said. "We need to know who saw her last and when."

Amaury nodded. "I've already set several of my men to that task."

Gwen bit her lip. She'd forgotten for a moment that she and Gareth couldn't conduct this investigation however they chose.

Gareth turned to her. "I can finish up here."

"Gareth—"

"I have a different task for you, and one that might prove more entertaining than examining yet another dead body," Gareth said, in Welsh, for Gwen's ears alone.

"What do you want me to do?"

"I picked up two Welsh boys at the friary who hope to return with us to Wales." Gareth pointed towards the kitchen, relating how he'd met them. "They're being fed right now. Would you settle them at our camp?"

Gwen's eyes narrowed. "You're trying to get rid of me."

"Never." Gareth reached for her hand. "It occurs to me, however, that our lords might wish to join you for a late afternoon ride. It is important for them to know that their people are well settled."

"Yes, it is." Gwen lowered her voice further. "You still fear for the princes?"

"Even more now than before. I don't trust anyone here." Gareth shot a look at Amaury, who was directing two men on how best to move Rosalind's body to the chapel. "I need to make sure that they are not in any danger."

"Before I go, I need to tell you what I've learned," Gwen said. "Will you walk with me a moment?"

A wary look came into Gareth's eyes, but he followed Gwen back to the kitchen, to a corner by the door where they could converse with one another out of the way of the kitchen staff's prying ears. In quick whispers, Gwen told Gareth of the discussion in Prior Rhys's room, and then Gareth related his conversation with Philippe.

"How did this get so complicated so quickly?" Gwen said. "You didn't tell Philippe about the emerald, did you?"

Gareth shook his head. "I couldn't, not without Prince Hywel's permission. And I wouldn't have done so even with it, once I realized how much I distrusted the man. He's the empress's spy! In addition, if Alard has committed treason—or plans to—I don't see how the gem fits into it. It was *David* who carried it, and Alard killed him. It's the one thing that doesn't make sense."

"The one thing?" Gwen gave a laugh. "None of this makes sense."

Gareth pulled on his upper lip. "Could it be that the gem was meant as payment from King Stephen to Alard for his service?"

"The only way the gem could be payment to Alard," Gwen said, "is if David was bringing it to him, which makes David a traitor too."

"That's not what Philippe said."

"Philippe may be lying about many things," Gwen said. "Perhaps Alard is a traitor. I don't care either way who wins the English crown. It means nothing to me, but I won't condemn a man without evidence. Truthfully, we don't even have evidence that Alard murdered David."

Gareth's brows came together. "Alard tossed him over the battlement."

"That doesn't mean he was the one who throttled him," Gwen said. "Or stabbed him, for that matter."

Gareth shook his head. "I don't know what to believe. Maybe it's better to believe nothing for now, until we can gather more information. All I have so far is three bodies, a spy ring, and a castle full of suspects."

"We will figure it out," Gwen said.

Gareth pulled Gwen to him for a quick hug. "We will. Now—off with you!"

Gareth headed back to the pantry, and Gwen threaded her way across the kitchen to where the two boys sat at a small table, stuffing their faces with fresh bread spread with butter and honey. One of them swiped at his mouth, leaving a smear of butter across his cheek.

Gwen planted herself in front of them. "I'm Gwen, Gareth's wife."

The smaller boy swallowed. "I'm Dai, Miss, and this is my brother, Llelo."

"Gareth said you'd like to come with us to the princes' camp."

They both bobbed their heads fervently. Dai said, "Yes, please," while Llelo rubbed at his buttered cheek, smearing it even more.

The boys reminded Gwen of her brother, Gwalchmai. They had the same dark hair and eyes—although her younger brother had rarely looked at her with as solemn an expression as Llelo wore now. As the eldest, Llelo would have felt responsible for his little brother and held the pair together when their father died, like Gwen had done with Gwalchmai at the death of their mother.

"If I bring you with me, you must do as you're told," Gwen said. "I expect none of the mischief I hear you inflicted on those poor monks."

"Yes, Miss," Dai said, his arm across Llelo's shoulder, stretching so he could reach.

Without further ado, Gwen took the boys with her into the great hall, looking for the princes, but when she saw no sign of them, she led the way upstairs to their room. They weren't there either, though Llelo and Dai enjoyed examining the privy at the end of the corridor. The vent under the seat opened right into the river below them. Finally, Gwen found Hywel and Rhun in the bailey, accompanied by Evan and Gruffydd. The princes were conversing with Ranulf, so Gwen waited with the boys until Ranulf departed. Hywel beckoned Gwen closer.

"What have we here?"

"Two rapscallions," Gwen said, "but they are Welsh rapscallions, and Gareth has taken them on as his responsibility for now."

Hywel took Llelo's chin in his hand. "Where's your father?"

"Dead," Llelo said.

"Where did Gareth find them?" Hywel said, glancing over at Gwen.

"At the friary," Gwen said. "Given that we have custody of them, Gareth suggested that this would be a good time to ride to the camp. All of us together."

133

"Where is Gareth?" Rhun said.

"He has another body to examine, a woman this time," Gwen said and gave a brief summary of what she knew about it.

Hywel laughed. "That should keep him entertained." He glanced at his brother, who nodded.

"The evening meal won't occur until the sun sets. If we ride now, we can return before then," Rhun said. "Earl Robert has promised us a place at the high table."

The two princes went to mount their horses, but just as Hywel put his foot into his stirrup and was preparing to swing himself into the saddle, a man came through the front door to the keep. "My lords!" He hustled across the courtyard and arrived, breathless, at Hywel's side. "My lords! Earl Robert asks that you attend him."

Slowly, Hywel lowered himself back to the ground. He glanced at his brother, who stepped closer to the messenger.

"Did he say why?" Rhun said.

"He would like to speak with you about several matters that he did not have time to discuss earlier," the messenger said.

"Can't it wait?" Hywel said.

The messenger bowed. "I apologize, my lords. I have spoken only as I was bidden."

Rhun studied the bowed head of the messenger and then nodded. "We will come."

"Thank you, my lords." The messenger clasped his hands together in front of him and waited.

Hywel sighed. "It seems we will not ride to the camp today." He put an arm around Gwen's shoulder and walked her to her horse. Hywel made a show of helping her mount, even as he spoke quickly to Evan and Gruffydd, who at his grave expression had clustered around him. "Evan, when you reach the camp, send two riders to my father immediately. Perhaps this is nothing; perhaps all is well. But I would have him on the alert to the fact that we may be prisoners in Earl Robert's court."

"It is a journey of several days, my lord," Evan said.

"It is necessary." Then Hywel turned to Gruffydd. "Let Evan escort Gwen and the boys to the camp. I need you to find Gareth and bring him to me. Tell him to leave the body for now."

"Yes, my lord," Gruffydd said.

Hywel patted Gwen's leg. "I will speak to Gareth and then send him to the camp to be with you. You two are going to have to be my eyes and ears outside of Newcastle, now more than ever. You must find Alard. He is the key to understanding all of this."

Gwen didn't ask the prince how she was supposed to do that, just nodded.

"Evan, when you've accomplished your task, return to me here. At the very least, the evening meal should prove interesting." Hywel strode away across the courtyard towards the keep with his brother at his side. With Evan riding with her, Gruffydd on a quest to find Gareth, and Prior Rhys incapacitated, the two princes were alone and without a guard. Gwen didn't like to see that, even for a short while.

"I'll bring more men back with me," Evan said as Dai clambered up behind him and Llelo found a seat behind Gwen. "Each hour we've been in Newcastle has been worse than the one before."

"That's what Gareth said."

Gwen had thought that leaving Newcastle would ease some of the tension in her shoulders, but as they rode towards the Welsh camp, her anxiety only increased. She hated leaving Gareth and the princes behind in enemy territory, surrounded by foreign soldiers and murderers. It felt as if her husband was more in harm's way at Newcastle than when he fought in battle.

"They can take care of themselves," Evan said, reading her thoughts.

"I know." Gwen glanced at him. She did know it, but she couldn't suppress the nausea she felt at leaving her husband behind. To distract herself, she reached behind her to pat Llelo's leg to gain his attention. "How did you meet Gareth?"

"We saw him enter through the main gate," Llelo said. "I knew he was Welsh the moment I saw him."

"By his clothes, you mean?" Gwen said.

She sensed Llelo's shrug. "Saxons hunch their shoulders and bob their heads as Normans pass. Gareth didn't."

Gwen smiled. Welsh prejudices against Saxons and Normans were as fixed as Saxon or Norman ones about them. "Gareth said that you told him of a meeting between that Norman lord, Philippe, and a stranger in the garden of the friary."

"I did," Llelo said.

"Do you know the name of the man he met?" Gwen said.

"It was one of the dead men." Llelo snapped his fingers. "John."

Overhearing, Evan swung his head around to look at Llelo. "How do you know that?"

"He was a Saxon, right?" Dai said, joining the conversation. "When he met with Philippe, he pushed back his hood and we saw his yellow hair and beard."

"I believe you saw Philippe meet with a Saxon, but how do you know he's the same one who is now dead?" Gwen said.

"Earlier in the day, he came to the friary, asking to see Philippe," Dai said. "We overheard his conversation with the gatekeeper."

"And then we heard about it again while we waited for Sir Gareth to finish his meeting with Philippe," Llelo said. "One of the monks who likes to gossip told the gatekeeper that John was dead and that he was the same John who'd come by earlier."

God bless curious boys. "Did you overhear what John and Philippe discussed?" Gwen said.

"Not everything." Dai glanced at Llelo, who nodded his encouragement. "Just something about *keeping an eye* on someone John knew, his brother, I think."

"Did you get a name?" Gwen said.

"He called him Alard," Dai said.

13

Gareth

It was very late by the time Gareth found his bed. Gwen lay in his arms but was having as much difficulty sleeping as he was.

"What are you thinking?" he said.

Gwen turned slightly and lifted her head so she could look at him, though her face was shadowed. He could make out little more than her shape in the dark because the only light in the tent came from the firelight and torches outside.

They were lucky to have their own tent. Most of their companions slept outside on the ground, grouped around the campfires that would burn all night. The princes had brought four cartloads of goods into England, but only half a dozen tents. The rest of the space in the carts had been taken up by provisions.

Hywel and Rhun's tent was empty, as was the one for Prior Rhys, since the young monk, Tomos, who'd accompanied the prior on the journey, had gone to the castle to wait on him.

"I've been thinking about what we've so far failed to understand," Gwen said.

"That would be just about everything, wouldn't it?" Gareth found the end of Gwen's night braid and tugged on it.

"Well, yes. But it's more than that. It's Mari's involvement, honestly, that has me flummoxed."

"Why?" Gareth said.

"You don't find it odd that Prior Rhys reported to Mari's father when he worked for Empress Maud?" Gwen said.

Gareth shrugged. "Every man, other than the king himself, serves a man of greater rank, and from what I know of Rhys on our short acquaintance, he was very good at his job."

"But Mari's father—"

"All men have pasts; you know that." Gareth hugged Gwen close. "Rhys escaped to the monastery when his work sickened him beyond endurance. Given what I know of the man, I can believe that series of events."

"I don't disagree," Gwen said.

"So what bothers you about his story?" Gareth said.

"I want to know what happened that drove him away. He never said, and when I asked, he took the conversation in a different direction. He spoke of Alard and the other horsemen as his brothers. You didn't hear him, but the decision to leave was a hard one. The monastery didn't call him. Something changed in his life to drive him toward it."

Gareth surveyed the ceiling of their tent. "Ralph's death."

"Certainly that was part of it, though that's not exactly what he said." Gwen pushed off Gareth's chest to sit cross-legged on the pallet, a blanket around her shoulders. He couldn't see her face properly, but he knew what she looked like: beautiful as always, and intent. He would have drawn her down to kiss her, but she would have wiggled away. His wife didn't like to be distracted when she was thinking. "Could Prior Rhys have killed Ralph? Is that why he fled?"

"That would be awkward, if true." Gareth ran both hands through his hair. Sleep had never been further off. "Prior Rhys was a warrior. He'd killed before. How much would it have bothered him to kill a man if he had a good reason?"

"What reason could that be?" Gwen said. "We're talking about Mari's *father*."

"A man we've never met," Gareth said. "How well did Mari even know him if he served the empress?"

"I'm going to *pin* her down about what she knows about him if it's the last thing I do," Gwen said.

"Let me talk to Prince Hywel first," Gareth said. "Sometimes asking direct questions isn't the best way."

"It's what I'm good at," Gwen said.

Gareth couldn't argue with that.

"Besides, though she wouldn't talk about it, something about the way he died meant that he left her with no dowry," Gwen said.

"It isn't because of how he died. Gwen, her father was Norman; even though he had been well-born, he was a younger son, so what wealth of his own he had would have been minimal. By Norman law, when Mari's mother married Ralph, all her property became his, and when he died, with no son to inherit, all of his property went to his elder brother's son. Women cannot own anything in England like they can in Wales. That's the main reason the English throne is in dispute in the first place."

"It doesn't seem right," Gwen said.

"Maybe you'll get along with Empress Maud after all," Gareth said.

"Did you tell Amaury that his fourth horseman isn't dead?" Gwen said, changing the subject.

"I did not," Gareth said. "Until I'm sure it's relevant, I'd rather not expose Prior Rhys's secrets. While I can work with Amaury, he reports to Philippe. I don't trust him at all."

"And you don't believe Philippe when he says Alard is a traitor?" Gwen said.

"I believe he intercepted a messenger, but if I were William of Ypres, would I commit such information to an intermediary?" Gareth said. "It could be a clever misdirection on William's part to incriminate an innocent man and deflect attention from the real villain."

"What about the dead woman?" Gwen said. "Why in all this does one of Alard's friends end up dead?"

"Because someone is tying up loose ends," Gareth said. "Rosalind knew Alard well and could have been questioned, perhaps even exonerated him."

"What if he has more friends out there?" Gwen said.

"I hope for his sake that he doesn't," Gareth said. "I would prefer not to face more murders tomorrow."

Gwen rested her elbows on her knees and her chin in both hands. "Where's the emerald, by the way?"

Gareth reached under his pillow, pulled out his purse, and shook it.

"Why did Rhun give it back to you?"

"If he is to be stuck inside the castle, the last thing he wanted was to keep it with him," Gareth said.

Gwen took in a deep breath and let it out. "I accept that. I wish we knew for whom it was intended and if that person will come looking for it."

"We don't even know if the man who took his body was looking for it," Gareth said. "If you're guess was correct that Alard didn't murder David, perhaps there was something about the way he died that would implicate someone. That someone could have taken the body."

"Like Prince Hywel hid King Anarawd's body last summer before you could examine it?" Gwen said.

"Exactly," Gareth said.

"These aren't questions we can answer tonight." Gwen snuggled down beside him again. "I wish we were back in Aber and the emerald was stored in the treasury."

"The camp is well-guarded. I wouldn't have let you sleep here, even with me, if I didn't think we'd be safe tonight," Gareth said. "I would never put you in danger, not even for Prince Hywel's sake."

"I know." Gwen yawned. "You need to sleep. These problems will still be with us in the morning."

"I just wish I knew whom I could trust."

Gareth lay awake a long while after that, though Gwen fell asleep almost immediately. As he listened to her breathe, Gareth stared into the darkness, cursing himself for keeping the emerald with him. Even if he'd spoken reassuringly to Gwen, he could believe that the man who took David's body wanted the gem and would wonder if she'd found it, especially once he saw the torn seam. Gareth's stomach roiled at the possible danger to Gwen. The list of tasks that he had to accomplish before he could take his sleeping wife home stretched before him, each item more insurmountable than the one before it.

Gareth eventually fell asleep, and as it turned out, the rest of the night passed without incident. He woke with the emerald still under his pillow, though as Gwen had pointed out, his double duty remained: to keep his wife safe, and to discover who murdered David and the others. Unfortunately, he had no real idea how he was going to do either.

Gwen opened her eyes. "We should at least inspect the farmhouse."

Gareth pushed onto one elbow to look down on her. He loved the fact that she woke up alert, as if sleep had been merely a moment's pause in her existence. "What farmhouse?" he said.

"Didn't I mention it last night? Prior Rhys told us that the four horsemen used to meet at a farmhouse. He thought it was possible that they had continued to use it. I assumed that was why Prince Hywel wanted you here last night instead of in the   castle."

Gareth gaped at his wife. "No—neither he nor you mentioned it."

"The emerald distracted me," Gwen said.

"Is the farmhouse far?

"All Prior Rhys said was that it lies in a wood to the south of the Lyme Brook," Gwen said.

"Who else knows about this?"

"Prior Rhys, of course, and Hywel and Mari. They were in the room when he spoke of it," Gwen said. "Nobody else."

"Why wasn't that the first place we hunted for Alard?" Gareth said.

"Hywel asked that too, but Prior Rhys said that the farmhouse had been kept a secret. After Rhys left, perhaps the remaining horsemen chose not to tell anyone else. If they had—Amaury, Philippe, Earl Robert—don't you think one of them would have said?"

"I would hope so," Gareth said, "but who knows the lengths to which these Normans will go to hide the truth? Philippe, certainly, would consider it just another secret to keep from me. But you're right, we should have a look."

"I get to come with you?"

"I'm not letting you out of my sight if I can possibly help it," Gareth said. "Besides, I'm smart enough to know that you might have an insight or two once we get there, if we get there."

Gwen didn't ask any more questions. She slipped her dress over her head, and Gareth rose to his feet to pull on his breeches. Then he stopped, one leg on, and said, "It may be that we'll find Alard there. We'll need to be careful not to scare him off."

"So just the two of us should go." Gwen laced up her boots. "Besides which, Hywel might object to including anyone else in the investigation if we don't need to, and Evan and Gruffydd must attend the princes."

Gareth lifted the tent flap. By the dampness on the ground, a light rain had fallen in the night, but the morning had dawned clear with only a few clouds skittering across the sky. Gareth and Gwen found Evan sitting in front of one of the cooking fires with Llelo and Dai, who perked up at their approach. Gareth affectionately cuffed each boy upside the head and then sent them off to fetch breakfast. Gareth and Gwen settled on a log beside Evan.

"What news do you have?" Gareth said.

Evan quirked a smile. "You mean because some of us put work before sleep?"

Gareth snorted laughter. "That would be Gwen, not me." He laughed again when Gwen elbowed him in the ribs.

"Nothing new," Evan said. "You and I tucked the princes in safe last night, and Gruffydd sent word a moment ago that all is well. I'm to report to Prince Hywel within the hour. How about you?"

"Prince Hywel instructed Gwen and me to question as many people as we could today—not in the castle, but in the village itself—all the while staying out of Philippe's way. But Gwen and I have a more important task to do first." Gareth glanced at his wife. "Gwen reports that Alard may have had a base—a farmhouse—to retreat to, south of the Lyme Brook. She and I are going to find it."

Evan raised his eyebrows. "I will tell the prince. You shouldn't go alone, you know."

Gareth looked around the encampment and repeated what Gwen had concluded. "I'll have Gwen with me, and I'm not sure that we should involve any of the other men in this if we don't have to. The fewer who know the details and can speak of them to someone else, the better."

"Some men do have too loose lips, even when instructed to keep silent," Evan agreed. "But if Alard finds you there, it could be dangerous."

"I want to talk to him, not capture him," Gareth said. "That is more likely to happen if Gwen and I go alone. He's a spy. He'll be on the watch for any threat, and he should recognize both of us from yesterday at Newcastle."

Evan gave way, if grudgingly, and only after another wary look. "Return before dark or I'll be sending out a search party."

"We will." Gareth clapped Evan on the shoulder.

After a quick breakfast and a warning to the boys to behave themselves and not get too much underfoot, Gareth and Gwen mounted their horses. Prior Rhys's description of the farmhouse wasn't detailed, but Gareth had looked at the lay of the land from the top of Newcastle's wall walk the day before and had some idea of where to start their quest.

Instead of following the road that would take them to Newcastle along the north side of the Lyme Brook, they crossed the water at a ford and found a path that ran on the south side of the brook, always following its course but at times wandering a hundred yards or more from it. A mile into their journey, the castle rose up on their left. When Gareth and Gwen trotted their horses past it, Gwen eyed the battlement. "Alard climbed down from there, did he? That was brave."

"I would have said 'desperate', but the grin he gave me when he dropped into the brook makes me think he's not the desperate type," Gareth said. "The move was calculated and looked easy."

Now the path turned strongly southeast, away from the Lyme Brook, and as they continued along it, Gareth looked for a sign that someone might live in the woods that closed them in on both sides. The brush and trees—fast-growing alders mostly—provided a nearly impenetrable barrier.

"Where are we, Gareth?" Gwen wiped her brow. They'd left the brook behind, along with the cooler air associated with it. The day was getting hot.

"The friary lands are ahead of us," Gareth said. "We'll skirt them to the south."

The path curved again, following the border of a cultivated field. The vegetation on either side of the path grew thicker. England wasn't as well forested as Wales, but many Norman lords had their own private forests for hunting grounds. Gareth speculated that Earl Robert had set aside this particular wood as his own. The terrain wasn't flat here anyway and wouldn't have been useful for farmland.

"I feel like we've ridden for miles," Gwen said. "How are we going to find the farmhouse Prior Rhys meant? It could be anywhere."

"It has to be near enough to the castle to be accessible but far enough away so as not to invite comment or to be easily stumbled over. But I agree in part. I don't think we should ride much farther east or south. We're getting too far from Newcastle's domains."

At last, Gareth reined in and surveyed the landscape from the saddle. "This isn't right."

"I've thought so for some time," Gwen said.

"Prior Rhys said a farmhouse, but perhaps that doesn't mean the same thing to him as it does to me," Gareth said.

"We just have to get around these trees," Gwen said. "These are as thick as many Welsh woods."

"That is exactly what I was thinking," Gareth said. "Come on!" He urged his horse, riding fast now and not worrying about finding a pathway into the woods. Then, with the day already approaching noon, the trees came to an abrupt end, while the path continued southeast into the customary rolling English countryside.

"Now that's more like it," Gwen said. "There are plenty of farmhouses here."

"But perhaps not the one we're looking for." Gareth turned his horse and headed off the trail, riding due south before curving back west, around the woods.

Gwen followed him without question, even as the growth became thicker, with the same alders as before, albeit with a higher concentration of oak mixed in. The brush wasn't quite as thick either, but this time there was no trail to follow.

"What are you thinking now?" Gwen said.

"I'm thinking that this farmhouse has been deliberately hidden." Gareth dismounted and began shouldering his way through the brush, clearing a path for Gwen, who followed. Strands of hair had come loose from her bun, framing her face. He thought she looked pretty.

After walking only ten yards, the brush thinned out, and a little farther on, the woods opened up, allowing sunlight to stream through the canopy. Gareth halted, and Gwen was able to come up beside him.

"Those trees back there were very strange," Gwen said. "They form a shield, as if they're walling this peaceful woods in."

"Listen." Gareth held up a hand.

The little wind that was blowing moaned among the trees. "That's an eerie sound." Gwen turned this way and that as she listened.

"I've never been in a haunted wood before," Gareth said.

Gwen looked sharply at him. "Do you think it is?"

"No," Gareth said. "Of course not. But someone means us to think so."

He could feel Gwen relax beside him. "You had me worried there for a moment. I could believe in ghosts if I'd ever encountered one."

Gareth squeezed Gwen's hand. "Even if spirits were here, I don't believe they would hurt us. But I'm inclined to believe people are responsible."

Gwen's brow furrowed. "You mean someone is making those noises?"

"Some*thing*, Gwen," Gareth said. "Think about it: the winding pathway, the thick forest which hides access to this pleasant wood, the moaning. It all adds up to an attempt to prevent people from coming here and, if they do find their way through these woods, ensuring that they leave quickly."

Gwen cocked her head and then handed the reins of her horse to Gareth. She walked twenty feet from him, halted at the base of a pine tree, and looked up. "The sound is louder here."

"Can you see something that could be making it? Wind chimes, perhaps?" Gareth said.

"There!" She pointed a finger. "And over there too!"

"Imagine what it might be like to come here on a gloomy winter day or in the dark," Gareth said.

Gwen spun around to look at Gareth. "Do you think, then, that those alders were planted on purpose? That they really are meant to be a shield or a fence?"

"If we find the farmhouse close by, I would say 'definitely'," Gareth said. "But let's find it first."

They continued walking, and even Gareth had to admit that occasionally the sound of the wind in the trees sent a chill down his spine. Gwen renewed her hold on his hand. They were heading northwest now and had just crested a small rise when they both halted at once.

A wooden house was nestled in a clearing with its back to a copse of trees. A creek ran past it on the west side, heading north to the Lyme Brook. Gareth was surprised to have found the farmhouse this easily, though five hours of looking might not qualify as 'easy' to some.

"We would never have known about this if Prior Rhys hadn't told you," Gareth said.

"The trees grow thicker again on the other side of the house." Gwen lifted a hand to indicate where she meant. "A traveler faces them no matter where he starts." She glanced at Gareth and then at the farmhouse. "Much easier to just continue along the main path, don't you think?"

"Between the eerie sounds and the thick trees, I'd agree that few would want to come here." Gareth looped the horses' reins around a tree branch and crept a few paces forward, keeping a screen of bushes between them and the house.

Gwen followed him and studied the house some more. "It has the look of being long abandoned."

"It does." Gareth didn't enter the clearing but crouched in the brush and pulled Gwen down beside him. "But then, like everything else, its appearance could be a carefully cultivated façade. We should stay here to watch for a while."

Gwen glanced up at him. "You're disturbed by the way things have fallen out, aren't you?"

"What makes you say that?" Gareth said, though even as he asked the question, he knew that she was right.

"Is it the spying?" she said. "Or that we're in England? It can't be the deception because people always lie to you."

"They do always lie." The words came out harsher than he intended, and he moderated his tone. "I think it's rather that the forces at play are so much more powerful than I'm used to, and the stakes are so much higher. King Owain rules Gwynedd and reaches his hand—uninvited at times—into other parts of Wales, but the war that Stephen and Maud are fighting is tearing England apart. I feel as if our troubles here make up only one piece of that larger whole. I need to get it right before Prince Henry dies."

"You are an honorable man, Gareth ap Rhys," Gwen said.

Gareth was glad to hear his wife say that because he tried to be. He didn't always succeed.

"You brought the emerald, didn't you? What if someone is inside—?"

Gareth was shaking his head before she finished. "Don't worry. It's safe."

"No place is safe," Gwen said, "and no one is safe."

"As safe as I can make it," Gareth said. "It's in my boot." Taking a leaf from David's book, Gareth had wrapped the emerald in a cloth and stuffed it near the smallest toe in his boot. "Truth be told, it's driving me mad, but it was the best I could think of at the time."

"You certainly were wise not to leave it in our tent," Gwen said. "I wish Prince Rhun still had it."

"At least he didn't give it to you."

"I would have been the better choice," Gwen said. "Nobody would think I had it."

"Except for the man who took David's body!" Gareth shook his head. "Gwen, be reasonable."

"Which is why he should have given it to me," Gwen said. "Perhaps another woman might have kept the gem to herself, but more likely I would have told you, and you would have told the princes, which is exactly what did happen. We were predictable. Giving it to me would have been unexpected."

"Clearly, everything we've done so far is predictable, or we would have captured Alard by now." Gareth rubbed at his forehead. "Let's not overthink this or give the person behind whatever is happening too much credit. We need to continue as we've been, and let him catch up to us if he can."

"You mean he's not a sorcerer," Gwen said. "He can't see the future."

"I wish I could," Gareth said.

"I do worry about the princes," Gwen said.

"They are guarded," Gareth said, though even as he said it, he began to worry about them himself. Then he shook his head. He had to trust Hywel, just as he knew Hywel trusted him to do his job and do it right.

"I suppose for us to stand sentry outside their room wouldn't help anyone, since Gruffydd is already doing it," Gwen said.

"I fear for them, but then, I feared for them as soon as we left Wales. We should have turned around and gone home the moment David's body hit the ground at your feet."

"That was never going to happen," Gwen said. "Never. And you know it. You and Hywel were not going to let this go."

Gareth grunted his agreement. "We have spent too long poking our noses into other people's business to stop now."

"Just as long as nobody *else* knows about the emerald," Gwen said, "I'm hoping we'll be all right for now."

"Our traitor seems to have extensive resources," Gareth said, "but unless Prince Rhun told Earl Robert in my absence, the emerald's existence remains the knowledge of you, me, Mari, and the princes."

"Good," Gwen said. "Earl Robert's obligations are to his sister, and I certainly don't trust *her*."

Gareth took a deep breath. "Let's find out what kind of man Alard really is." He straightened and entered the clearing. Nobody stirred in the farmhouse. Gareth didn't know whether to be glad or disappointed. They reached the door, two inches thick and solid oak with heavy iron fittings. The farmhouse wasn't as ramshackle as it had initially looked. Gareth pointed at the door and then put a finger to his lips.

Gwen nodded, and Gareth pushed on the door. It was unlatched and swung open on silent hinges.

Gareth stepped into the main room, Gwen following close behind him. He had drawn his belt knife rather than his sword because it was better for fighting in confined spaces. Two steps into the room, however, he relaxed.

"It's empty," Gwen said, disappointment in her voice.

Gareth looked around the room. "Who leaves two chairs and a table in an empty and unguarded house?" He stowed his knife. "I was hoping for more."

"You were hoping someone would be here to greet us," Gwen said. "Alard, as you suggested back at the camp?"

Gareth laughed under his breath. "I'm not ashamed to say that I assumed it. And at this point, any sign of him would have been better than no sign." He went to a ladder that led up to a loft. It took up half the width of the main room with a single rail to prevent someone from falling to the floor below. From a point halfway up the ladder, Gareth was tall enough to see into the whole loft. It was completely bare, without even a bed or blanket, just blank floorboards.

"It's empty up here, too." Gareth swept his fingers along the wooden planks and came up with a layer of dust. "Empty a long while."

"Someone left us a lantern." Gwen pointed to a side wall where it hung on a hook. She lifted it to examine the wick and showed it to Gareth, who'd come back down the ladder. "The farmhouse isn't quite as abandoned as it looks if someone left a lantern full of oil and a freshly trimmed wick."

"That's more like it." Gareth was back to wary, but more hopeful too. Whoever had left the lantern hadn't chosen to occupy the house but had left it in good order. It might be deserted, with dust in the loft, but it hadn't been allowed to fall into actual disrepair.

He could tell by how closely the wooden planks were fitted together that the place was well-built. That craftsmanship, along with the rudimentary fireplace that vented out the far wall, spoke of a degree of wealth unusual for English farmers. Someone had taken care to build a home that would stand for many years. Peasant huts in Wales had a dirt floor with a fire pit in the center and a hole in the ceiling to let out the smoke. Most Saxon peasants lived similarly.

Gareth knelt and put his cheek to the boards so his eyes could follow the line of the floor all the way to the door. His brow furrowed. "Someone *has* been here recently. The floor has been swept clean of footprints and dust."

"Do you think that whoever was here last thought so far ahead that he didn't want you—or anyone—to see where he walked in his own house?" Gwen said.

"These are spies, Gwen. They are trained to think many moves ahead and to go to seemingly unnecessary extremes as a matter of course." Gareth got to his feet and stood in the center of the floor, gazing around the room. "He's hidden something here, and his footprints would have revealed where it was."

Gareth waved a hand, and they both began an inspection of the house, Gwen starting on the opposite side of the room from Gareth. When he reached the table, Gareth pulled it away from where it was positioned, slightly to the left of the center of the house, and studied the floor beneath where it had been, looking for a trap door.

Meanwhile, Gwen trailed her hand along the right-hand wall of the house. "Perhaps he's hidden a treasure somewhere in the walls. It may be that one section is unusually thick, but we wouldn't know it by looking from the inside."

"If we find nothing in here, we'll walk around the outside," Gareth said.

Gwen bent to the floor. "I think I've found something."

Gareth reached her in three strides and crouched to look at what she showed him. An inch from the wall, the floor had been scratched. It looked as if someone had dug into the wood with a knife.

"Take a step back." Gareth put a hand on Gwen's shoulder, and they observed that portion of the floor together.

"You can see the join," Gwen said. "It's well done. Look— it follows the grain of the wood."

"The planks are rough enough that you wouldn't notice unless you were looking." Gareth paused. "That's good work, Gwen."

Gwen smiled. "As you said, we're dealing with spies, right? Too bad Hywel isn't here. He would love this." Taking out her belt knife, she slid it into the crack near the wall and worked the blade back and forth.

A small square of wood lifted up, revealing an iron ring underneath. Gareth found himself grinning as he reached for it. Before he could pull on it, however, Gwen stopped him with a hand to his arm. "What if this is its own trap?"

Gareth pulled back his hand. "You think a crossbow is set to fire at me the moment I pull on this?"

Gwen settled back on her heels. "No. That would be silly. Prior Rhys said they used this place."

Gareth pulled on the ring. He couldn't get it to budge.

"Wait," Gwen said. "Maybe we have to pull up more of the flooring first."

Gareth nodded and stuck the blade of his knife between what appeared to be two layers of flooring: a top layer, three feet on a side, hid a trap door built into the bottom layer underneath.

With the top panel set aside, Gareth again grasped the ring and pulled. Up came the trap door, and Gareth and Gwen inspected the dark space below them. Gareth got onto his knees and bent forward to stick his head into the hole. "I can't see anything."

"Now we know what the lantern is for," Gwen said.

"And why there's a ladder leading to an unused loft," Gareth said.

While Gwen lit the lantern, Gareth lowered the ladder into the hole. The floor below had been dug deep and the top of the ladder barely reached the level of the upper floor. The pair exchanged a glance and Gareth shrugged. He stepped onto the first rung.

"Take it slowly," Gwen said.

"I'll be fine."

Ten feet down, Gareth reached the cellar floor and looked upwards to Gwen, still framed in the square hole with the light coming in from the open door behind her. He gestured for her to climb down too. She handed him the lantern, and when she reached the ground, she gasped.

Gareth didn't gasp, but he was no less surprised than Gwen. After he set the lantern on a narrow table, they both spun slowly around, taking in the shelves, crates, and trunks filled with an assortment of goods from clothing to weapons. "I know several lords who would be envious of what we've found here," he said.

"Why did they dig the cellar so deep?" Gwen said. "With the river nearby, I would have thought they'd have hit water."

Gareth put a hand to the dirt wall. His fingers came away dry. "Apparently they know something we don't."

Armor and weaponry, including bows, crossbows and axes, lined one wall. An entire barrelful of arrows rested in one corner. A single wooden chair sat at an angle in another. Gareth's eyes narrowed. He grabbed the lantern and went to inspect the chair. The arms were worn in places, as if ropes had rubbed them, and the ground beneath the chair was discolored. He bent closer.

"Are those bloodstains?" Gwen pointed to the seat of the chair.

"I know why the ceiling is so high," Gareth said.

"Why?" Gwen looked from the chair to him.

Gareth stretched, trying to touch the ceiling, but even jumping, he couldn't reach it. "This is meant to be a place to question and hold prisoners, in addition to keeping supplies."

Gwen shivered. "Just as long as we don't get trapped down here." She lifted up the lid of a nearby trunk and pulled out the robes of a priest. "Why would they have this—" And then she broke off and nodded. "Because they're spies."

"They've kept everything in excellent condition," Gareth said.

"Before yesterday, three of the horsemen still lived," Gwen said. "They must have used it often, and given that they left the door unlocked, had confidence that nobody but they would ever come here."

"Or the door was left open as a trap for us," Gareth said.

Gwen glanced at him. "What? How can you say that so calmly? Do you really think so?"

"I hope so." Gareth smiled at Gwen's stunned expression.

Then she frowned at him. "You could have told me what you were thinking."

"I didn't want to speak of it in case I was wrong." Gareth looked around the room, struck by the order, the neatness. The men who spent time here had cared about their work.

"I feel like I'm prying. Alard isn't here. We should go—" Gwen broke off.

"What—?" Gareth spun around. The bottom of the ladder was already five feet off the floor. Gareth leapt towards it, his fingers just brushing at the last rung before it was pulled out of reach.

Gareth looked upwards. Gwen moved to stand beside him, but Gareth put out his hand to keep her back. He pulled his sword from its sheath, though it would be of little use against the air between them and whoever had pulled up the ladder. Still, having it in his hand made him feel more confident.

Then Alard came to stand at the edge of the trap door and look down on them. He wore a wry smile and was as untouchable as when he'd hung from the rope above the Lyme

Brook. He had his own lantern, and between the two, the farmhouse was lit up like day.

Gareth could have thrown his knife, maybe even hurt the man badly, but that would have defeated the entire purpose of this exercise, not to mention leaving him and Gwen still in the cellar. Given that Alard had trapped them down here instead of killing them, Gareth was hoping for talk, which was all he'd wanted in the first place.

"So, it is the Welshman who comes. I am Alard, servant of Empress Maud, but you knew that already."

Gareth nodded. "What do you want?"

"To talk to you."

"Why?" Gareth said, though that was what he had wanted too.

"I have many questions that need answering, and the only way for me to clear my name is to encourage someone other than Ranulf or Philippe, someone from the outside, to find me answers," Alard said. "I trust nobody's motives but yours."

Gareth sheathed his sword. That was quite a declaration, coming from a lifelong spy. He decided to be as friendly as possible until he had a reason not to. Alard had all the advantages currently. It might pay to play nice. "Why do you name Ranulf? What does he have to do with this?"

"He is Earl Robert's son-in-law, and certain tasks fall to him—unsavory tasks—because he excels at making problems go away," Alard said. "I knew Earl Robert would place the investigation of David's death in his hands, and he and I have no love for each other."

"Why is that?" Gwen said.

"His allegiance is to Robert only. He cares nothing for the empress. I don't trust him."

"It is my impression that what Ranulf cares most about is his own power and status," Gareth said.

"That too," Alard admitted.

"You may have questions, but we also have them—and they need answers," Gareth said. "First and foremost, did you murder David?"

"No," Alard said.

Gareth scoffed. "Then how did he die if you didn't kill him?"

"I didn't say I didn't kill him," Alard said. "I did. But it wasn't murder. He came at me, and I had no choice. He was my friend and I killed him, with regret and in self-defense."

"You had to throttle *and* stab him?" Gwen said. Gareth was glad Gwen wasn't cowed by the Norman spy and was asking some of the questions. Alard might take them better coming from a woman who seemed no threat to him.

Alard unhooked his cloak to show Gwen his neck. It was mottled with bruises. "My side is bandaged—it's a wound from David's knife. Do you need to see that too?"

Gareth remembered the splashes of blood on the leaves beside the brook. "That won't be necessary. What about John?"

"I didn't kill him either," Alard said. "He was dead before I came out of the brook."

Gareth pursed his lips. "Then who murdered him?"

"I cannot say," Alard said.

"Can't or won't?" Gwen said.

Alard's chin firmed, and for a moment he looked like he was going to walk away. Gareth changed the subject before they lost him. "What were you doing in Newcastle in the first place?"

Alard gestured to the farmhouse. "This is our base. I always return here. And in this case, David asked to meet me. Knowing he might think *my* loyalty was in question, I became concerned about *his*, so I suggested a public place for our meeting. When he didn't show, I took the opportunity to observe your arrival. A Welsh delegation is an unusual enough sight for me to want to inspect it personally, and that is all I was doing on the wall walk until David came up behind me and caught me unawares."

"How sloppy of you," Gwen said under her breath, in Welsh and for Gareth's ears alone.

Gareth clasped her hand in his, and she looked down, hiding a smile. "Why would David want to kill you?" Gareth said.

"I assume he'd been told that I was a traitor. I wanted to speak with him, hoping that he would give me the benefit of the doubt." Alard sighed and looked away again. "Apparently not."

"I'm not sure that I believe you," Gareth said. "You left yourself an escape route by rope from the battlement. That smacks of planning, not happenstance."

"I always leave myself an escape route," Alard said.

Gareth coughed a laugh, his fist to his mouth, and granted Alard his point.

"When you chased me, I knew I had made the right choice to drop David at your feet," Alard said. "Did you know that he was a traitor to your King Owain?"

"Prince Hywel knew it as soon as Earl Ranulf claimed him as his man," Gareth said.

"Good," Alard said. "That was as I hoped."

"You should know that one of the reasons we're here listening to you at all is because you have at least one friend who wanted to hear your side before he passed judgment," Gareth said.

"Who's that?"

"Amaury, a retainer of the Earl of Chester," Gareth said.

Some of the tension around Alard's eyes eased, and he nodded. "I always admired his intelligence, though he has too much honor to make a good spy."

"We know about the four horsemen," Gwen said.

Gareth managed not to smirk when Alard raised his eyebrows. "Then you know I am the only one left."

Gareth regarded Alard steadily, careful not to give Prior Rhys away. But then as Alard gazed back at him, his focus caused Gareth to think again. "I would prefer we don't tell each other lies. Too many men have lied to me already since we arrived at Newcastle."

Alard rubbed his chin. "So I did see what I thought I saw in the bailey yesterday."

"What did you think you saw?" Gwen said.

"Peter, with the Welsh princes. I was busy with David at the time and later decided my eyes had deceived me. I'm guessing that it is through his knowledge that you learned of this farmhouse."

Gareth canted his head, without giving anything more away.

"Does Peter think ill of me too?" Alard said.

"He did not share his opinion of you with us," Gwen said. "You do understand that the accusations against you go beyond murder? That both Earl Ranulf and your spymaster, Philippe, have named you traitor to the empress?"

"I'd been told that was the way of it." Alard crouched near the hole, hanging his hands between his knees and looking more relaxed than before. "I have no illusions of my own importance, great or small, but it explains the effort expended to hunt me."

"There's more, however, that you're not telling us," Gareth said.

Alard's jaw worked. "You wouldn't believe me."

Gareth gestured to the contents of the room. "I wouldn't have believed this until I saw it. Tell me. You may find me surprisingly open-minded."

"You do have a captive audience," Gwen said. "You are accused of murder and apparently sentenced to die without a trial. At this point, telling us the truth may be your only hope. You have nothing to lose."

Alard clicked his tongue, not yet nodding his agreement, but then he said, "Yes. You read me right. Besides which, you have information I need. Perhaps we can help each other."

"Is that why you chose to dump David at our feet instead of leaving him on the wall walk?" Gwen said.

"That is exactly why," Alard said.

"You got our attention," Gareth said. "I'll give you that."

"Surely some of it had to be unwanted," Gwen said.

"It was the price I chose to pay. I can take care of myself." Alard leaned forward. "You must be wary of Philippe most of all. If he sent David to kill me, then it is he who is the most dangerous—to you and to me. It is he who betrays the empress."

Gareth didn't trust Philippe either, but somehow the idea that Philippe was the traitor was troubling. "The man is dying. Why would he betray the empress now? He has nothing to gain."

"Dying men can be traitors if it means leaving their loved ones well-provided-for," Alard said.

"Philippe accuses you, and you accuse Philippe," Gwen said. "Why should we believe you over him? You murdered your fellow horseman."

"As I said, I defended myself only after Philippe sent David to kill me," Alard said.

"He denies doing any such thing," Gareth said.

"He would," Alard said.

"But why?" Gwen said. "What would he gain by lying about a thing like that?"

"Trapping us here so we'll listen to your story is not the act of an innocent man either," Gareth said.

"It is the act of a desperate one," Alard said, belying Gareth's earlier assumption. "I have served the empress my whole life. I would not betray her. Not ever."

"Yet Philippe believes you have," Gwen said, "and you accuse him when he has served her just as long."

Alard straightened. "I don't know what is going on. I don't know what he believes me to be planning. I only know that he is laying someone else's treachery at my feet."

"Philippe claims that your aim is to murder Prince Henry." It was on the tip of Gareth's tongue to mention the messenger from William de Ypres, but he didn't, not yet. He wanted to see if Alard had already heard of him.

Alard absorbed that news with an impassive expression, but it took him a moment to answer. "I spend much of my time in France. If I were planning to murder Henry, I would have done it there."

"According to Philippe, Prince Henry has been in England since the Christmas feast," Gareth said.

That, of all Gareth's news, rocked Alard back on his heels. He cursed in French and paced away from the hole. He returned before Gareth could start to worry that he wasn't coming back. "The empress swore to me that she would not allow her son to come to England!"

"Philippe says that he's been living in Bristol and is on his way here now," Gareth said. "He arrives in two days' time."

"It should have been my job to protect him." Alard glared at Gareth. "Does the empress know of this plot against him? Does she believe I am at its center and that is why she sent me to cool my heels in Scotland at the court of King David while she brought her son across the channel?"

"That I cannot tell you," Gareth said.

Alard paced away from the hole again, muttering to himself. "That must be it. That's why she did not call me to her side as I expected."

"It would have made more sense to do so, actually," Gwen said.

Alard spun back to the trap door. "What did you say?"

"If the empress believed you to be a traitor, all she had to do was summon you and arrest you in her receiving room," Gwen said. "There would have been no need to send David or John to kill you."

"My wife has a point," Gareth said. "Much here does not add up."

Alard bent forward, his hands on his knees. "You *must* get to the truth, for all our sakes."

"Let us out and we will do what we can," Gwen said.

"Our conversation has been productive, but still, I cannot have you following me. If you would just give me a moment—" Alard broke off and looked towards the door. Gareth couldn't hear anything, but he was in a deep cellar. The corners of Alard's mouth turned down.

"Wait!" Gareth said.

But Alard was already striding to the door, his boots resounding hollowly on the floor. He went through it and did not return.

14

Gwen

Stunned at Alard's abrupt departure and hoping for his quick return, Gwen kept her eyes on the opening in the ceiling. "What just happened?"

Gareth put his arm around her. "Don't worry. We'll get out of here."

Gwen rested her cheek against his chest. "I know we will. I'm not worried about that." She gestured to the weaponry in the storeroom. "We can dig our way out if it comes to that. But I'm still confused as to what, exactly, Alard was telling us and what he hopes we can do for him."

"Nothing more than discovering the real reason Philippe has accused Alard of treason, finding out who stole David's body, and saving Prince Henry," Gareth said, grinning.

"Is that all?" Gwen laughed and then tucked her hand into Gareth's. His attention remained on the floor above them. They both strained to listen for any sound of Alard's return. It suddenly struck Gwen that having the trap door open exposed them to anyone who might come along.

"Did you hear what drew Alard away?" Gwen said.

"No," Gareth said, "but I don't think he's coming back."

"You know what we never got him to tell us?" Gwen said.

"Who helped him out of the brook, I know," Gareth said. "Believe me, I'm kicking myself right now."

Gwen cast around the room, looking for something that would help them to escape. Nothing came to mind, short of digging through the dirt that formed the walls of the house and tunneling up to ground level. Unfortunately, a stone foundation supported the farmhouse. It wouldn't be easy getting around that.

"Help me move the table."

Gwen laughed as she took up one end of the table. "I would have cooled my heels down here for hours before I thought of something so simple." They maneuvered the table underneath the hole. The tabletop was a little more than two feet off the ground, so when Gareth stood on it and stretched, his fingers could just reach the opening.

"Come here." Gareth gestured that Gwen should join him on the table.

Gwen put her knee on the tabletop, but as soon as she got both feet under her, the table gave an ominous *creak*. Gareth froze, bent forward with one hand on her arm and the other reaching for her waist.

"Just take it slow," Gareth said.

Gwen carefully stood, and then Gareth crouched so she could clamber onto his shoulders, her skirt scrunched up around her thighs. When he straightened to his full height, her head poked through the trapdoor. She grasped the edge of the hole with both hands—and then screamed as Gareth suddenly disappeared out from under her. The table legs had given way, dumping him to the ground and leaving Gwen hanging from the opening.

"Gareth!"

She looked down. He knelt on the dirt floor, his hand on his left shoulder and his head bent. Gwen twisted her hips, fighting to maintain her hold on the edge of the floor, but even that movement cost her whatever grip she had, and she fell. She landed in a heap beside Gareth, letting herself roll onto her side to better take the force of the fall. As she sat up, she realized that she'd hurt her ankle. Gareth hovered over her. "I'm so sorry!"

"What happened to you? Are you all right?" she said. They faced each other, both still on the floor, getting back their breath.

Gareth continued to rub at his left shoulder, and then he rotated his arm, working at the muscle and joint. "I'm fine. Stupid, but fine."

"You couldn't know the table was going to break in that instant," Gwen said. "I almost made it out of the cellar."

Gareth grimaced as he moved to help her upright. "I shouldn't have risked you at all. I should have pulled myself up. At the very least, I should have caught you before you fell."

Gwen rotated her ankle; it wasn't broken. "Why didn't you? What's wrong with your shoulder?"

Gareth twitched his shoulder again. "It gives me trouble when I ask it to bear my full weight. It has for a while."

"Why didn't you say something?" Gwen stared at her husband, appalled. "I could have been working on it with a salve all this time."

Gareth shrugged. "You know how it is. I have aches and pains much of the time that come from working with the men. It seemed a small thing." He made a rueful face at Gwen's continued glare. "It won't happen again."

"Especially not if it means that we're stuck here all night." Gwen scrutinized the trap door, which looked farther away than ever.

"Let's look through what the horsemen have left us," Gareth said. "I already have a few ideas about what might get us up there."

But Gwen couldn't see a way. They had rope but nothing to tie it to. None of the trunks were as large as the table, and they were built even less sturdily. The lone chair couldn't get Gareth close enough to the hole to grasp the edge and his weakened shoulder meant he couldn't pull himself through the hole even if he could reach it.

"Why don't you lift me up to stand on your shoulders?" Gwen said.

Gareth observed the hole ruefully. "I could manage that, but your ankle isn't quite right." Gwen made a face and paced around the cellar with determination. Every time she put her foot down, she winced. Gareth found a length of cloth and wrapped her ankle tightly, which helped.

"You sit here. I have an idea." Gareth found a length of rope and took three spears from the rack on the wall.

Gwen sat in the chair with her foot elevated on a trunk and watched him. Then she said, "What's going to happen when we get home?" She'd thought about asking him this a hundred times since they'd left Wales but never quite managed to get the words out. It wasn't that she thought he wouldn't answer, or would be angry, but that she hadn't decided if she really wanted to know.

"What do you mean?" Gareth sat cross-legged on the floor and began to tie a knot in the rope at every foot. When Gwen didn't answer right away, he lifted his head. "You're talking about my duties to Prince Hywel, aren't you?"

Gwen nodded and within the space of a single breath found her throat constricting. It was a stupid time to be in tears and a stupid thing to be in tears about. Gareth put down his rope and crouched in front of her, rubbing a thumb along one of her cheeks and coming away with a salty droplet. He kissed her forehead and then her lips.

"Likely I will go south with the prince," Gareth said. "I do not yet know if I can bring you with me."

"I don't want to be parted from you," Gwen said.

"I know. And I want to be with you. But whether or not it can happen will depend on how restless our Norman and Welsh neighbors in Ceredigion continue to be. It would be one thing to bring you south if I am to assume my regular duties over Prince Hywel's *teulu*. It's quite another to bring you into an ongoing war. The castle at Aberystwyth has burned twice already."

Gwen found that she could look into Gareth's eyes. "What's wrong with our Welsh allies? Is King Cadell not the ally King Owain hoped for?"

"He has settled into his inheritance," Gareth said, returning to his work. He put the three spears together and began to wind the rope around them. "And he has voiced his opinion that Gwynedd should have no hold in Deheubarth."

"Anarawd gave Ceredigion to Gwynedd as thanks for King Owain's help in the 1136 war," Gwen said.

"That's a nice way to think about it," Gareth said flatly, "but the truth is rather that Owain and Cadwaladr annexed it. I do not believe Anarawd was given a choice in the matter. His father was dead—"

"—because Anarawd himself murdered him," Gwen said.

"Yes, but nobody but Prince Hywel knew it at the time," Gareth said. "Regardless, as the new king of Deheubarth, put there by King Owain, he was in no position to argue. That was years ago, and seeing how Anarawd is dead too—" Gareth broke off.

They didn't need to speak of what had happened last August, since solving that case had brought the two of them together, and neither of them was in any danger of forgetting. Prince Cadwaladr had paid mercenaries from Ireland to murder Anarawd and had then abducted Gwen when he thought she was getting close to uncovering his secret. While King Owain had punished Cadwaladr by taking Ceredigion from him, he hadn't given the region to Cadell, Anarawd's heir and brother, but to his son, Prince Hywel.

"I need the chair, *cariad*." Gareth put his hand to the rail at the back. "How's the ankle?"

"Better." Gwen rotated it and found to her surprise that it was better. She stood and let Gareth take the chair. He put it under the hole. In his right hand he held the three six-foot spears, now tied tightly together with a long length of rope.

"You just needed to sit and let some of the swelling go down." Gareth stood on the chair and tossed what he'd created through the hole so it landed with a thud on farmhouse floor. Then he tugged the spears back towards him at an angle and ended up with the spears across the hole and the rope hanging from their center like a candle maker with a fresh wick.

"That's very clever of you," Gwen said, admiring his creation.

Gareth laughed. "Prince Hywel counts on me to figure things like this out." He waved an arm at Gwen, who got up on the chair with him. "I don't know how much weight the spears can hold. A great deal I would think, but if I stand under you and help you up, can you climb this rope?"

"Of course." Gwen hadn't climbed a rope since she was ten—Hywel's doing, naturally—but she reached up to grasp a higher knot and began to shimmy up it. The knots really helped, though she found that, proportionate to her adult body, her arms were far less strong than they had been when she was a girl.

She reached the top and hung suspended, catching her breath. "Now what?" She looked down at Gareth.

"I'm going to put the palms of my hands on the soles of your feet while you haul yourself up over the edge," Gareth said.

It sounded easy when he said it, and as it turned out, it wasn't as difficult as she had thought it might be before she started. A moment later, she lay on her back on the floor of the farmhouse, gasping a little for breath but happy to be out of the cellar.

"Are you all right?" Gareth said.

"Just getting the ladder." Gwen pushed it across the floor to the trapdoor and tipped it downward. Then Gareth climbed out too.

"Excellent," he said. "Let's put everything back the way it was and get out of here."

Gwen agreed with that plan and marveled at how perfectly crafted the house had been, such that when the floorboards were properly arranged again, it looked again as if the cellar wasn't even there. They left the farmhouse, collected the horses, and led them west through the screen of trees. They arrived on the path—and walked right into Llelo and Dai.

15

Gareth

"A merry chase you've led us on, my lord," Dai said, his grin a mile wide.

Llelo and Dai bounced up and down before them, accompanied by a third boy, who towered above them. It was Prior Rhys's servant, Tomos, to whom Gareth had never spoken more than a few words. Hardly older than the boys, he was as thin as a flag pole and dressed in a monk's robe. His brow was furrowed in concern.

Not so Dai and Llelo.

Gareth studied the boys, his hands on his hips. "Llelo. Dai. It's nice to see you. You, too, Brother Tomos."

Tomos nodded his head. "My lord."

"What are you doing here?" Gwen said.

"Not that we aren't pleased to see you whole and well," Gareth said, softening Gwen's stance, "but you were supposed to stay in the camp."

The boys looked at each other, and then Dai answered for his brother, as he often did, even though he was the younger of the two. "We're sorry we disobeyed, but we knew we had to find you."

Gareth's eyes narrowed. "Why would you be looking for us?"

"It is my fault entirely," Tomos said.

"Llelo thought something might be wrong," Dai said. "He was almost in tears just thinking about what might have happened to you."

Llelo shoved at his little brother's shoulder. "Shut it, Dai. That's not it at all. It's the fault of that guard on duty, Ieuan. Tomos came with a message from Prior Rhys, which he said was important. He had already tried to find Evan, Gruffydd, or the princes, but they were nowhere to be seen."

Tomos nodded. "They weren't in their rooms or in the hall."

Gareth made a growling noise low in his throat. "Ieuan was supposed to refer anyone who needed me to Evan."

"We know," Llelo said. "Dai and I overheard you this morning. But Ieuan did nothing! He didn't even try to find you!"

"What was the message?" Gwen said.

Tomos cleared his throat. "Prior Rhys asked that you come to him at Newcastle."

"Did he say why?" Gwen said.

"He didn't tell me, though I asked." Tomos shook his head. "I was to find you and bring you as soon as I could. When

183

Ieuan didn't know where you were, I would have returned to Newcastle then and there, but the boys convinced me that you might be in danger."

"What of the other men? Did you try to speak to someone else?" Gwen said.

Tomos cleared his throat. "The boys seemed to think your mission required secrecy. I see my mistake now, but they convinced me that we'd be better off searching for you on our own."

"Nobody listens to boys." Dai's lower lip stuck out.

Gareth rubbed at his chin. "So you took matters into your own hands."

Dai said, "We did the right thing, didn't we?"

"I didn't know what else to do but to stay with them," Tomos said, continuing his apology. "I feared they would try to find you whether I came with them or not."

Gareth turned to his wife. "There's no point in speculating what Prior Rhys wanted. We should simply return to the castle."

"What about Ieuan?" Dai said.

"I will deal with him when I see him." Gareth checked the sky. "We've been gone *all day*. I don't understand what's happening here."

"How did you get here?" Gwen said.

"Tomos rode. We ran," Dai said.

Gareth laughed and ruffled his hair, no more able to stay angry at the boys than Gwen.

"Do you know Ieuan well? Could he be some kind of traitor, too?" Gwen said, as Gareth boosted her into her saddle. "Or a spy?"

"He's been attached to Prince Rhun's company since last autumn." Gareth adjusted Gwen's foot in her stirrup. "It was foolish of me not to have been on the lookout for treachery in our own camp. I just don't know what else I could have done to avert it."

"I've felt lost since we entered Newcastle," Gwen said. "I think our problem is simply that we're in England."

"Why do you say that?" Llelo said.

"The rules aren't the same," Gwen said, "and I don't just mean that our laws are different from the ones the people live by here. If David had been murdered at Aber, we know exactly what would have happened: King Owain would have turned to Hywel, who would have turned to Gareth. We would have questioned everyone in the castle and systematically chipped away at the lies to get to the truth. But here ... ever since yesterday morning, we've been fumbling about in the dark, with no authority, no ability to question anyone properly, and yet we're still involved with spies and multiple murders. It feels all wrong."

Gareth patted her leg. "I fear it's going to get worse before it gets better. I can send you home if would you prefer it."

Gwen wrinkled her nose at him. "And leave you to settle this yourself? I don't think so."

"It's a genuine offer." Gareth tossed Llelo up to ride behind Gwen, mounted his horse, and pulled Dai up behind him. "I would feel better if you were home, but I'm concerned about you getting there."

"Which is why you aren't going to send me away," Gwen said.

"If he sent you, he'd probably send us too," Llelo said from behind her. "We don't want to go either."

Gwen put out a hand to Gareth. "Alard could be watching us right now."

"I don't think so," Gareth said. "He heard something, or sensed someone approaching, and either met them or fled from them. I have the feeling that in his mind, the farmhouse has served its purpose. Besides which, I don't find the idea that Alard is spying on us as worrisome as I might have when we woke up this morning. He wants something from us, and as long as we appear to be doing as he asks—"

"—though not because he asked it," Gwen said.

"—then we're safe from him," Gareth said. "In fact, I would be more surprised if he didn't find a way to keep an eye on us than if he did. He can't ask questions himself at this point, and it's his name, not ours, that needs clearing."

"What about the safety of Prince Henry?" Gwen said.

"Prince Henry is a concern, but what happens to him is almost entirely out of our hands," Gareth said. "If his mother and Earl Robert don't have him well protected, they're fools."

"You already thought she was foolish for allowing him to come to England in the first place," Gwen said.

"True, though for all that she's his mother, it might not have been entirely up to her." Gareth grinned at the trio of young boys with them: strong-willed sons were rather thick on the ground at present.

They'd come out of the wood on its western side and followed the trail the boys had taken from the camp. Reversing their steps, they now approached the Lyme Brook at a point almost equidistant between their encampment and the castle. Gareth stopped at the ford they would need to cross to return to the castle. "Tomos, I need you to escort the boys back to camp."

"But sir! I must see to Prior Rhys!" Tomos said.

"Not today." Gareth said, putting as much authority as he could into his voice. He poked Dai's leg. "This is where you get off, boys."

Llelo and Dai slid to the ground.

"What? No complaints?" Gwen said.

Dai shook his head. "You're going to the castle. I don't want to enter there. We might never get out again."

187

"And why would that be?" Gareth said.

"Too many Saxons," Llelo said.

Gareth laughed. "I can't disagree. Be off with you, then."

The boys took off running, but Tomos still hesitated. "My lord—"

Gwen leaned in. "Thank you for taking them under your wing when we couldn't—and for listening to them. I would feel better if you stayed with them."

Tomos swallowed, his Adam's apple bobbing up and down. "My duty is to my master."

"We will see to him," Gareth said. "I want you out of harm's way."

Tomos bowed his head. "Yes, my lord." He spurred his horse after Llelo and Dai.

Once Gareth and Gwen were sure the boys were well on their way, they trotted their horses across the ford and turned their heads towards Newcastle. As they approached the gateway, the sun low in the sky behind them, Gareth found himself a little ahead of Gwen. She'd slowed, and he pulled up to wait for her to come abreast. "I feel as reluctant as those boys," she said.

"You could have gone back to the camp with them," Gareth said. "You could go now."

"And wish away the evening waiting for you to return?" Gwen said. "Anything I face in there is better than that."

"We'll see if you still think so by the time the sun sets," Gareth said. "At least we have some news for Hywel."

"I'm glad we heard Alard's side of the story," Gwen said, "though it doesn't make me trust these Normans any more than I did before."

Gareth laughed. "You didn't trust them at all before." He reached out and squeezed her hand.

They passed under the gatehouse. Gruffydd had been keeping an eye out for them, because he came to meet them as they reined in. "Thanks be to God, you're here."

"We feared something was wrong. What is it?" Gareth tossed his reins to the stable boy who waited for them and dropped to the ground. He caught Gwen as she dismounted.

"Prior Rhys and Mari have disappeared," Gruffydd said.

Gareth's expression darkened while the blood drained from Gwen's face. Gareth pulled her to him in a brief hug. "We'll find them. Don't worry."

His words of comfort could only be a kindness. She couldn't help but worry and he knew it, but she came with him up the steps to the keep, limping a little on her wounded ankle.

"This way." Gruffydd eyed Gareth as they crossed the anteroom. "What happened to you?"

"It's a long story," Gareth said. "Who saw them last and at what time?"

"A maid brought Prior Rhys a meal some time after noon," Gruffydd said, "but no one has seen them since."

189

"That must have been about the time he sent a message to you, Gareth," Gwen said.

Gruffydd knocked on a door and entered at Hywel's command. They found themselves in a room Gareth hadn't seen before, not that he'd spent very much time in Newcastle so far. It was decorated with a table and several spindle chairs but little else. No fire burned in the grate, and the shutter was open to the eastern sky. They had no more than an hour until sunset.

At their entrance, Hywel, who'd been looking out the window, turned to face them. "At last. We were just about to send out a search party for you."

"We're safe," Gareth said. "What has happened to Prior Rhys and Mari?"

"We don't know," Rhun said, rising from one of the chairs. "The maid reports that when she brought him a tray of food, the prior was sitting up in bed, awake, with Mari beside him. Nobody has seen either of them since then."

"Could this have something to do with Alard?"

Gareth glanced towards the voice. Sir Amaury leaned against the wall in the corner of the room.

"How could it?" Gwen said.

"Prince Hywel has informed me of Prior Rhys's former identity as one of the horsemen," Amaury said. "Perhaps he went to meet Alard?"

190

"Alard may have contacted Prior Rhys," Gareth said, "but I find it unlikely that Alard abducted them. If they went with them, they did so of their own accord."

"How would you know that?" Amaury took a step forward.

"Because of the hour," Gareth said. "When did the maid say she brought the tray?"

"All she remembered was that the bell had rung for *sext* some time before, but not for *none*," Prince Rhun said, referring to the mid-afternoon toll of the chapel bell, which at the friary would have called the monks to prayer.

Gwen tugged on Gareth's sleeve and spoke in Welsh. "We were at the farmhouse by then, and likely, so was Alard."

"You went to the farmhouse?" Hywel said, in the same language. "The horsemen's farmhouse?"

Gareth nodded. "Gwen told me of it, and she and I decided that we would find it this morning."

Amaury joined their little circle, his brow furrowed. "What are you saying? Speak French so I can understand!"

Gareth pursed his lips, sorry that he had angered Amaury. He'd never seen the Norman knight so worked up. "Gwen and I went looking for Alard today. Instead, Alard found us."

"You spoke to him? What did he say?" Amaury said.

"A great deal," Gareth said. "He insists that while he did kill David, it was because David tried to murder him. He also claims to still be loyal to Maud."

"He would say that," Prince Hywel said.

"As would any man, guilty or not," Gareth said.

"But we believed him—at least enough to keep digging deeper," Gwen said.

Amaury looked at Gareth warily. "Is that why you let him go?"

"I wasn't in a position to gainsay him when he wanted to leave," Gareth said.

With a nod, Amaury bowed. "If you'll excuse me, I must report to Philippe and instruct my men. We should continue the search for Prior Rhys and Mari outside the castle." Amaury departed.

"I've looked everywhere inside Newcastle," Hywel's brow remain furrowed, "even to the point of inspecting the barrels in the cellar for bodies instead of drink."

"Why didn't you tell Amaury about the farmhouse, Gareth?" Gwen said.

"Because he has superiors," Gareth said. "I didn't feel it was my place to reveal that particular secret if Alard and the other horsemen had kept it for so long: not to Amaury, not to Philippe, not to anyone." He looked at Prince Hywel. "I'm surprised you told him that Prior Rhys was a horseman."

"I needed something to reveal," Hywel said, "to encourage his confidence in us. It was either that or speak of the emerald."

"This investigation would be less complicated if everybody would just tell the truth," Gwen said.

"Heaven forfend!" Hywel said. "How unusual that would be!"

"Whatever has happened to Prior Rhys and Mari," Gwen said, "at least we know that Rhys never intended to disappear without telling someone where he was going."

"How so?" Prince Rhun said.

"After he was unable to find you or your brother, Gruffydd, or Evan, he sent Tomos to the camp to find me," Gareth said. "We weren't there, and your man, Ieuan, never passed on the message."

"What?" Prince Rhun said. "Could you be mistaken?"

Gareth shook his head. "Now it seems we have a traitor among us too."

16

Hywel

Hywel was concerned about Mari's absence. Of course he was. But he was also concerned by the fact that he was *concerned*. It had been a long time since he'd paid attention to any woman for more than one night. The trouble with Mari was that he hadn't paid attention to her for any night—and every one of his friends, companions, brothers, and the rest—would have his head if he had.

To add to his difficulties, he had to be courteous and diplomatic to a castle full of Normans, any one of whom he would gladly have faced on a battlefield for the sheer pleasure of spilling Norman blood.

Just this morning, Rhun had lectured him about respecting the opinions of others, even when their beliefs differed from his own. Hywel had nodded politely, but rare was the time when Hywel's internal thoughts coincided with his outward expression. If he spoke what he thought, he would jeopardize everything his father had built in Gwynedd.

So he didn't.

Hywel eyed Gareth and Amaury, who had finally returned from seeing to his men so they could begin the search for Mari and Prior Rhys. Gareth was one of the few men with whom Hywel felt he could share his opinions to any degree. But knowing that Amaury had lied about the empress's presence, even if ordered to by Philippe, made Hywel distrust every word coming from Amaury's mouth.

"My lord." Gareth turned to Hywel. "Amaury suggests that we begin the search along the river."

"In case they drowned?" Hywel said. "Rhys is a wounded man and Mari couldn't have gone ten paces with him outside the castle without someone noticing."

Amaury coughed. "The castle is very busy. There's the postern gate, though we checked with the guard and he saw nothing."

"I assume he wasn't drunk?" Gareth said.

"Or bribed?" Hywel said.

Amaury ran a hand through his hair. "You don't think much of the discipline of my men, do you?"

"Most men can be bought if the price is right," Hywel said.

"Perhaps the wall walk—" Amaury stopped, his face flushing.

"Do you suggest she descended by rope like Alard? Don't be absurd." Hywel knew he was being rude, but he had no patience for this. Mari had been gone most of the day, and

195

Hywel felt like it was his fault. He had deliberately not gone to check on her because of his conflicting emotions, busying himself with meeting and greeting the dozens of Norman noblemen here at Newcastle. And now she'd disappeared to God knew where.

"Mari would go down that rope if she had to, but I can't see her doing it in broad daylight," Gwen said. "Someone would have noticed. Certainly, Prior Rhys would have been in no condition to do so."

"Is there another way out of the castle besides the two gates?" Hywel said.

Gwen peered at Amaury. "You've just had an idea. What is it?"

"There is another way, but I can't imagine..."

Hywel glared at him. To his credit, Amaury didn't wilt under his gaze, and Hywel's estimation of the man went up a notch.

"The tunnel," Amaury said.

"What tunnel?" Rhun said.

"You're not supposed to know about it," Amaury said, "and Philippe will surely have my head for telling you. It runs north from underneath the old motte. Earl Robert started his work on the expansion of Newcastle before he knew of it and decided to continue despite the hole it created in his defenses. It isn't so different from a postern gate except that access to it is more hidden."

"Would Prior Rhys have known of it?" Hywel said.

"Rhys has lived a quiet life since he joined the monastery, or so I understand," Rhun said, "but from what I've seen of the man, he always has his eyes open, watching, even if he's too much of a man of God to pass judgment. I would be surprised if he didn't know of it."

With Rhun's observation, Hywel reminded himself—and not for the first time—that just because his brother thought the best of everyone didn't mean that he was simple. He had a strategic intellect that observed everything, even if he, like Prior Rhys, kept his judgments to himself.

Amaury looked nonplussed. "I don't know about that, but I can tell you that while the initial entrance to the tunnel was in the old keep, built by the original owner of the castle, another entrance was added after the tunnel was explored and enlarged."

"Where's the entrance?" Gareth said.

"I can show you," Amaury said. "It leads away from the river."

"As you would expect," Hywel said, "else it would be full of water year round."

Amaury shrugged. "Earl Robert has great plans for the defenses of the castle, including the construction of a moat, but in order to do that, the tunnel will be drowned."

"I can see how the earl would have to weigh the cost of one verses the benefit of the other," Hywel said. "Will you lead us to it now?"

Amaury didn't answer. He seemed to be warring with himself as to what to do.

"You've told us about it," Gwen said, "and it's too late to take the knowledge back."

Amaury clenched his jaw and then jerked his head in a nod. "I am tasked with discovering the truth about David's death. Earl Robert will forgive me for following where that investigation leads."

"Thank you. Not every man would have your courage to do what was right, even if it means countering a direct order." Hywel bent his neck. "We appreciate your candor."

"I suggest you stay here, my lords," Gareth said to Hywel and Rhun. "It would be better if neither of you involved yourself further in this, for your own safety and in pursuit of amicable relations between Gwynedd and England."

Hywel scoffed. "How could those words have possibly come from your mouth?"

Gareth had the grace to look abashed. "I apologize for suggesting it, my lord, but it *would* be better if you stayed here. Evening is coming on. What if Earl Robert invites you to his table?"

"Then he'll just have to eat with Rhun." Hywel turned to his brother. "You can tell him I'm indisposed."

Rhun nodded. He enjoyed an adventure as much as Hywel, but he was the elder son and took his responsibilities seriously. He knew Hywel would tell him all about it when he got back.

"He doesn't have to know that it won't mean what it usually means," Rhun said in Welsh.

Hywel's eyes narrowed at his brother, suppressing a sudden anger that what Rhun had said was all too true. His reputation among the ladies was well known. While he hadn't always been as circumspect with his women as he might have, he was growing wiser in his old age. Hywel took in a breath and let his shoulders relax. Rhun was right. It was likely that Hywel's reputation had preceded him and would serve him in this instance.

All things being equal, Hywel didn't care one bit about what any Norman might think of him, but he hated to feel at a disadvantage or to be looked down upon. It was bad enough that among Normans, Rhun and he possessed a lesser status because they were born illegitimate. At Newcastle, however, the circumstances of their birth were never mentioned because Earl Robert was a bastard too, and that put them all on equal footing, at least in this.

Hywel gestured to Amaury. "Lead on."

Amaury did, taking them into the basement of the northwest tower of the curtain wall. As they approached the entrance to the tunnel, the two soldiers who guarded it rose to their feet and stood at attention. They'd been sitting at a table. At the sight of Amaury, one of them said, "Sir."

"Has anyone passed this way on your watch?" Amaury said.

"No, sir," the man said.

Hywel looked closer at the man. He'd been looking down, which wasn't unusual for a subordinate. "How long have you been on duty?"

"Since *none*, my lord," the man said, again with downcast eyes.

"We would like to pass this way," Amaury said. "No one is to follow us, is that clear?"

"Yes, my lord," the man said.

The second man had remained silent, his chin up, staring at the wall behind Amaury. He was inordinately tall, which meant that Hywel, who wasn't a short man, had to look up to see into his face as he passed him. The man kept his face impassive. Hywel walked by them and entered the tunnel.

"These English lie too well," he said to Gwen in Welsh.

"It's because they're used to it," Gwen said.

They'd both been speaking in a low voice, but even so, their voices had echoed down the passage. If someone else was down here, he and Gwen had given away their position.

"The time the guard gave us tells us nothing," Gareth said, overhearing, "since we don't know what time Mari and Prior Rhys left his room."

"We know it was after he sent Tomos to Gareth," Gwen said. "I wish he could have spoken to any of you who remained at the castle. Where did you spend the day such that he couldn't find you?"

Hywel let out a sharp burst of air, cursing under his breath for the hundredth time since he'd discovered Mari's absence. "Evan watched my back as I wooed different Norman lords. Rhun and Gruffydd rode to the Earl of Chester's camp and returned to the castle only moments before you arrived. With everyone coming and going so often, I can see why Tomos gave up and rode to find Gareth, but I wish he'd tried harder to find me."

"He's just a boy," Gwen said. "My hope is that Mari and Prior Rhys simply gave up on his return and left the castle of their own volition."

"That is my hope too," Hywel said.

The tunnel looked nothing like the tunnels underneath Aber Castle. Although Hywel's father maintained them and kept them clear of debris, he couldn't keep back the damp, and the ceiling ran only a few inches above Hywel's head. Here, the tunnel was natural, not dug out of the dirt, made by God and of solid stone. The ceiling arched above Hywel's head, curving this way and that as the tunnel meandered downwards from the entrance.

"You said there was more than one passage?" Gwen said.

"I did." Amaury plucked a lantern from where it hung on the wall and handed it to Gareth while he lit a second one. "But only one comes out the other side."

"I assume you know the right one?" Gareth said.

"I do," Amaury said.

"Before we begin, allow me to walk a little ahead and check for footprints," Gareth said.

He held his lantern and cat-walked forward twenty paces, holding the light close to the ground. He went a little further and then came back. "I can't be sure what I'm seeing because I want to see footprints. I'll walk ahead with Amaury because once we pass by, our feet will obscure the prints of those who went before us."

Clear water dripped from the ceiling, reflecting the light of the lanterns off the golden stones that surrounded them. The companions followed Amaury for a quarter of an hour, twisting through this tunnel and that before finally heading upwards again. Hywel could hear Gareth counting his paces in front of him. For Hywel's part, he'd already built a mental map of their journey and could have returned on his own, even in the dark. His senses told him that the tunnel had skirted the village of Newcastle to the west and come out the other side.

Amaury lowered his lantern and stopped. Ahead, a faint light cut through the darkness. "We're almost there."

"I haven't seen any sign so far of Mari and Prior Rhys," Gareth said. "I apologize, my lord, if this was a fool's errand."

"We had to know," Hywel said. "We haven't come out in one piece yet, either."

Gareth took Gwen's hand and now paced with her just behind Hywel. "What are the chances this turns bad?"

Amaury's brows came together. "Why would you even say that?"

Gareth gave a mocking laugh. "Stick with Gwen and me. You'll see."

Hywel smirked, and they exited the tunnel. Like the entrance back at the castle, this one was located in a damp basement. Then his smile faded as he saw the two guards who were supposed to be protecting the tunnel. They sat on benches at a table, heads down on their arms, unmoving.

Gareth shot Amaury a grim smile. "See what I mean? It's inevitable." He released Gwen and put a finger to the neck of the first man. "He's alive."

"This one is too," Gwen said from the opposite side of the table. "His pulse is faint, but present."

"My impulse is to send you back to the castle for help, Gwen, but I don't want you going off on your own," Hywel said.

"We should just go on," Gwen said.

Amaury gestured towards the inclined corridor leading out of the guardroom. "Earl Robert took this over when he claimed Newcastle. We are underneath an old country chapel, long abandoned in favor of St. Giles."

Hywel looked up. The foundations of the church had been grafted onto the natural stones. Thick wooden beams grew from floor to ceiling to support what was above them.

Amaury had already started walking and Hywel followed, but then he stopped when Gwen hesitated, her hand on her stomach. "Are you all right?"

"I'm fine," Gwen said.

"Then let's move. We need to find Mari." Hywel continued on without waiting for her. He'd learned over the years that there were few situations he couldn't handle merely by declaring that he could. Even at fourteen, when his father sent him to roust one of his knights who'd betrayed him, Hywel had sat on his horse, watching the man's steading burn, while a feeling of cold certainty settled onto his shoulders and wrapped itself around him like a cloak. He'd worn that mantle ever since. Hywel could always do what had to be done.

But the anxious feeling he'd felt in his chest ever since he'd learned of Mari's disappearance had him concerned that his surety had abandoned him.

The passage opened into the crypt of the church. Stone sarcophagi had been placed on ledges on either side of the passage. Twenty feet long at most, it ended at a door. "This opens onto a stairway which rises behind the altar in the choir."

"Do you hear voices?" Gwen said, her ear to the wooden panel.

Hywel didn't stop. It was time to move this along. He didn't want to be reckless, but he heard the voices too, and one of them sounded like Mari's. He pulled on the door, which was closed but not locked, and stepped through it, his sword extended. As Amaury had indicated would happen, he stood on a stone slab at the bottom of a set of stairs that rose above him to his own height, approximately six feet.

Gareth had come through the door just behind him, and together they took the stairs up two at a time. They came out behind the altar and turned toward the voices, which were coming from an alcove to their right. Hywel hadn't been able to see the alcove at first due to the pillars that ran from floor to ceiling—or had once done when the chapel had a ceiling.

Amaury hadn't been misleading them when he'd said the chapel was abandoned. Most of the roof was gone, along with three-quarters of the walls. All that was left of the nave were the pillars, the stone altar, and the wall at the back of the church. The chapel had become hardly more than a grassy clearing, though flagstones still poked through the grass near the altar.

Three people stared at them from the former alcove: Mari, Prior Rhys, and a third man Hywel didn't recognize. "*Cariad*, are you all right?" Hywel strode towards Mari and caught her up in his arms before she could answer.

Mari hugged him back, and then he reluctantly released her.

"I'm-I'm fine." Mari's eyes were wide as she clutched his arms.

She then glanced at the third man, a worried expression on her face. Given his greying hair and the lines on his forehead and around his eyes, the stranger was at least twenty years older than Mari and Hywel, similar in age to Prior Rhys, who stood next to him.

"How did you find us?" While Rhys's face was very pale and he clutched his cloak around his shoulders, he didn't waver on his feet. "Did Gareth get my message?"

Hywel gestured to Amaury, who had entered the chapel with Gwen and joined them in the alcove. "Eventually," Hywel said.

"We didn't know where you'd gone, of course, but I thought this was a place worth looking," Amaury said.

Mari released Hywel's hand to hug Gwen and give her a peck on the cheek. "We were very worried," Gwen said.

"I'm sorry to have frightened you," Mari said.

"Mari wanted to tell you where she was going, my lord," Rhys said to Hywel, "but neither she nor Tomos could find you. I did the best I could by sending a message to Gareth."

Hywel made a gesture of dismissal, accepting the apology even though his instinct was the opposite. "All is forgiven if you tell me why."

Mari took in a deep breath. "My lord Hywel, may I introduce you to my father, Ralph de Lacy."

THE FOURTH HORSEMAN

17

Gwen

The older man beside Prior Rhys bowed low. "My lord."

Gwen's hand went to her mouth. Mari gave her a tremulous smile, and Gwen noticed the dried tear tracks on her cheeks that looked to be renewed at any moment.

Hywel was looking daggers at Ralph. "We thought you were dead. You let Mari believe you were dead."

Gwen blinked at the fierceness in Hywel's voice. He was *angry*.

Ralph bowed his head. "I have been serving my empress."

"You left your daughter to fend for herself," Hywel said, "while you've been alive this whole time?"

"I made sure she was cared for—"

"You let her think she no longer had a father!" Hywel's hands clenched into fists.

Ralph didn't flinch or raise his voice. "It was necessary."

Mari put a hand on Hywel's arm and spoke in rapid Welsh. "Thank you, my lord. But it's all right."

"It isn't all right." Hywel was still glaring at Ralph. "Why did you do it? How could you do it? And why reveal yourself now?"

"What I did then, I did out of loyalty to my sovereign, just as I serve her now by coming forward," Ralph said. "As I was just saying to Peter—I mean, Rhys—I have learned of a plot that threatens Prince Henry's life. Saving him is more important than continuing my deception."

"We know of the plot," Amaury said. Gwen glanced at him, curious that like Hywel, his hands were clenching and unclenching as if he were struggling to control his emotions.

"Where have you been all this time?" Gareth said.

"Like Rhys, I changed my name, though instead of retreating to a monastery, I made my way to the court of King Stephen."

"But not because you switched sides?" Gwen said. "You've continued to work for the empress?"

"Yes."

Hywel made an impatient gesture with his hand. "Tell us about this plot and how you discovered it."

"It was a matter of following the emeralds," Ralph said. "I understand you know of them too."

Hywel's arm came around Mari's waist, and he looked down at her. It looked like he'd managed to rein in his temper, because his words were soft, "I wouldn't have had you mention the emerald to your father."

"He knew about the gems already but not for whom they were destined," Mari said. "It seemed important that we pool our information before it was too late."

Hywel nodded and then looked back to Ralph. "Tell us what you do know."

"William de Ypres, King Stephen's spymaster, has been paying off men in the empress's retinue since Stephen was crowned king," Ralph said. "It was to discover who these traitors were that I joined King Stephen's service in the first place."

"How did that come about?" Gareth said. "How did you convince King Stephen of your loyalty?"

"Earl Robert arranged for me to be attached to Ranulf when he was still a member of the King's company. When Ranulf defected to the empress a few years later, I stayed, having established myself as a loyal retainer."

Gareth nodded. "And yet you chose this moment to jeopardize everything for which you've worked so hard?"

Ralph sniffed. "William of Ypres found someone close to the empress who agreed to murder Prince Henry for the payment of four emeralds. I had no choice but to come in the hope that I'd be in time to stop him. I hadn't realized that Prince Henry was due to arrive at Newcastle so soon until my daughter told me of it."

"Why not send a message?" Hywel said.

"I did not dare in case it was intercepted. It has been many years since I lived among Earl Robert's men, and I didn't know whom I could trust. My instincts told me that other than my friend, Alard, I might be able to tell only the empress herself of what I'd learned. When I got word that she would be arriving at Newcastle tomorrow, I resolved to come myself."

Gwen pursed her lips. That was a chain of events she could actually understand.

Ralph continued, "But in the hours since I arrived, David and John have died, Alard is accused of murdering them, my own daughter and former friend are involved somehow— and nobody is at all concerned about the welfare of the prince."

"That would be because we had no idea who might be behind such a plot if that man is not Alard," Gareth said, "and he has strongly asserted his innocence in this matter."

"Was it you on the wall walk with him when we first arrived?" Gwen said. "Was it you who met Alard by the river ... and killed John?"

Ralph's mouth twitched, hinting at a smile, though Gwen couldn't see how taking a man's life could ever be amusing. "I hoped nobody had seen me, either at the castle or beside the river. I was very careful to leave no signs of myself."

"You left boot prints," Gareth said.

"You understand that my first act, after I left King Stephen's court, would have been to contact Alard? He was the only one, besides Rhys and the empress herself, who knew of my mission all these years. Alard and I met in secret every few months—though I hadn't seen him since he was sent to Scotland."

"And the real traitor?" Hywel said.

"I don't know who's behind the plot. The man is surely high up in the empress's ranks," Ralph said.

Amaury stepped into the ring around Ralph. "We need to know everything you do." The Norman's face was both intent and anxious. "Begin with the emeralds, if you will." Then his brow furrowed, and he turned to Hywel. "Tell me, my lord, how is it that you know of them?"

Hywel said: "Could it be Ranulf who is betraying the Empress?"

"I don't know," Ralph said.

"I would know if the traitor was Ranulf," Amaury said, irritation rising in his voice. Hywel had ignored his questions in favor of interrogating Ralph. "I am the castellan at Chester, after all—"

Thwtt!

An arrow whipped by Gwen's cheek and lodged in a pillar to the right of Ralph. It had come so close to her she'd felt the feathers on her skin. Then Amaury staggered and fell to one knee, an arrow high in his chest, near his left collarbone. Gwen gasped, without even the presence of mind to dive to the ground. Fortunately, Gareth, Hywel, and Prior Rhys moved instead: Gareth to throw himself on top of Gwen and bring her to the ground, Hywel to do the same for Mari, and Prior Rhys to clutch at Amaury and cover his body with his own.

"Stay down, all of you!" Gareth said, though he himself lifted his head and gazed around the chapel.

Gwen turned her head to one side. Mari lay in the grass with Hywel crouched over her. She looked at Gwen with wide eyes. "Are you hurt?" Gwen said.

Mari shook her head.

"Where is Ralph?" Hywel said, looking right and left, much like Gareth.

"I don't know!" Gareth moved off of Gwen, cursing under his breath, though he still kept a hand on her shoulder to keep her down. He swiveled on the toe of his boot, scanning their surroundings.

"We need to get the women to safety," Hywel said.

"I know. Come this way." Gareth grabbed Gwen's arm to help her up and urged her towards the back of the altar and the stairs that led down to the crypt. "Stay here."

A moment later, Mari crouched beside her. "What about Amaury?" Gwen said.

Hywel scuttled to where Prior Rhys held the Norman knight in his arms. "How is he?" Hywel said.

"Bleeding, but breathing," Rhys said. "If we can get him help, I don't think the wound has to be fatal. I don't dare withdraw the arrow, however, until we have a way to stop the flow of blood."

"Don't worry about me," Amaury said, his voice low and guttural. "Find Ralph."

"We can do both." Gareth jogged to Rhys's side. Gwen's stomach roiled again, afraid she'd see an arrow appear in his chest.

Hywel glanced towards Mari and Gwen. "I'm sorry, Mari. I don't see your father."

"Likely, the archer is long gone, too," Gareth said.

"You and I should go for help, Gwen. Gareth and Hywel can track my father and the shooter." Mari's face was very pale, but she wasn't in tears.

"That's the best suggestion I've heard all day," Hywel said. "Go, Mari. Now. Through the tunnel."

Gwen caught Mari's arm before she dashed away. "Do you know the tunnel well enough to find your way back? Because I don't."

Mari looked to Hywel, who said, "It would be safer, surely."

"Not if we got lost," Gwen said.

"She's right, my lord," Gareth said. "The archer wasn't after the women. I want them safe, too, but getting lost underneath Newcastle is surely not the best way to accomplish that."

"Send them to the friary for help. Amaury's life depends upon it." Rhys pointed to an arrow lying in the grass ten feet from him. "The archer may not have accomplished what he came for, but he would know better than to remain in his roost this long."

Gareth bent to pick up the arrow. He looked at it and then held it out to Hywel. "There's blood on it."

"Do you think the arrow hit my father?" Mari's voice went high.

Hywel strode to her. "He was well enough to run, and he's an old soldier. He'll be all right."

"They should do as Rhys suggests," Gareth said. "The healer at the friary can send a cart and bandages for Amaury. Perhaps if your father is injured, he will take refuge there as well. You and I, my lord, should do what we can from here."

Mari bobbed her head in jerky agreement. Gwen took her elbow, and the two women set off at a half-run. Their skirts hindered the movement of their legs, but they discarded modesty and lifted their hems, following an overgrown track that started at the front of the abandoned chapel and ran southeast. Gwen wasn't sure if she couldn't feel her ankle because she hadn't injured it very badly or if her anxiety was blocking out the pain.

"Do you know the way to the friary?" Mari said.

Gwen gestured ahead of them. "That's Newcastle there." She could see one of the many towers poking above the trees to the southwest. "I'm following my nose, but the tunnel dumped us out to the north of the town. We might be on the friary lands already without knowing it." Gwen glanced at her friend. "Are you all right?"

"I wouldn't even know," Mari said.

"How did you end up in that clearing with your father and Prior Rhys?"

"A man sent by my father came for us," Mari said. "He was very straightforward about what he wanted. He simply handed me a letter written in my father's hand, asking for Prior Rhys and me to come to him. Prior Rhys didn't want to leave until he'd told someone where we were going. He sent a message to Gareth through his servant, Tomos."

"Unfortunately, we were not at the camp to get it," Gwen said.

Mari nodded. "We'd only talked for a few moments before you arrived."

"But you've been gone for hours," Gwen said. "What have you been doing all this time?"

"Once we arrived at the chapel, the messenger told us that my father would show himself only when he was sure that we hadn't been followed."

Gwen shook her head. "Perhaps he waited too long, given that the archer got so close. Was it he who subdued the two guards at the tunnel's exit?"

"What guards?" Mari said. "What do you mean subdued?"

Gwen pinched her lips together. "I'll tell you later. It's more important to know the rest of what your father said to you."

"We had so little time before you came," Mari said. "He did apologize for leaving me alone."

"Did he tell you why?" Gwen said.

The track led them into the friary from the rear, through the gardens. By now the sun had gone down behind the hills to the west, but Gwen could still see well enough to navigate.

After a short pause, Mari said, "He said disappearing was the only way to protect me."

"From what?" Gwen said. The two women slowed to a walk as they pushed through a gate between an orchard and the kitchen garden.

"I don't know." Mari shrugged. "I'm surprised to find myself calmer than I ever would have expected about it. I can't change my father. I can't change the past. Let's get to the healer."

Gwen and Mari hustled through the garden and almost ran into a brother bending over an herb bed with a hoe, pulling at a last few weeds before the onset of full dark. He straightened. "May I help you?" He was youngish—thirty perhaps—and had kilted his robe so the hem didn't trail in the dirt while he worked. Another man hoed the garden ten feet away. He wore breeches and a shirt, which meant he was a lay brother, not a monk.

"A man has been shot, one of the knights in Earl Ranulf's company," Gwen said without preamble. "We need a stretcher, bandages, and the healer if you have one."

"I am Matthias, the herbalist." Then he pointed at the second man. "Find me three others to help." He turned back to Gwen. "Where?"

"The old chapel." Gwen gestured to the northwest. "Do you know it?"

Matthias's brows drew together in an expression of concern, but he nodded. The other man ran off, still holding his hoe, and Matthias followed, headed towards the center of the monastery. Mari and Gwen trotted after him.

Gwen had seen larger monasteries, but none richer than this friary. The stained glass in the windows, the slate roofs, the well-tended grounds, and the bustle in the courtyard all pointed to considerable wealth. Maybe all monasteries in England were better supported than their Welsh counterparts, but either way, Gwen had hope that their infirmary would be well-stocked, and more importantly, that this healer was knowledgeable. He certainly exuded confidence.

Gwen and Mari arrived in the courtyard, breathless, and pulled up at a sign from the healer. "Wait here."

Gwen bent over, her hands on her knees. She couldn't remember the last time she'd run as far as this. She tried to calculate the relationship of the castle to the friary to the chapel and decided that the three locations formed an uneven triangle, with the chapel at the northernmost point.

Matthias had disappeared, but he came hustling back a quarter of an hour later with another monk. "A cart will meet us on the track that leads to the chapel. Take me to your man."

Breath or no breath, Mari and Gwen set off again. And it was only after they arrived back at the chapel that Gwen remembered Mari's father. She had forgotten to ask about him, and she and Mari had seen no sign of him.

18

Gareth

Gareth watched Mari and Gwen go and then crouched beside Amaury to take his hand. The Norman knight's eyes glinted beneath half-closed lids. "I live, Sir Gareth," he said.

"Don't speak," Prior Rhys said.

Hywel touched Gareth's shoulder, and Gareth moved with him a short distance away. "We need to track both Ralph and the archer. I'd like to know that the latter, at least, is long gone."

"That will be my task," Gareth said, and then added, "I wouldn't have let the women go if I thought they were in danger."

"I know. I'm not worried about them." Hywel glanced to where Amaury lay. The knight's chest rose and fell. "Someone really didn't want Ralph to talk to us."

"He's a poor shot," Gareth said, "I'll say that for him."

"That he used a longbow, not a crossbow, makes him a Welshman," Hywel said.

"Any Welshman whose aim is that bad isn't worthy of the name," Gareth said. "Too bad for Amaury."

"It will be dark soon. Meet me back here before an hour passes," Hywel said.

"Yes, my lord," Gareth said.

That Amaury still lived was one of the few pieces of good news in the last two days. Gareth's comment to Gwen that this investigation got worse with each hour that passed continued to prove true. Bad enough that someone had attacked Gwen and struck Prior Rhys on the head; bad enough that three people had died. A lone archer roaming free in the countryside, against whom it was nearly impossible to defend, left Gareth with an ache behind his eyes. If Prince Henry were to come to Newcastle, they *might* be able to protect him inside the castle. But outside the castle, he'd be an easy target. A mediocre archer could hit a target at a hundred yards, and an excellent archer at four hundred.

Judging the direction from which the arrows had come, the archer had been hiding in the trees to the east of the chapel. An overgrown clearing surrounded the ruin, so it was a matter of crossing a field of patchy grass and scrub to get to the trees. Gareth made his way towards them, keeping to the bushes as best he could. He assumed the archer had fled, but he wasn't going to bet his life on it.

Gareth looked back. He could just see Prior Rhys, still bent of Amaury and fewer than a hundred yards away. The archer could have easily shot them from this place. Gareth inspected the ground at his feet but couldn't make out any specific tracks. He moved along the fringe of the trees, glancing every now and again towards Rhys to make sure he didn't need help. Another few yards along, Gareth came to an old oak. Something bumped into his forehead, and he stopped. Looking up, he saw the knotted end of a rope hanging from the lowest branch, which was at least twelve feet in the air. He hadn't noticed it at first because he'd been looking at the ground.

Gareth tugged on the rope. It didn't give way. Its fibers weren't worn or marred with dirt, as would have occurred if it had been hanging in the tree for a while. Gareth knew he needed to get up there. Even though his shoulder hurt more than he wanted to admit, he gritted his teeth and grasped the rope, climbing hand over hand until he reached the branch onto which the rope had been tied. He pulled himself onto it and sat, rolling his shoulders and shaking out his left arm to loosen it and ease the pain. At last he stood, finding his balance, and slid his feet towards the cleft where the branch met the tree. When he reached it, he looked back.

The whole chapel was laid out before him, perfectly visible through a natural break in the oak's growth that left an eight-foot-wide gap in the branches. Gareth mimed shooting off a bow and revised his estimation of the archer's ability upward. With the oak branch as an unstable platform, hitting Ralph or

Amaury would have meant achieving a tougher shot than if the archer had been standing on the ground.

The only signs that someone might have stood where Gareth himself was standing were scuff marks on the branch, possibly from the archer's boots. Now that Gareth knew what to look for, he climbed out of the tree and found more boot prints in the dirt below the branch. He circled around the tree and began to track the archer away from the chapel, heading east. The soft earth meant the man wasn't hard to follow. The archer had made no attempt to hide his retreat. But another quarter of a mile on, the woods and the prints ended at a deeply rutted, dirt road.

Gareth pulled up and bent to the last boot print. From that point, he moved in a gradually widening circle until he reached the base of another tree where he found the hoof prints of a single horse. Gareth stepped into the road, which carried on due north for a time before being lost in the hills in the distance. Going the other way, the road headed south before curving west. Gareth had never been here before, but the width of the road suggested to him that if he were to follow it, it might take him all the way back to Newcastle.

Suddenly, he heard the thud of a horse's hooves, coming from the south. Gareth's first instinct was to move toward the sound, but then he thought better of that action and retreated to the woods. Soon a riderless horse appeared, pounding down the road towards Gareth. He stepped from the trees, his hands up, making himself as large as possible to slow the racing horse. "Whoa! Whoa!"

The horse had been panicked, but he wasn't wild. Gareth caught his bridle and ran with him a few yards until the horse stopped, breathing hard and whickering.

"That's a good boy." Gareth patted the horse's neck and ran his hands down his legs. The horse was uninjured, but something had to have spooked him to have sent him racing away from his master. Still holding the reins, Gareth walked around to the horse's other side—and noticed the longbow strapped to the saddle bags.

Gareth was already almost through the hour that Hywel had given him, but it was worth the extra time to find where this horse might have left his master. Gareth swung himself into the saddle and directed the horse's head back down the road in the direction from which it had just come. Two hundred yards on, as the road curved west from Gareth's initial position, which was now hidden behind him, Gareth found a dead man. He lay in the brush beside the road, his throat cut.

Damn was the mildest curse Gareth spit out as he dismounted and crouched by the body. Blood still trickled from the man's neck, indicating he'd been killed very recently, and Gareth swiveled on his toes, wondering if he was in danger too. The road was empty of movement, however, and Gareth decided he should just get to work.

He studied the dead man, noting his slender build, well-worn clothing, and cheap leather armor. Then he picked up the man's left hand. The bruising at the wrist indicated that someone had grasped it tightly, even wrenched it. The man's other wrist was undamaged, but something wasn't right with his fingers. Gareth didn't realize what it was until he compared the dead man's fingers to his own. Gareth didn't shoot his bow often, but despite the finger tabs he always wore when shooting, his right hand had callouses from pulling at the bowstring. This man's fingers did not.

Gareth ran his hand through his hair, wondering what the hell it meant. Questions mounted in his mind, not the least of which was whether or not this man was even the archer Gareth had been seeking. The lack of callouses said he wasn't, but the bow on the horse's back said that he was. Furthermore, whatever the man's identity, Gareth wanted to know who had sent him, why had he sent him, and who had killed him. Gareth glanced back the way he'd come, imagining the series of events that had resulted in this death:

The archer fails to kill Ralph, shooting Amaury instead, and without a good angle of fire, gives up and flees to the edge of the woods where he left his horse. He rides south and west (back to Newcastle?) where he encounters another man, perhaps his superior, perhaps someone sent to silence him. One of the men dies but cannot control the horse, which races away. The killer hears Gareth calling to the horse, realizes he is out of time, and flees himself.

Gareth rummaged through the saddle bags, looking for something he could wrap the body with, and came up with a cloak. It was finer than he would have liked to waste on a dead man, but it wasn't his, and he felt that he was out of time and too exposed out here on the road. Although the killer could be a mile away from here by now, he could also be watching Gareth from the trees, waiting for his chance to strike. In the dusk, he would then have all the time he might need to hide both both bodies.

Gareth laid the cloak on the ground and rolled the body into it, all the while trying to look in every direction at once. The blood had mostly stopped seeping from the dead man's wound when he'd lain in the ditch, but as soon as Gareth moved him, the bleeding started again. He'd leave a trail behind him that a blind man could follow.

After untying the quiver and bow from the saddle bags and slinging them on his own back, Gareth threw the body over the horse. Then he took the reins and began walking, not back the way he'd come but towards Newcastle. Fifty yards on, he left the road for the woods. Because had the newly risen moon to guide him by its light and location, he decided that he was better off finding his way back to the chapel by dead reckoning than taking the road to wherever it led.

After a quarter of a mile, Gareth reached a narrow track. He was about to turn onto it when he heard voices coming towards him. A moment later, a cart creaked into view, along with a number of other people on foot. Among them, Gareth recognized his wife.

Gareth lifted a hand in greeting and Hywel, who'd been walking beside one of the monks, quickened his steps to outpace the cart. "Your hour was up long since," said the prince. "Gwen would have had my head if something had happened to you."

"I apologize, my lord, but I couldn't leave him in the road." Gareth gestured to the body on the back of the horse.

Hywel eyed the dead man and then the bow on Gareth's back. "I gather that's what remains of our archer?"

"I don't know who he is," Gareth said, not ready to draw any firm conclusion yet.

"Did you kill him?"

Gareth barked a laugh, unoffended by Hywel's question. "Not I. Someone else killed him moments before I found him, but I didn't see who it was."

Hywel swept a hand through his hair. "The dead are going to be stacked up like firewood in the chapel before we're through."

"Gareth!" Gwen hopped down from the cart when it reached him, and he caught her up in his arms.

"I'm all right," he said.

"I had to trust that you would be," Gwen said.

"How is Amaury?"

The cart carrying the Norman knight passed them by. He lay in the bed, the arrow still rising from his left shoulder. The prior sat in the cart with Amaury, while Mari perched beside him on the rail.

"He's alive," Gwen said. "The healer, Matthias, says the wound isn't as serious as all that, even though it has bled heavily. Even Prior Rhys is reluctantly optimistic."

"We'll take care of him," said a man in monk's robes, walking behind the cart.

"Mari keeps saying that this is her fault because she agreed to meet with her father," Gwen said.

"It is Rhys who should have known better," Gareth said.

Hywel scoffed. "As if he could have done anything else. Mari was going to see her father, with or without him."

"Any luck finding Ralph, my lord?" Gareth said.

"No," Hywel said. "He took to horseback within a dozen yards of the chapel. I couldn't follow him."

"So he's lost to us, too, until he chooses to come in," Gareth said.

"He could be going to the farmhouse," Gwen said.

"He could, but I don't see us waiting for him there on the off-chance he decides to appear," Gareth said. "Unless it was Ralph himself who killed our dead friend, here."

"Possible," Hywel said, "but how likely?"

"I have no idea," Gareth said.

"All we know of him is what he has chosen to tell us, much like Alard," Gwen said.

"We have yet another killer to chase," Gareth said. "We can't afford to hunt for Ralph and Alard, not when they clearly don't want to be found."

"Which reminds me," Hywel said, "you've not yet told me all that you learned from Alard."

As the three companions followed the cart towards the friary, Gareth relayed the gist of their conversation with the empress's horseman. When he'd finished, Hywel came to a halt, standing with one arm across his chest and a finger tapping his chin. "I'm inclined to believe Alard when he says that he killed David in self-defense."

"Alard told the truth about not killing John, too," Gwen said.

Gareth scoffed. "He told the truth, which is to say that Ralph killed him before Alard could get to him."

"We heard all sorts of truths today," Hywel said. "It may even be true that David didn't steal that emerald; he may be a traitor—one of several, apparently—and was given it."

"I would say so, too," Gareth said. "To my mind, however, we've cleared Alard's name."

"Given that both John and David are dead, is the threat to Prince Henry over?" Gwen said.

"I wouldn't assume that," Gareth said. "We have three emeralds unaccounted for."

"My guess, and you know how much I hate guessing," Hywel said, "is that once David was dead, our culprit didn't want anyone to find the emerald among his possessions. He took the body from the chapel so he could retrieve it at his leisure."

Hywel gazed down the road that led to the friary, lost in thought. The cart had disappeared, and Gareth shifted, hoping the movement would prod his prince into action. The dead man hung over the horse, which continued to calmly crop the grass. But the body was cooling, and Gareth wanted to get it inside before it stiffened.

"I wish my father were here," Hywel said. "He would know how to talk to Earl Robert—and whether we should talk to him at all."

"I think you have no choice but to speak to him," Gwen said. "None of what we have discovered will matter if Prince Henry   dies."

19

Hywel

"What do we do now, my lord?" Gareth said as they entered Newcastle's bailey, which was nearly deserted for the first time since the day they arrived.

"I feel honor-bound to speak to the earl and to tell him what we know," Hywel said, dismounting from his borrowed horse and then reaching up to help Mari down from hers. "Immediately."

"Hywel, you cannot. It's past midnight; it's too late to meet with him tonight," she said.

"My father would want to be woken."

"Earl Robert is not your father, my lord," Gareth said.

Which was only too true. Hywel had hoped to keep the emerald. It would make a fine addition to his father's treasury—and his father would have remembered always that Hywel had brought it to him. But events had overtaken them, and they could no longer keep it a secret.

Gareth was right, however, that it was very late. Hywel would have spoken to Philippe back at the friary if the old spy hadn't taken to his bed and given instructions that he wasn't to be disturbed, even for something as important as this. Speaking to the steward of Newcastle wasn't going to be sufficient either. It was Earl Robert or nobody. Hywel would have to wait until morning.

"You should sleep while you can, my lord," Mari said.

He patted her hand as it rested on his arm. "Of course." Hywel just wished Mari would be sleeping beside him instead of Rhun.

Evan came down the steps to the keep to meet them. "I'm very glad to see you, my lord."

"Where's my brother?"

"In your rooms, my lord. Gruffydd is with him."

"Good." Hywel turned to Gareth. "I assume your plan is to return to the friary tonight?"

"Yes, my lord," Gareth said. "I left Gwen asleep in their guest hall. I will speak to Philippe first thing in the morning and then report to you."

"Try to get some sleep yourself," Hywel said, and at the skeptical look that crossed Gareth's face, added, "That's an order."

"Yes, my lord."

* * * * *

The next morning, Hywel and Rhun appeared in the great hall well before the time most of the inhabitants of the castle chose to rise and asked for an audience with the earl. Perhaps Philippe had already sent a message with some of the details of the events of the previous night, because the steward showed them immediately into his receiving room.

As they entered, the earl sat with his elbow on the arm of his chair, a finger to his lips. The table in front of him was clear of documents. No fire burned in the grate, even on this cool morning, which Hywel took to be a sign of Earl Robert's celebrated toughness. He was a warrior who didn't need to be coddled.

Hywel and Rhun hadn't spoken at length with Earl Robert since that first morning. They'd assumed others had been keeping him apprised of the progress of the investigation, but they still told him everything they'd learned in the hours since David's body had fallen at Gwen's feet. The earl seemed to accept it all with equanimity, even the resurrection of Ralph and Prior Rhys. But when they mentioned the gems, the Earl leaned forward and began tapping his fingers on the table in irritation.

"The emeralds were meant for Alard, clearly," Earl Robert said.

Earl Robert's instant assumption set Hywel back on his heels, since it went against everything Hywel had just relayed. "Alard insists that he remains loyal to the empress."

233

Earl Robert's eyes narrowed. "Your man should have arrested him so he could have been questioned."

"Gareth was at something of a disadvantage at the time," Hywel said. "Alard came upon him when Gareth was with his wife. He could not both protect her and capture Alard."

Earl Robert pulled on his lower lip. "Philippe says Alard is the traitor, and I trust his instincts. He has been with the empress longer than Alard—almost as long as I have, in point of fact."

"Long acquaintance is no barrier to animosity," Rhun said.

Hywel agreed with Rhun and could have said, *look at my Uncle Cadwaladr.*

"Is that an accusation of Philippe?" Earl Robert said. "I'm shocked that you would even think it. He's dying. What would he gain by switching camps now?"

"I cannot answer that. I tried to speak to him after we brought Amaury to the friary, but he was indisposed," Hywel said. "But I must point out that Philippe is a spy. He lives and breathes lies as much as Alard does."

Earl Robert sat back in his chair, his hands clasped before his lips, and contemplated the two Welsh princes. "May I see the gem?"

Accepting that they were moving on from the topic of the traitor's identity, Hywel removed the emerald from his scrip—having retrieved it the night before from Gareth—and placed it on the table between them. Earl Robert leaned forward, turning the emerald over with one finger. "Gwen found this in David's cloak?"

"Yes, my lord," Rhun said.

Hywel cleared his throat. "When we spoke with you shortly after David's death, you implied that you didn't know him, but as one of your sister's four horsemen, you did know who he was, did you not?"

Robert looked up at Hywel and then back to the gem. "I did."

When Earl Robert didn't continue speaking, Hywel realized he'd received the only apology for being lied to he was going to get.

The earl turned the gem over on the table one more time and then flicked it towards Hywel in an act of dismissal. "This is poor specimen. Keep it."

Hywel eyed him carefully and didn't pick up the gem. "My lord?"

"It is payment from an enemy to a traitor. Its very existence sullies my house."

Such an attitude was completely foreign to Hywel. Gems and gold meant wealth, which led to power. But when the earl didn't retract his statement, Hywel reached out a hand and picked up the emerald. "Of course." He handed it to Rhun, who stowed it in his scrip.

Earl Robert breathed deeply in and out through his nose. "Whether or not Alard is a traitor or friend, it is now definite that not only do I have one traitor to my sister's cause, I have several."

"You have at least three," Hywel said. "I understand the delicacy with which I must speak on this matter, but while David owed the empress his ultimate allegiance, of late he'd worked within Ranulf's retinue. It was Ranulf who first told you that Alard was a traitor, and he has an army of men loyal to him, many of whom would do his bidding regardless of what he asked. Can you be sure of his loyalties?"

"I apologize for my brother's impertinence, my lord." Rhun kicked Hywel under the table. Hywel wasn't bothered. Rhun was far more concerned about the social niceties than he was, and Hywel had asked what needed asking.

Earl Robert didn't answer either of them right away, and the two princes let the silence draw out. Then Earl Robert seemed to shake himself. "As you indicated, it is not always easy to know where a man's loyalty lies, but I believe that my son-in-law is faithful to me and to my sister."

That was what Amaury had said, too. Hywel bowed his head. "I apologize, my lord. I felt it necessary to ask."

"Ranulf's thoughts do tend to focus on himself," Earl Robert said. "You would not be the clever young man I understand you to be if you didn't wonder about Ranulf. But I believe you must look elsewhere for your current traitor."

"Yes, my lord," Hywel said.

"When does Prince Henry arrive?" Rhun said.

"Tomorrow," Earl Robert said.

"And the empress arrives today?" Hywel said.

"She's already here."

* * * * *

Mari hadn't been far from Hywel's thoughts from the moment she'd put a hand on his arm and asked for Gwen's whereabouts that first day at Newcastle, but he'd managed to push his feelings for her to the back of his mind during his conversation with Earl Robert.

They came back full bore, however, when he saw her standing in the hallway with the look of someone who was prepared to wait, her eyes downcast and her hands folded in front of her. He was barely able to prevent his tongue from hanging out of his mouth when he looked at her. He wanted her in his bed that very instant, all the more so because she looked every inch the Norman lady, aloof and untouchable. A snide comment rose to his lips that he instantly swallowed. He didn't feel snide about her at all and didn't want to hold her at arm's length any longer. He wasn't angry at Mari. He was irritated at Earl Robert for not stopping this traitor long before, at society for its overbearing morals, and at himself for wanting her—not necessarily in that order.

"Mari, what are you doing here?"

"I came to find you," she said.

"Is it about Amaury?" Hywel said.

"Amaury is doing well. The bleeding is contained, and the healer says the arrow didn't puncture a lung. So he should continue to irritate you for many years to come, my lord." Mari cast a quick glance at him as she spoke those last words, a smile on her lips, before looking down again.

"Are you ... mocking me?" Hywel bent slightly at the waist, trying to see into her face.

Mari continued to stare down at her feet, but Hywel could have sworn that her mouth twitched. Hywel found his hand coming up to her arm, itching to touch her, and then he put his finger under her chin and lifted it. As he had supposed, she was smiling. He dropped his hand. "Why do you think I don't like Amaury?"

"He is both too opaque and too transparent for you," she said.

Hywel bit his lip. He hadn't considered Amaury in that light before and wouldn't have put it that way, but Mari was right.

When he'd touched her, he'd moved closer than propriety allowed, especially in so public a space, and would have moved away again, except that Mari chose that moment to touch his hand. Her blue eyes regarded him with a clear certainty that caused his heart to skip a beat, and he held her hand tightly in his.

Hywel cleared his throat. "Did you come here to speak to me about Amaury or was there something else?"

"It's my father. I don't know what to think about him."

Hywel pursed his lips. "I'm sorry, Mari. I don't know that I can be of help to you in this because I don't know what to think of him either."

"I want to believe that he thought he was doing the right thing, but to have abandoned me, his only daughter ..." She bowed her head again, and this time when Hywel lifted her chin, he saw tears.

With is other hand, he rubbed gently at Mari's arm, the smooth fabric of her dress teasing his thumb. "We'll find him and you two can have a chance to talk, long and in private. Until then, you don't have to decide anything about him at all. While he valued you less than his obligation to the empress, that is a tale many men might tell. He still loves you, that is plain, or he would not have gone to such lengths to meet you."

"Last night before retiring to bed, I spoke with Uncle Goronwy. He had no idea that my father had been alive all this time. He's had no contact with him."

Hywel's thumb stopped moving. "You told Goronwy that your father was alive?"

"Yes, of course. Wasn't I supposed to?"

Hywel took in a breath and let it out. The whole castle might know of Ralph's resurrection by now, and there was nothing he could do about it. "I forget that you aren't used to keeping secrets."

"My father is loyal to the empress, and by appearing here, he has exposed himself for who he is," Mari said. "Honestly, it never occurred to me that he would try to return to King Stephen after this."

Hywel found his irritation turning to admiration. "You are as devious as your father."

"Excuse me?" Mari said.

"You come to me all quiet and obedient, but you told Goronwy about your father on purpose, to prevent him from leaving you again."

Mari's mouth fell open. "I didn't—"

Hywel scoffed. "Don't lie to me." Then he sobered and grasped both of her arms to pull her closer. He looked down at her, their faces only inches apart. "Never lie to me."

Mari licked her lips. "Gwen told me to stay away from you."

Hywel felt the floorboards shift beneath his feet at the change of tone. "I won't pretend not to know what you're talking about. Gwen is right. You should stay away from me."

"Gwen isn't right. She doesn't know you like I do," Mari said.

240

Hywel couldn't swallow around his suddenly dry throat. He desperately wanted to crush Mari against him and kiss her. "How so?"

"I'm not saying that you are a good man in the way a priest is a good man, but I've watched you for years, you know, ever since I came to Uncle Goronwy's house. When you make up your mind about something, you follow it through. You demand the truth from others, and you don't lie to yourself either. And if you want something badly enough, you move heaven and earth to get it."

Hywel looked left and right, willing nobody to be watching them so he wouldn't have to step away from her. "I'm not that honorable."

"I didn't say you were honorable. In fact, I'm almost hoping you're not." And with that, Mari went up on her tiptoes, pecked Hywel once on the lips—and fled.

Hywel found himself standing alone in the corridor, still feeling the soft pressure of her lips on his and genuine laughter bubbling up in his chest.

20

Gwen

The bells for *sext*, the mid-day prayer, came and went as Gwen sat with Amaury and held his hand, though the Norman knight didn't know it. He had survived the night and was neither dead nor fevered, just asleep. Gwen looked over at Gareth, who stood speaking with the healer. Gareth had been busy at the friary all morning: he'd spent an hour in consultation with Philippe, examined the bodies of both John and the archer, and questioned anyone else who had been willing to give him a moment of his time.

At Gwen's glance, Gareth finished his conversation with Matthias and walked to the bedside. "I'm glad to see Amaury alive, but we should return to the castle."

"Will Amaury be safe here?" Gwen said.

"Guards are posted around the friary because the empress is now in residence. Philippe assures me that, if the arrow was meant for Amaury, he will be well-protected here."

Gwen was still concerned. "I feel as if we've missed something."

"I know," Gareth said. "We started out many steps behind the traitor, which is usual, of course, but few weeks have ever gone as badly awry as this one, and I don't feel like we're catching up."

"Prince Cadwaladr was such an easy villain," Gwen said. "In Gwynedd, his name is synonymous with treachery. But here, it's different. There are too many possible culprits, and either our informants don't tell us the truth, or the traitor gets to them before we do and silences them."

"Or they're dead, or are accused of murder and treason themselves," Gareth said.

"You mean Alard?"

"Alard and Ralph," Gareth said. "Neither of them has survived this long by being stupid. I'd rather be working with them than hunting them."

"Are we hunting Ralph?" Gwen said.

"Philippe seems to think we should be," Gareth said. "While I wish we'd learned more about what he knows in the few moments we had with him, he refuses to come in, and there's nothing I can do about it."

"Perhaps Ralph is afraid he might accidently betray Alard, by word or deed," Gwen said. "Philippe hasn't changed his mind about Alard, even with the new evidence we've discovered."

Gareth scoffed. "Philippe thinks Alard was the archer."

Gwen stared at him. "How does that make sense?"

"The dead man was one of Philippe's. Philippe claims that his man came upon Alard and died trying to bring him in. Naturally, Philippe says the horse, bow, and arrow were Alard's." Gareth shrugged. "It would explain the lack of callouses on the dead man's fingers."

"It might explain that but nothing else," Gwen said. "The idea is so absurd, I can almost see how Philippe could believe it."

"I don't want to speak more about this here. It's time we went back to the castle, and we can talk on the way." Gareth took Gwen's arm and led her out of the infirmary. They crossed the courtyard to the gatehouse and started down the road to the castle. Gwen was glad that she had boots on instead of her slippers, which were back in her tent at the Welsh camp, but she still took two steps for every one of Gareth's.

"Let's think about the series of events we have here," Gareth said, settling into a loose-hipped stride beside Gwen. "Four emeralds come to Newcastle, sent by William of Ypres. David acquires one, either for services rendered, about to be rendered, or by theft, which I still haven't ruled out entirely. Regardless of how or why, he attacks Alard, who kills him in self-defense, or so he says, and then Ralph kills John for the same reason. We don't know if John ever had an emerald on him. He didn't when I examined him."

"After Ralph killed John, he could have taken the emerald," Gwen said.

"Are you suggesting that Ralph could be our traitor?" Gareth laughed. "Ralph knew of the emeralds, obviously, since they are what brought him to Newcastle in the first place. I suppose he could have arranged for the archer to shoot Amaury, knowing we'd assume the arrows were meant for him."

"Philippe could construct a good argument for why Ralph is the traitor," Gwen said. "I know Ralph is Mari's father, but faking his own death is surely an extreme act, even for a spy."

"Prior Rhys did it, too," Gareth said.

Gwen nodded. "And we like him and want to trust him, so why not give the same benefit of the doubt to Mari's father?"

Gareth shrugged. "We don't know him."

"At least we have a little more information than we did. Ralph is extremely lucky that no one recognized him before now," Gwen said. "I don't see how he managed to continue this deception for so long."

"It's been anarchy in England for the last five years, and the distance from Chester to Kent is greater than ever," Gareth said. "You know as well as I do how many hundreds of men are associated with each royal court. If Ralph changed his appearance and kept to himself, he could pass as another man and make himself scarce during the few times the two sides have met in council."

"Wales is a much smaller place," Gwen admitted, "and although I've traveled the length and breadth of it, I have hardly met any noblemen from the south."

"I haven't either."

They were approaching the outskirts of Newcastle, and the entrance to the castle lay ahead of them to the left of the road. "I am worried about Mari," Gwen said. "The resurrection of her father has shaken her."

"I can't imagine what I would be thinking if one of my parents rose from the dead," Gareth said.

"Ralph more than rose from the dead," Gwen said. "He rose and then disappeared again almost immediately after. Mari doesn't know if she will ever see him again. I just hope she doesn't do something reckless."

Gareth pulled up near the castle gate. "What do you mean?"

"Mari is smart but vulnerable, and ... well ... Hywel is very handsome."

"Prince Hywel knows that Mari is not a girl he can take to his bed and then toss aside afterwards," Gareth said.

"He might know it, but I'm not sure she does," Gwen said. "When she climbed into that cart with Amaury, I saw a wildness in her eyes. She wanted to be involved in the investigation, but I don't think she was prepared for any of what has happened."

"None of us were," Gareth said.

"But you and I are used to it."

Gareth put an arm around Gwen's shoulders. "Am I a bad husband for putting my wife into a situation where that could possibly be true?"

"At least working on an investigation allows us to stay together," Gwen said. "Hywel is used to relying on us."

"Make way! Make way for Empress Maud!" a man shouted from the top of the gatehouse tower.

Gareth and Gwen hustled through the gatehouse and into the outer bailey. If they'd waited any longer, they would have been run over by the cavalcade of horsemen riding after them.

"I'm hungry." Gwen checked the position of the sun in the sky. "Are we to dine in the hall?"

"Hywel said we should," Gareth said, "and I wouldn't want to miss it. All the world will be on display today."

* * * * *

The gossip about Empress Maud was that she was arrogant and vindictive, with a stubborn streak bordering on pig-headedness. And that was exactly how she behaved when she arrived at the castle. When it was time to eat, the empress swept into the great hall with her entourage, paraded between the tables as all the guests bowed low, and didn't look at any of the noblemen in the hall but her brother, who went down on one knee before her.

Even once she reached him, she barely acknowledged his obeisance, waving a hand dismissively as she passed him, and then didn't give him leave to rise until she'd reached her chair. Given that he was the most powerful man in England besides King Stephen, not to mention the only reason Maud hadn't been defeated in this war already, Gwen thought she should have treated him better. She said as much to Gareth.

"This isn't Wales, Gwen. The empress believes she is England's intended queen and that God works through her."

"Some of the Welsh kings would like to think that," Gwen said.

"Why else fight so hard and so long?" Gareth said. "Her support dwindles, and yet she continues, Earl Robert at her side."

"She has too much pride to do anything different," Gwen said, "and she sees herself as holding the crown in trust for her son."

They were sitting in the middle of one of the numerous tables in the hall. So many people needed to be fed that the steward of the castle had made it clear that the diners at the lower tables were to eat on a rotating basis. When they were done eating, Gareth and Gwen would have to give up their seats to someone else.

The pair across from them, a knight and his wife from Chester, excused themselves, and Evan and Gruffydd sat down in their seats, immediately setting to their food. A moment later, another seat opened up and Prior Rhys joined them. Gwen hadn't seen Rhys since last evening at the chapel.

"Have you been to see Amaury today?" she said.

"I've just come from the friary," Rhys said. "Amaury wakes to sleep again, but I am hopeful for a full recovery. The friary's infirmary is well-stocked with herbs, and Matthias is knowledgeable."

"It's the onset of a fever we must worry about—"

"I know," Prior Rhys said, not letting Gwen finish, but then he softened his tone. "I am worried too, but Amaury's wound is high in his left shoulder and did little more than damage his tissues. He is in God's hands, and God is good."

Gwen nodded, wanting to believe that Rhys was right. He joined Evan and Gruffydd in their meal, and Gwen let him eat without interruption. She turned away to observe the high table. "Not much in the way of joy up there," she said to Gareth.

Gareth glanced up the hall and then took a longer second look. "Where are the princes?"

"We're here," said Prince Rhun, as he and Hywel appeared on either side of Gareth and Gwen, Mari in tow.

Everybody made room for them. "We thought it best to make ourselves scarce," Hywel said. "The empress is in a very bad mood."

"Likely, someone has told her about the horsemen," Gwen said.

Mari squeezed in between Hywel and Gwen. Her eyes were bright and her color high. Gwen glanced at her and then past her to Hywel, who had grabbed a trencher and begun piling food on it to share with Mari.

"How are you?" Gwen said.

"Very well," Mari said, absently, as Hywel distracted her with a hunk of bread dipped in gravy. She took it and then turned to look at Gwen more fully. "Really, I'm fine."

"Have you heard from your father?" Gwen watched Mari's face closely, but Mari simply shook her head. Her cheerful mood, despite the lack of news about her father, confused Gwen—until Hywel leaned in to whisper something in Mari's ear.

Mari giggled.

Gwen's heart sank. While she worried that Hywel wasn't capable of being faithful to any woman and would ultimately break her friend's heart, Gwen had to acknowledge Mari's delight at the attention Hywel was giving her. It was nice to see Mari happy. Hywel was charming and funny, and when he trained his attention on a girl, she felt as if nobody else existed in the world for him but her. That didn't make him someone to get involved with, however, not for Gwen once upon a time, and not for Mari now. Mari, however, wasn't behaving like a girl who believed that.

At the same time, circumstances had been different for Gwen. Her station as the daughter of a bard, even King Owain's court bard, meant that all she could have been to Hywel was his lover. Mari could become his wife.

Gareth put a hand on Gwen's thigh. "Let it go, Gwen," he said in a low voice. "Mari is your friend, but Prince Hywel is our master. Whatever happens between them cannot be our concern."

Gwen ground her teeth together but nodded, looking down at the trencher she shared with Gareth. As usual, he'd eaten three-quarters of what they'd put on it. She nibbled on a piece of bread, contemplating the dishes before them and wondering if she could feign interest in more food to provide an excuse for staying longer at the meal and keeping an eye on Mari.

As she reached out to spoon more food onto the trencher, the door to the hall swung open. A man in a travel-stained cloak strode through it, followed by three other men. Hywel leaned forward to look down the table at Rhun, who nodded. Both princes stood, and then Prince Hywel tapped Gareth's shoulder, his eyes on the messenger as he marched down the hall towards the high table. "We may need you." When the other men made to rise as well, the prince added, "Stay with Mari and Gwen. If the news isn't good, I'll want you to escort them to our camp."

"Yes, my lord," Evan said.

251

But if Hywel had intended to make his way towards the high table, he was thwarted by the sudden crowd of men who had the same idea as he did and who blocked the aisle between their table and the wall. All they could do was watch the messenger. Gareth put his head next to Gwen's. "For him to enter the hall this way means that something important has happened and the empress doesn't mind everyone knowing about it."

"What do you mean?" Mari said, looking first at Gareth, and then over to Hywel, who stood with his arms folded across his chest, his jaw tight. "The messenger has just arrived."

"So it is meant to appear," Gareth said, "but our empress hates surprises and her retainers know that. He would have reported first to her personal steward, who would have then told her the news. At that point, she would have decided whether or not to share it with the hall. Watch her face. She won't be surprised by what he has to say."

The messenger went down on one knee before the dais, as seemed to be required in the empress's presence. She stood from her position at the center of the high table and raised a hand. "Rise and speak."

"I have news of a great victory, my queen. Four days ago, King Stephen's forces attacked Lincoln Castle, but they have already been defeated. King Stephen has skulked away like a dog with his tail between his legs!"

Ranulf, whose half-brother held Lincoln for the empress, leapt to his feet. In the uproar that followed, he came around the table, grasped the messenger's cloak at the shoulders, and shook him. "Tell me! Tell me everything!"

Ranulf's words cut through the chatter among the tables, and in an instant the crowd quieted, neighbor shushing neighbor as they strained to listen.

"It was a miracle, my lord," the messenger said, clearly reveling in the information he could impart. "Eighty of King Stephen's men were killed when a siege tower collapsed. The rest of his army departed in the night."

Ranulf swung around to look not at the empress, whose face held a supercilious smile, but at Earl Robert. The earl hadn't risen to his feet and merely looked back at his son-in-law while plucking at his lower lip with two fingers. Though Ranulf's reaction seemed genuine, and the empress glowed at the news, Earl Robert wasn't even trying to feign surprise. "That is good news indeed," he said.

"My empress," Ranulf bowed before Maud, "I must ride to Lincoln immediately to support my brother in case Stephen returns. With your permission."

Empress Maud waved a hand in a magnanimous gesture. "Of course."

Ranulf strode off the dais, heading towards a far door, as if he would leave Newcastle that instant. Maybe he meant to.

SARAH WOODBURY

After a moment, with similar permission from his sister, given with a wave of her hand, Earl Robert followed Ranulf.

"I wish I could be a fly on the wall to overhear the conversation those two are about to have," Mari said.

Gwen couldn't disagree. "What does this mean for our investigation?"

"I have no idea." Gareth turned to Hywel. "What say you, my lord?"

"With Ranulf leaving, Amaury wounded, and Earl Robert focused on Prince Henry's arrival, we may be the only ones left interested in asking questions," Hywel said.

Gareth rubbed his chin. "That's unfortunate, because I still have far too many of them."

21

Gareth

"I need you to see to Mari's safety," Hywel said.

Gareth had already seen to Gwen's, without engendering much in the way of protest from her. She'd looked exhausted, and Prior Rhys had claimed that it would be his pleasure to escort her back to the camp. Gareth had watched her go with some trepidation, but with some relief too. She was out of it for the night. He hoped.

Gareth looked at his lord. "Of course."

Hywel glanced to where Mari still sat with Rhun, Gruffydd, and Evan. "The empress may well keep us occupied for hours. I need you to escort Mari to the women's solar, and then do what you can to continue the investigation." He pursed his lips. "There are too many killers here altogether."

"We are all killers when we choose to be," Gareth said.

"Exactly my point." Hywel had been looking around the hall as he was speaking but now turned his gaze fully on Gareth. "What's wrong with you tonight?"

"Excuse me?"

"You spent most of the meal glaring at me."

"Gwen is concerned ..." Gareth snapped his mouth shut, knowing instantly that he shouldn't have brought Gwen into this.

"This is about Mari, is that it?"

"Yes, my lord," Gareth said, taking refuge in formality.

Hywel snorted under his breath. "What does Gwen think I'm going to do to Mari?"

Gareth cleared his throat. "I—"

"Don't answer that. Gwen is a married woman now, but even before that, my liaisons never concerned her." Hywel narrowed his eyes at Gareth. "Does she—do you—think so little of me as to believe that I would harm Mari in any way?"

Gareth found himself coloring. This had become a disconcertingly frank conversation. "She did not ask me to speak to you. I urged her to accept your relationship with Mari. You are our liege lord and we have no business interfering."

"How kind of you to be so understanding." Hywel studied Gareth for a moment and then looked at Mari. His expression softened.

Gareth recognized what was in his lord's eyes, for Gareth felt the same when he looked at Gwen.

"I haven't felt this way about a woman since ..." Hywel didn't finish his sentence, but Gareth didn't need him to. He'd been among those who'd had to pick up the pieces three years ago after Hywel had lost his lover and her babe. Love and loss were entwined in Hywel's world as much as they were in Gareth's.

Hywel turned back to Gareth. "My intentions are honorable, my friend." He clapped Gareth on the shoulder. "I'd appreciate it if you would put Gwen's mind at rest."

"Yes, my lord," Gareth said, relieved that he'd escaped the conversation unscathed.

Gareth escorted Mari upstairs as Hywel requested and then felt himself at loose ends, unsure of how to proceed at such a late hour. The princes were occupied with the empress, Gruffydd in attendance, and at Hywel's insistence, Evan was posted in the hallway outside the women's solar until Hywel could come to check on Mari himself. Gareth found himself in the bailey, where the crowd was just as large as ever. Half the knights in Newcastle were being housed in the town because there was no more room in the friary or the castle.

Gareth decided he would check on Amaury. Taking his horse's reins from the stable boy, he headed for the gatehouse. Such was the crush of men and horses entering and exiting that Gareth was jostled several times. The third time someone elbowed him in the back, he turned, trying to control his temper, and found himself facing a man who studied him with keen eyes from underneath his hood. It was Alard.

Gareth faced front again and continued walking, very aware of how closely Alard was following him. While Alard kept his face averted, Gareth lifted a hand to the guard watching the entrance, who by now knew him by sight. The guard, trained to stop men from entering the castle as opposed to leaving it, waved them through.

Gareth paced a dozen yards away from the castle entrance before he turned on the Norman spy. "What are you doing here? What if someone had recognized you?"

"Now that Empress Maud has arrived at Newcastle, I must speak with her, to plead my case. I hoped that you could get me in to see her."

"Not I," Gareth said. "Abandon the idea. Earl Robert's orders are to arrest you if we can or to kill you if you resist."

"I must try."

"She's meeting with her brother and counselors right now, including my princes. You'll never get past the guards at the door, not even if I accompany you. Such is the feeling against you that I fear they would cut you down and say you were killed trying to escape."

Alard cursed and kicked at a clod of dirt in the road. "Might Prince Hywel defend me?"

"All of us have been defending you," Gareth said. "It has done no good."

"Has the empress spoken yet with Philippe?"

"You should assume that she has," Gareth said. "During the evening meal, before the messenger arrived from Lincoln, her expression could have curdled milk."

Alard looked down at the ground. "Once the empress gets an idea in her head, it is nearly impossible to unfix it. I am a condemned man."

"You've been a condemned man for some time now. You may have had hope, but I wouldn't view your current situation as changed in any way." Gareth turned away and began walking down the road to the friary, leading his horse. Alard fell into step beside him, behaving as if he wasn't a hunted man and could walk wherever he pleased. Because Alard appeared unconcerned about getting under cover, Gareth didn't broach the subject.

Huts clustered to the left of the road, and the bell at St. Giles, the village church, tolled for compline. Most of the village's huts and its market stood between the church and the castle, with the friary on the southeastern outskirts. As they left the village behind, the entrance to the friary came into view, lit with torches.

"You're taking a risk, not turning me in," Alard said.

Gareth kept walking. "Am I? My obligation is to my prince and after that to my king."

"The empress might not see it that way," Alard said. "If you were to arrest me, it might raise her estimation of your princes; she might favor them."

Gareth pulled up. "Is that really what you think of us?"

Alard licked his lips. He hadn't pushed back his hood, even in the dark of the road, and the lower half of his face was all Gareth could see. "What do you mean?"

A party of knights rode by them, heading for the friary. Alard took a step towards the trees that lined the right side of the road, turning his head away so he wouldn't be recognized.

Once the horsemen were past, Gareth started walking again. He shook his head, thinking about Alard's query. At times, the difference between his mindset and a Norman's was vast and unbridgeable.

Alard took a couple of extra steps at a trot to catch up. "I apologize, Sir Gareth, if I offended you, but I don't see the offense."

"Prince Hywel and Rhun didn't come to Newcastle to curry favor," Gareth said. "There is nothing that Earl Robert or the empress can do for them that will aid them, other than rein in some of their more belligerent lords whose lands abut Gwynedd. They don't want a place in the royal court. They don't need the empress's favor."

"I see," Alard said.

Gareth wasn't sure that he really did, so he explained further: "We came here at Earl Robert's request. King Owain hopes for an alliance of some kind, but would rather have none than appear as a petitioner. The King of Gwynedd wants peace and the freedom to govern his domains without interference from England. Prince Hywel and Rhun are ambassadors, not supplicants."

Alard nodded. "I might suggest that you are naïve, but I do not wish to offend again. Still, you owe me nothing either. Why *not* turn me in?"

"If Prince Hywel returns to Gwynedd without learning the truth of these events," Gareth said, "his father will be disappointed."

Alard made to scoff, but when Gareth didn't amend his statement, he swallowed it back down. "You're serious?"

Gareth shrugged. "At the very least, Prince Hywel wants to shed light on David's death so that his father can calculate the size of his losses. It is David's death, however, that seems to be the least of anyone else's concerns."

"David attacked me; I killed him," Alard said. "What more do you need to know?"

"But why did he attack you?" Gareth said. "Who sent him?"

"Philippe, of course."

"Philippe told me forthrightly that he didn't," Gareth said.

Alard rubbed his chin. "Why would he lie about something like that?"

"Thus, my point," Gareth said.

"Philippe is a dying man," Alard said, as if it was something he was loath to admit. "His mind isn't what it once was."

"Are you suggesting he doesn't remember sending David after you?" Gareth said.

"No ... no. You're right. He's lying."

"I wouldn't be so sure." The voice came from the trees to the right of the road, and then Ralph stepped out in front of Gareth and Alard.

Gareth was getting used to the way these spies appeared out of nowhere. "You were waiting for us." He turned to Alard. "Were you really trying to see the empress, or did you merely use me as a means to exit Newcastle safely?"

"Does it matter?" Alard said softly.

"I suppose not." Gareth looked at Ralph. "Now that you're here, I'd like to finish our conversation from the chapel. It's long past time I knew all that you know."

Ralph and Alard exchanged a look, which in the darkness Gareth couldn't interpret, but they seemed to decide to go along with what Gareth wanted for now.

"Alard and I have known each other a long time," Ralph said. "When I came to him with the news of the plot against Prince Henry, he and I agreed to pool our resources to learn what we could about it. Since I no longer existed—and almost immediately he learned that he was a wanted man—our task was made doubly difficult."

"I knew that if I wasn't the traitor, someone else had to be," Alard said, "but I didn't know who that might be. When David asked to meet me, I agreed and suggested the castle, whose inhabitants had swelled sufficiently in number for me to lose myself among them. David had lied about wanting to talk, however, because he attacked me on the wall walk without warning."

Ralph nodded. "I came too late to see anything but the end."

"While Alard escaped by rope, you made your way downstream to meet him, is that right?" Gareth said.

"Yes," Ralph said.

"Why didn't you mention the emeralds when we spoke at the farmhouse?" Gareth said to Alard.

Alard's brow furrowed. "I was gathering information while imparting as little as possible. Since I didn't have the emeralds, and I didn't know at the time that David had been given one, it wasn't something I was willing to discuss with a possible enemy. I certainly never thought that *you* might have one."

Gareth nodded, admitting that he would have behaved no differently. He looked at Ralph. "Yet you chose to speak of the gems at the chapel. Why?"

"Alard's situation had grown even more imperiled," said Ralph. "I needed your help."

"It was a good choice to trust us, given that we now appear to be your only hope," Gareth said, unable to keep an edge of bitterness out of his voice.

Ralph gazed west towards the castle. "Perhaps Earl Robert—" He stopped and then shook his head, dismissing the thought.

"Robert wants the truth," Gareth said, "but not at the expense of men and time he doesn't feel he has. I get the sense that he is a very pragmatic man."

"That he is," Alard said.

"Unlike his sister," Ralph said, as if stating an obvious truth. Then he lifted his chin. "You should come with us to find Philippe now and get to the bottom of this."

"Back at the abandoned chapel, you said that only Alard and Prior Rhys knew you were still alive, but that was a lie," Gareth said. "Philippe must have known all this time, too."

"He did."

"But he didn't think to ask you—the man imbedded in King Stephen's court—if you had come to the same conclusions about Alard as he had?" Gareth said.

"He may have," Ralph said, "but since Alard was my liaison and Philippe no longer trusted him, such a discussion could only be held in person. Philippe is too ill to travel, and he would never have jeopardized my mission by summoning me here."

Gareth ran a hand through his hair. "The friary must be in an uproar now that the empress has arrived. How are you going to get past all those people who not only know you, but who work for Philippe and know that Alard is the man he most wants to find?"

"If you came with us—" Alard said.

Gareth closed his eyes. These men had no sense of self-preservation.

"What would you have us do instead?" Alard said. "Return to the farmhouse for our safety or find our way to the Welsh camp?"

"Nobody there knows who you are except for Gwen and Prior Rhys," Gareth said.

"We cannot hide," Alard said, "not while Prince Henry remains in danger."

Gareth hated his choices, but they weren't going to change just because he wanted them to. He sighed. "We'll go in the back way, across the fields."

"Thank you," Ralph said.

They left the road, threading their way between the village and the adjacent fields which belonged to the friary. They followed the line of the hill upon which St. Giles Church perched until the wall that surrounded the abbey proper gave way to field markers and a split rail fence. It was a matter of a moment to hop the fence and then take a pathway between the fields. They could see well enough without a torch, since the sky remained clear and the moon had risen. May was one of the driest months of the year in England. Gareth was glad he'd left off his cloak.

As they approached the herb garden, Gareth slowed and put out a hand to his companions. "You know the friary better than I. Which sleeping chamber is Philippe's?"

"I would think Philippe would be the last person you would want to see!"

The voice boomed from behind them, and the three companions swung around to find ten men, with swords at the ready, boxing them in against a hedge. Philippe himself stepped out from between two of his men.

If anything, Philippe looked worse than he had that morning in his office. The torchlight cast his face in an unhealthy-looking, yellowish glow, and Gareth felt he could see right through Philippe's skin to the tissue and blood beneath. Worn though he was, Phillipe stood straight and didn't take the arm of the man next to him, even though the soldier held out his elbow in case Philippe needed it.

"Seize him!" Philippe pointed at Alard, who'd flung back the hood of his cloak, no longer trying to hide.

Philippe's men moved at the same time Gareth did, leaping in front of Alard, sword out. "No. Stay back!"

Philippe's men pulled up, just outside of Gareth's reach. Philippe didn't have any archers with him, so Gareth had no fear of being felled from a distance. "What are you doing, Sir Gareth?" Philippe said.

"I could ask the same of you," Gareth said. "I gather you had me followed?" At Philippe's nod, Gareth added, "We came only to talk."

Philippe pointed a shaky hand at Alard. "That man is a traitor."

"I do not believe that he is," Gareth said, "and if you give us a chance to talk about it, I think you will no longer believe it either."

"You cannot accept anything he says," Philippe said. "He lies as a matter of course."

"And you don't?"

Philippe's mouth twitched, and Gareth could have sworn the man said 'touché' under his breath.

Then Ralph pushed back his hood and stepped forward. "We really have just come to talk, Philippe."

Philippe gritted his teeth. "I'd hoped you'd gone back to London. You are not needed here. Your position is too important to risk over one man's life."

"Even if that life belongs to Prince Henry?" Ralph said.

"It is Alard who threatens it." Philippe glared at Ralph. "Amaury told me that you were here. You are mistaken that your presence might make me trust Alard. Perhaps living so long in Stephen's court has turned you, too. Your loyalty to the empress could be questioned."

267

"You are a stubborn old man, Philippe. You need to listen to me." Ralph gestured to Alard and Gareth. "To us."

"It is you who will not listen, despite what is right in front of you. I have proof that Alard conspires with William of Ypres," Philippe said.

Along with Gareth, Ralph had pulled out his sword but now he sheathed it. "We come in peace." Then he took a knife from each boot, along with two throwing knives that he'd secreted at his wrists, and dropped them on the ground. With his arsenal forsaken, Ralph held out both hands palm up to Philippe and walked forward to stand in front of Gareth, who still stood in front of Alard.

"Have your men put up their swords. You have us at your mercy if you want to throw us in chains," Ralph said.

Philippe said nothing for a count of five, and then he nodded at his men. "Leave us. Stay within hailing distance."

His men muttered among themselves but did as he asked, backing several dozen paces away from where Philippe, Ralph, Gareth, and Alard stood together. Gareth straightened but didn't sheath his sword. Alard stepped out from behind him.

"Sir." Alard put his heels together and bowed slightly at the waist. It was more of a salute, one soldier to another, than a true obeisance. "I am not a traitor. Not to you, not to Empress Maud."

"You killed David," Philippe said.

"He came after me with a knife after you sent him to kill me," Alard said. "I had no choice."

"I did not send him," Philippe said, "neither him nor John. I didn't even know you had returned from Scotland."

"I didn't report in to you because Ralph had already contacted me with the news of the existence of the emeralds, and that you believed me to be a traitor," Alard said. "I determined that it was in everyone's best interests, not the least my own, that I remained free."

"We both cannot be telling the truth." Philippe looked hard at Alard. "I know I am; therefore you are not."

"Why are you so resistant to sense?" Alard said.

Philippe tsked through his teeth. "I'd shared the evidence against you with David. When he saw you, he must have decided to take matters into his own hands."

"What were your orders regarding Alard, then?" Gareth said. "If everyone knew that he'd betrayed the empress, wasn't that as good as a death sentence among you?"

"I wanted him captured, not killed, until I could speak to the empress myself," Philippe said. "I didn't want Alard dead because then I would have had difficulty convincing her that he had betrayed her. With him alive, she could question him herself."

"What about John?" Ralph said. "Philippe, both David and John encountered Alard within an hour of his arrival at

Newcastle and tried to kill him. They were taking orders from someone."

Philippe shrugged. "You are wrong. They were acting on their own volition. Alard was a brother to them, and he betrayed them. I cannot condone what they did, but neither can I blame them."

"What about the emeralds?" Ralph said. "One was found in David's possession."

Philippe sneered. "Found by him!" He threw out a hand to point at Gareth. "A fact that Sir Gareth kept hidden from me. More likely, the Welsh have been conspiring with Alard all along to lay the blame at David's feet so that the emerald could go to King Owain."

Gareth almost laughed, marveling at how easy it was for Philippe to construct a case against him out of nothing. "The gem had been sewn into the seam of David's cloak."

But Philippe wasn't listening. "Enough of this talk!" He pointed at Alard. "Seize him!"

Gareth raised his sword, prepared to defend Alard, but Ralph made a sharp gesture with one hand. "Stop!"

And to Gareth's surprise, Philippe's men did. Maybe it was because they had listened to the conversation and weren't as sure of Alard's guilt as Philippe, or maybe it was because Ralph had once been their master, before Philippe. Regardless of the reason, when Philippe staggered, his hand clutching at his chest, it was Alard and Ralph who caught his arms and maneuvered him to a bench set against the wall of the garden hut.

Gareth went down on one knee before the old spymaster. "Four emeralds came to Newcastle. David had one. Do you really think Alard would have come here, even to clear his name, if he had the other three in his possession?"

"He hopes to ingratiate himself again, to get close to Prince Henry so he can murder him," Philippe said, his voice a wheeze.

"Who stole David's body from the chapel?" Gareth said. "Did you order it?"

Philippe's brow furrowed. "Of course not."

"Are you suggesting that Alard returned to the castle, subdued Gwen and Prior Rhys, and murdered his friend, Rosalind, all without anyone recognizing him?" Gareth said.

Philippe's jaw clenched, and he didn't answer.

"If you accept that he could not have done those things, then you have to acknowledge that someone else is the traitor," Gareth said. "I believe you are an honorable enough man to admit when you are wrong." When Philippe didn't answer, Gareth sat beside him. "I need you to answer a few more questions for me, and then I will not trouble you again."

"You want more?" Though Philippe's voice trembled, a hint of amusement appeared in it as well. "What is it?"

"We have a chain of events that we must follow, threads that have been woven together that we must unravel. You say that you didn't send David and John after Alard."

Philippe nodded but didn't speak, preserving his energy. His sudden attack seemed to be easing, and he rested his head against the wall at his back.

"You also say that you didn't order someone to steal David's body and disable Prior Rhys," Gareth said.

"I did not."

Gareth rubbed his chin. "Do you know about the farmhouse?"

Alard stared hard at Gareth, but Philippe didn't seem to notice and said, "What farmhouse?"

Gareth rubbed his hands together. "Lastly, did you send that archer to the abandoned chapel last night?"

"No."

"Thank you." Gareth rose to his feet. He and Alard moved several paces away to allow Ralph to take Gareth's place and speak with Philippe, one old spy to another.

"My friend, the only evidence you have against Alard is the word of a messenger sent by William de Ypres," Ralph said. "If you entertain the idea that he played you false, in a deliberate attempt to mislead you, than everything else we have argued in Alard's defense must be true."

Philippe's breath came more easily, along with the encouragement they needed: "Go on."

"Thank the Virgin," Alard said in Gareth's ear. "He's beginning to listen."

"This means Philippe isn't our traitor either," Gareth said.

"I don't know if that makes me feel better or worse," Alard said. "I had convinced myself that he was the only one who had the means to assassinate Prince Henry."

"I never trusted him, of course," Gareth said, "but why didn't you?"

Alard's brow furrowed. "Who else has a finger in every pie? Who has the ambition and the reach?"

"I don't know. There's too much I still don't know."

"We must find the answers," Alard said. "Prince Henry's life depends on it, and I am more worried now than before. I have been taking orders from Philippe for years, and yet the events of the past few days have completely passed him by."

"I apologize for revealing the existence of the farmhouse," Gareth said. "You deliberately kept it a secret, did you not?"

Alard nodded.

"From everyone?" Gareth said.

"Only the four of us and Ralph knew of it." Alard paused. "And Ranulf, of course."

Gareth started. "Why Ranulf?"

"All this land, except for Newcastle itself, belongs to the Earl of Chester," Alard said. "We couldn't build on it without him knowing."

Gareth turned to look back at Philippe. Ralph sat next to him, and the two men were talking quietly. "A secret stops being a secret the moment you tell one person," Gareth said. "It occurs to me only now that if David was paid an emerald to betray you and the empress, what other of your secrets might he have told? And to whom?

22

Gwen

"I don't feel like sleeping yet," Gwen said to Prior Rhys when they reached the Welsh camp.

"I confess, I'm wide awake too." Prior Rhys helped Gwen dismount at the pickets and then crooked his elbow in invitation. "How's the ankle?"

"Fine." That wasn't exactly a lie. It mostly was fine. Gwen took Rhys's arm and began to stroll with him around the perimeter of the camp. As they walked, she could see Prior Rhys evaluating the layout of the encampment, his eyes flicking from the sentries, to the picketed horses, to the tents and fire circles. Old habits weren't easily put aside.

"I understand that Prince Henry will pass our camp on his way to the castle tomorrow morning; we should be able to join his party," Gwen said.

"It is my thought to get a little ahead of him," Rhys said. "I don't want his murder to happen on my watch."

"But you aren't a sentry," Gwen said. "It isn't your watch any longer, and yet you still feel responsible? Why?"

"In some way, I feel that everything that has happened this week stems from Ralph and me. If we hadn't left, if we had found another way, we might have stopped this before it started."

"That's a great many days to relive," Gwen said. "Think of all the good you've done at St. Asaph. If you hadn't been there last winter, Gareth might not be alive."

Prior Rhys patted Gwen's hand. "You comfort me."

"Besides, there are a hundred ways to murder a prince," Gwen said. "Perhaps tomorrow is not the day."

"No." Rhys shook his head. "There are a hundred ways, but only a few that are manageable without getting caught. That has to be the reason for the traitor's focus on Newcastle—and his craftiness. Whoever is behind this plot has been planning Prince Henry's death for some time. Those emeralds aren't payment for failure."

"I can see that," Gwen said, "but why hasn't our assassin tried to kill Prince Henry long before now?"

"Who's to say that he hasn't?" Prior Rhys said. "But I suspect he wasn't able to get close to Prince Henry in Bristol."

"Why not? Clearly, he has resources," Gwen said.

"Not enough to allow him to mingle with Prince Henry's usual retainers," Rhys said. "He is not of Henry's inner circle."

"So the person we're looking for is here at Newcastle because Prince Henry has finally left Bristol and is more exposed," Gwen said.

276

"That is what I suspect," Prior Rhys said.

"Then the assassin couldn't ever have been Alard," Gwen said. "He would have had access to Prince Henry many times over."

"He would have been more subtle about it too," Rhys said. "He's a spy."

"And yet, isn't it odd that of all the events that have occurred since we arrived, David's death was the only one accomplished in public."

Rhys fingered his bottom lip. "Perhaps that's been our mistake all along."

"How so?"

"In assuming the murderer is a spy," Rhys said, "I have taken it as a given that the threat to Prince Henry will come in secret—as poison, a knife in the darkness of his bedroom, or from a distance like that archer who shot Amaury. But what if the traitor isn't a spy?"

"Spy or not, the murderer will work in secret if wants to survive to spend his money," Gwen said.

"You're right. Perhaps I'm over-complicating matters," Rhys said.

"We may have already done all we can." They had come full circle, back to Gwen's tent, and as she stopped in front of it, Gwen canted her head. "Did you notice anything unusual in your inspection of the camp?"

Prior Rhys smiled. "What do you mean?"

"Our walk brought us conveniently close to every sentry," Gwen said. "They each stiffened to attention at your approach."

Prior Rhys waved a hand. "It isn't the first time I've walked the perimeter."

"Did you know the guard, Ieuan, who didn't pass on your message to Gareth?" Gwen said. "This is the first time any of us have been at the camp since yesterday morning. We should talk to him."

Rhys led Gwen to a fallen log near a brightly burning campfire. The night had turned cool, and Gwen rubbed her hands together in front of the blaze, glad for the warmth. She observed two women having an argument thirty feet away, near another campfire. One poked a finger in the other's face.

"Ieuan is one of Prince Rhun's men," Rhys said, ignoring the fight. "If you would sit a moment, I'll see if I can find him."

Gwen didn't protest to Prior Rhys that he should let her come with him. He was a churchman. If anyone could get information from a recalcitrant guard, it was he. As Gwen sat, several soldiers near the fire nodded to her. She recognized them as men under Gareth's command. One of the soldiers, a man named Rhodri, sat heavily at the end of Gwen's log, a good three feet away. "Will Sir Gareth be returning to the camp this evening? With both him and Evan gone, it has fallen to me to see to the men, and I have some questions."

"He told me he would spend the night here," Gwen said. "Are you concerned about something in particular?"

Rhodri had been whittling on a stick, turning it into a horse, though only the head had appeared so far. At Gwen's question, he looked up from his work. "I don't mind telling you that we are too exposed here, with too many women and servants and not enough soldiers. I don't trust these Normans."

One of his companions tossed a log on the fire. "We can't return to Wales soon enough for me."

"I share your sentiment," Gwen said, and then the sound of running feet had her turning around. Llelo and Dai plopped themselves on either side of her. She hugged them both, one arm around each boy.

Rhodri grinned. "Good boys you have there."

"They haven't been too much trouble?"

"Far from it," Rhodri said. "I wish they'd come to me before running off to look for you. I would have believed their tale and could have helped."

"We didn't know you then," Dai said. "We didn't know anyone we could trust, and Tomos didn't either."

"You did the best you could," Rhodri said. "Can't ask more than that."

Gwen was glad to see that the soldiers hadn't been bothered by the boys, though as she eyed her two charges, she was sure that there was more to their acceptable behavior than a sudden change of heart and conversion to obedience. She peered at Dai. "You have something to say to me. What is it?"

Dai glanced at Rhodri. "You didn't tell her?"

"The tale belongs to you," Rhodri said.

"That soldier, Ieuan, has run off," Llelo said, for once getting in ahead of his brother.

Dai gave him a sour look. "I was going to tell her!"

Llelo merely looked smug. "We followed him as far as we could, but he was on horseback, and we were running. We couldn't keep up on the road."

"Did he go west or east?" Gwen said.

"Neither," Dai said. "South."

Prior Rhys settled himself on the other side of Dai. "You two really are rapscallions, aren't you?" He ruffled Dai's hair.

Llelo and Dai straightened their shoulders at their own importance, and out of respect for Prior Rhys, whom they recognized as something more than a monk. They didn't lump him in among those they'd left at the friary in Newcastle.

"As soon as the boys reported Ieuan's absence, I sent men after him," Rhodri said. "They haven't returned, and I don't expect they'll catch him."

"Did you know Ieuan well?" Gwen said.

"No," Rhodri said. "Not before this journey."

"I did." One of the men raised his hand. "I fought with him down in Ceredigion."

"Did he strike you as one who might turn traitor?" Gwen said.

The man scratched at his sandy beard. "They say that any man can be bought if the price is right. I might have said that Ieuan's price would be cheaper than most." He nodded to Gwen. "Not much in the way of honor had Ieuan."

Rhodri rose to his feet. The other soldiers around the fire, who'd been listening to the conversation with open interest, stood with him. "Your orders, Sir," one said.

"See to the perimeter," Rhodri said.

The men dispersed, and Rhodri bowed slightly towards Gwen. "I must confer with Gruffydd's second on the disposition of the men for tonight. Until we know more about Ieuan's betrayal, we will remain on heightened alert. Please ask Sir Gareth to find me when he arrives, if I don't find him first." Gwen nodded, and Rhodri strode off.

Gwen looked over at Prior Rhys. "Llelo and Dai say Ieuan rode south. Do you think that's significant?"

"It is the direction from which Prince Henry will come." Prior Rhys got to his feet too. "Please stay here. I intend to confer further with Rhodri, and then may well return to Newcastle if I think the situation warrants it. The princes should know of what has transpired here today."

Once again, Gwen found that she couldn't argue with the old prior like she might have if Gareth or Hywel had been the one doing the asking. "Of course. Llelo and Dai will protect me, won't you, boys?"

Their eyes brightened in unison, and she couldn't regret the pleasure it gave them to be asked to take up a man's job. And just because she stayed here didn't mean she had nothing of importance to do. She felt in her boot for the emerald in the toe. She, Prince Rhun, and Gareth had been playing the shell game with the gem all day. Between Earl Robert, Ralph, and Amaury, too many Normans knew of it now. Hywel had sent it back to camp with Gwen for safekeeping, though she supposed that when Prior Rhys returned, she might include him in their little circle and give it to him.

Prior Rhys saluted the boys, following the path Rhodri had taken. The other men had dispersed to other duties, so Gwen tipped her head to Llelo and Dai. "I think the safest place for all of us to stay until Gareth returns is in my tent."

"I'll sleep across the doorway," Llelo said, claiming primacy as the eldest.

Dai's lower lip stuck out, but Gwen put an arm around his shoulders and leaned in to whisper in his ear. "Evil men are known best for coming in the back. You can sleep there."

Dai nodded, and Gwen felt the pull of her heart strings. They reminded her very much of her brother, Gwalchmai, left at home at Aber. She looked at them carefully. "Boys, has anyone ever taught you to sing?"

23

Hywel

Hywel groaned and tried to shift to a more comfortable position, but his hands were tightly tied behind him, and the back of the chair prevented him from moving more than an inch or two. That realization had him more awake in a hurry, and he blinked and blinked again, trying to adjust to the darkness around him. He wiggled his feet, which were tied at each ankle to the legs of a chair, and the toe of his boot hit something soft.

He heard a low moan.

Hywel forced down the panic that filled his throat. His eyes were growing used to the darkness, which wasn't as complete as he'd first thought. Light filtered through the floorboards above his head and through a square opening in the ceiling on the opposite end of the room. Footsteps paced above him, and then a man appeared in the opening, holding a lantern.

"So you're awake."

It was too late to feign sleep, but Hywel didn't answer—not that he could, given the gag in his mouth. The man came down the ladder, carrying the lantern, which illumined the cellar in which Hywel found himself. Mari lay on the floor at Hywel's feet, unconscious and no longer moaning. Her chest rose and fell as she breathed, and no blood showed on her clothing, which eased some of the tension in Hywel's shoulders. She was alive and, on the surface, unhurt.

Hywel tried to recall how they'd ended up here. He remembered talking with Mari in a quiet corner of one of the receiving rooms at Newcastle. He'd gone to find her after his meeting with the empress, which had been cordial, dull, and endless. Evan had brought them some wine and then ... Hywel could remember nothing after that. He had no idea how long he'd been unconscious, but from the light coming through the trap door, Hywel guessed that dawn had come and gone and the day was already passing.

Hywel didn't recognize the man who held the lantern high so he could see into Hywel's face and then tugged the gag from Hywel's mouth. "Go ahead and shout. No one will hear you."

Hywel tried to spit, but his mouth was dry and he couldn't make any saliva. "Do you know who I am?"

"Oh, I know." The man smiled. "You're one of the Welsh bastards." He shined the light around the chair on which Hywel was sitting. "See that blood? Yours'll join it soon enough if you don't cooperate."

"What do you want?"

"Me? Nothing. But my master? He didn't tell me exactly what he wanted from you, but he'll be along shortly to collect it."

Hywel groaned internally. He could guess what the man's master wanted: the emerald. Hywel had never had it on him, but either the killer didn't know that or thought he could torture its whereabouts out of Hywel.

While Hywel hoped he was strong enough to withstand whatever a torturer might mete out, he honestly didn't know what his limits were. Gareth had survived abuse last winter, and Hywel hoped he was man enough to do the same. But he didn't know. With Mari unconscious at his feet, he knew he had to get out of here before he found out.

As the man turned away, Hywel's mind wandered to a last aside he'd had with Prior Rhys, back at the castle. Hywel had asked him the real reason he'd joined their company on the journey to England. There'd been a pause, and then Rhys's voice had come softly. "It struck me as my duty to go, given my knowledge of the area. And perhaps, after all these years, as a gift. I have always felt it wise to accept the gifts God gives me."

With these last words, Prior Rhys's eyes had skated over to Mari and then back to Hywel. The old churchman had meant that Mari was a gift to Hywel, and as he sat in the chair, tied as he was, Hywel knew within himself that it was time he claimed the right to protect her.

The guard climbed the ladder, leaving the lantern on a hook by the trapdoor. Hywel was glad for the light, though he was disappointed to see the bottom of the ladder rising up.

From the trap door and ladder, to the stone and dirt foundation, to the chair in which he sat and the blood beneath, Hywel could guess now where he was: the farmhouse cellar. Gareth had described it to him at length, but other than those initial details, all else was changed. It must have taken several cartloads to clear out everything in the cellar but the chair. He wondered if all that work had been done in preparation for his abduction. He didn't exactly feel honored.

Hywel nudged Mari's shin with his toe, and this time her eyes popped open. "Where am I—?" Her voice went high in anguish and panic. "Hywel?"

"Shush, *cariad*. I'm here," he said. "We're at Prior Rhys's farmhouse, the one Gwen and Gareth found. We're going to be fine, but you need to keep quiet."

Mari gasped another few breaths but then breathed more easily as she gained control of herself.

"Good girl," Hywel said, his voice barely a whisper. "Now. How tightly are you tied?"

"Tightly—but only at my wrists and ankles." Mari lifted her hands to show him the rope that bound her hands in front of her. Hywel raised his eyes to say a prayer of gratitude that whoever had abducted them was an idiot.

"Can you sit up?" Hywel said.

"I think so." Mari rolled onto her stomach, bending at the waist and putting all of her weight onto her elbows until she could get her knees under her. The skirt of her dress made it difficult to move her legs, but she managed to scoot forward so she could kneel in front of Hywel. She lifted her hands to touch his cheek. "You're hurt."

"I hadn't noticed." It seemed as if someone had punched him a few times while he was asleep, just to make sure he stayed that way. "Can you wriggle around to the back of the chair and untie my hands?"

"I can try. These bonds are very tight; I can barely move my fingers."

Still, Mari tried to do as he asked. She tugged at the front of her dress with the fingers she could move, and managed to pull the hem out from beneath her knees. Even so, her legs got tangled up in her skirt the first time she tried to move. She squeaked as she lost her balance, falling forward with her forehead butting into Hywel's shoulder.

"It's all right," Hywel said, trying to shush her again. He wished he could put his arms around her to steady her.

"Sorry." By holding onto one arm of the chair and allowing Hywel's weight to counterbalance her own when she leaned back, Mari got her feet under her.

"Good girl," Hywel said again.

"Do you know how we got here?" Mari said. "My head hurts when I try to remember."

"I can't imagine I remember any more than you," Hywel said. "Evan brought us that wine and—"

"What do you think might have happened to Evan since he's not here with us?" Mari said, her eyes wide.

"Hopefully, he is asleep in an out-of-the-way place." Hywel prayed that Evan wasn't dead; he didn't even want to speak of it. To voice his fear would mean admitting it might be true. "If he wakes as we have, he will understand immediately that something has happened to us. He'll find my brother or Gareth and Gwen."

"All of whom you insisted were to make Prince Henry's safety their first priority," Mari said. "They'll be among those watching for him, and since we have no idea of the current time, he could be arriving at any moment!"

"I think we have to accept that we are out of this particular fight, Mari," Hywel said. "Control over whether or not Prince Henry lives or dies has moved beyond us."

"Do you know why we're even here?" Mari worked her way around the chair with little hops and bent to work at the rope that bound his hands. "We haven't figured anything out yet!"

"We're not here because the traitor is afraid of what we know," Hywel said. "We're here because he wants his emerald."

"As if you would tell him where it is," Mari said.

"I would tell him in a heartbeat if I thought it would get us out of here or if he threatened to hurt you if I didn't," Hywel said. "But how long after I told him do you think he'd let us live?"

Mari grunted as her fingers wrenched and slipped on his bonds. "Not long—"

A chair scraped the floor above them, and they both froze. They had been speaking very quietly, and even the sound of Mari's hopping had been muffled by the dirt floor, but they needed more time if they were to get free. They would get only one chance at this.

Hywel gave it a long count of ten before he shifted his shoulders, working to ease the strain on them from having his hands pulled so tightly behind his back.

"I feel like an animal waiting for slaughter," Mari said.

"I'm afraid too, *cariad*," Hywel said.

"How could this happen?" The last word would have been a wail if she hadn't spoken it right in his ear.

"I made a mistake," Hywel said. "I trusted the wrong person. I just wish I knew who that person was."

"We'll know before we die," Mari said. Her voice came out much more matter-of-fact this time. "We'll have that satisfaction, at least."

Hywel grunted his assent. "How's it going back there?"

"My fingers are very stiff. I wish I had a knife—" And then her fingers stiffened on his hands. "I do have a knife, a tiny one. Let me see if I can get it from my boot."

"Take your time." Hywel leaned back his head and closed his eyes, breathing in and out, searching for patience and not wanting to put any additional pressure on Mari. He could think of only one other woman who wouldn't have been reduced to tears to find herself bound and left to rot in a dark cellar—and who might carry a knife in her boot as a matter of course—and that was Gwen.

While he waited, he strained to hear more from the guard above them. He hoped it wasn't too much to ask that he could have fallen asleep.

"I've got it." She worked at the bonds some more, and it took long enough to slice through them that he guessed the blade wasn't as sharp as it could have been. "There," Mari said at last. The strand of rope fell to the ground.

Hywel brought his arms around in front of him, working one wrist and then the other to renew the circulation in his hands. Then he took the knife Mari handed him and began sawing through the rope that constrained his ankles.

He got his feet free and moved around the chair so he could crouch in front of Mari to free her hands. "We're going to have to trust that Gareth and Gwen will do what they can, and that what is meant to happen, will."

"You are very sensible," Mari said.

"I've had to be," Hywel said. "And I would return the compliment. While I regret that your father abandoned you for his work for the empress, your upbringing has made you strong. Capable."

Mari regarded him with a composed expression. It was on the tip of Hywel's tongue to speak of how he felt about her, but now that it came to it, he had no idea what to say. He'd had more women than he'd had any right to, wooing them with an eloquent tongue—or more often a song—and yet anything he thought to say to Mari sounded trite and insincere when he rehearsed it in his head. His default was to simply kiss her, but that might send the wrong message. She had kissed him, true, but she'd had no idea what she was doing.

He did. It was up to him to make this right.

"Why are you looking at me like that?" Mari said.

Now that her hands were free, she let Hywel ease her down to sit on the ground. She straightened her legs so her feet were in front of her and he could get to the rope that tied her ankles together.

"I was thinking about two things of equal importance," Hywel said. "The first is how we're going to get past that guard up there. The second—" He almost looked away but at the last moment told himself not to be a coward, "—the second is how to tell you that I love you."

The bonds around Mari's ankles loosened and dropped to the floor. Hywel grasped her hands and pulled her to her feet. He didn't let her go.

"Do you really?"

Hywel was glad his hands were no longer tied because he knew what to do with them. He slipped one around her waist and brushed a stray hair back from her face with the other. "I do."

"Why?" Mari said.

Hywel made to laugh but then swallowed it back, afraid the guard would hear him. The cellar wasn't the place for this, and it certainly wasn't the time, but now that the words were out, the rest was easy. "You may know that I haven't given any woman my full attention in a long while, but I don't think you know the reason for it."

Mari didn't speak, just remained focused on his face.

"After I lost a woman and her babe—our babe—three years ago, I swore I would never care that much about anyone ever again," Hywel said, remembering the path of self-destruction he'd followed for far too long after Branwen's death. "Although I meant it at the time, I know now that I was wrong to make that oath, and I cannot keep it, not if it means I can't have you."

Mari put the palm of her hand to his cheek. "Whether you admit it or not, you are a sweet man, Hywel ap Owain, and I love you too."

A bang from above had them jumping apart.

"Who are you?" their guard said.

A chair scraped on the floor, and then a different voice said, "I am someone about whom you should be very worried."

"Prior Rhys—" Mari breathed the name. Hywel would have recognized the prior's educated French accent anywhere.

Grunts, slaps, and thuds resounded throughout the house, and then Hywel heard a loud *thunk* as if something heavy had fallen to the floor.

Taking a chance, Hywel raced to the opening. "We're here!"

"My lord." Prior Rhys crouched above them, grinning and shaking his hand to ease its hurt. His knuckles were scraped red and bleeding.

"I'm glad you haven't forgotten how to fight," Hywel said.

"Son, I can't say that I'm glad I had to use my skills, but I'm certainly not sorry I have them," Rhys said. "Let's get you out of there. We have a traitor to catch."

24

Gwen

Gwen gripped Gareth's hand tightly as they stood with Prince Rhun, Gruffydd, and the two boys near the cluster of huts that lined the road to the west of the castle. They had converged together in the last quarter of an hour after Gareth and Gwen had ridden to Newcastle at the tail end of Prince Henry's entourage. Rhun and Gruffydd had come from the castle with the bad news that Evan, Mari, and Hywel were missing, and Llelo and Dai had run all the way from the Welsh camp to tell Gwen that Prior Rhys still couldn't be found. No one had seen him since she'd said good night to him and retired to her tent with the boys.

To top it off, Gwen was focusing very hard on not allowing the roiling in her stomach to overwhelm her completely. She'd woken every morning for the last week feeling as if she didn't want breakfast and would lose it if she ate it. At first, she'd told herself that her queasy feeling was due to anxiety over the trip or the progress of the investigation.

Yesterday, she'd decided that she'd eaten a bad piece of meat. But she couldn't deny the other changes in her body any longer.

While part of her wanted to shout from the highest tower in Newcastle that she was carrying Gareth's baby, she knew it would be better to wait to tell Gareth until they were alone, maybe even in their own bed at home. If her courses hadn't returned by then, she could be absolutely sure of her pregnancy, and Gareth wouldn't have so much else to worry about.

The entire village of Newcastle, not to mention the residents of the castle itself, had come out to greet Prince Henry as he arrived. The boy himself appeared innocent enough, waving as he passed, though he had to be uncomfortable wearing his fine clothes and thick ermine-trimmed cloak in the brightness of the early morning sun. On his head he wore a gold circlet, which wasn't quite his right, since his mother was uncrowned as yet. Gwen felt sorry for him for having a mother who insisted on full ceremony at every occasion.

"If Empress Maud and Earl Robert can't protect the prince, nobody can," Gareth said. Gwen and Gareth had tried to close the distance between them and the prince during the ride, but the boy's retainers had protected him, and it was reasonable to believe that they would continue to do so.

"I can accept that," Rhun said, "especially if it means we can turn our attention to what concerns us specifically: where my brother and Mari have gone."

"Where do we even begin to look?" Gwen said. A dozen worst-case scenarios were skipping through her head, each one more evil than the last and all of them ending in her friends' deaths.

"We could try the tunnel again," said Gareth. "Amaury said that other passages branched from the main one with plenty of places to hide a body if a man wanted to."

Rhun nodded. "That's a good place to start—"

"The prince! The prince!"

"No—" Gwen choked on the word as more shouts came from the gatehouse. A woman ran towards them, screaming and sobbing, her arms spread wide. "He's dead!"

Onlookers had overflowed the road when Prince Henry had ridden by. They'd begun to disperse once the parade was over but now surged towards the castle. At the same time, some inside the castle looked to flee, and they fought to get past each other at the gate.

Rhun let out a sharp breath and pointed at Gruffydd. "Begin your search for Prince Hywel in the village. Go from house to house if you have to. Perhaps someone noticed a cart—anything—leaving the castle that could have hidden two or three people." Gruffydd nodded and departed at a run.

Then Rhun put his hand on Gareth's shoulder. "It has to be chaos in the castle right now. With Ranulf gone and Amaury injured, Earl Robert needs men who can think. That's you."

"Surely you would be better suited to that task—"

"I've already searched the castle from top to bottom. My brother isn't there. Hywel's life is in danger, and I can be of no use to Earl Robert or the empress until he is found," Prince Rhun said.

"I will go with Gareth," Gwen said.

Rhun shook his head. "You should return to the camp."

"She can't go off on her own, not in this crowd," Gareth said, taking Gwen's hand. "I won't let her out of my sight."

"What about us?" Llelo and Dai had been standing behind Rhun, hopping from one foot to the other, waiting for their assignment.

Rhun swung around to look at them, but instead of sending them back to the camp like Gwen expected, he said, "You know the friary and its grounds better than most, I imagine. You will come with me to find Philippe and tell him what has happened."

"Yes, my lord!" the two boys sang in unison and then set off, sprinting down the road towards the friary.

Rhun turned back to Gareth and Gwen. "Come to us there when you can."

Gareth handed the prince the reins of his horse, upon which he and Gwen had ridden together from the camp. "Take him. It'll be faster."

More sure and decisive than Gwen had ever seen him, Rhun swung into the saddle and spurred the horse after the boys.

Gwen hurried beside Gareth towards the gatehouse, lifting her skirt so the hem wouldn't trip her up. Like a fool, she'd dressed in finery again, in honor of the coming of Prince Henry. She should have known better.

Shouts still erupted from the bailey, but the crowd wasn't shoving and heaving anymore, and as they came under the gatehouse, Gwen understood why: the guards had dropped the portcullis. Gwen and Gareth had to be let in by the wicket gate. Gareth pointed at one of the guards as he passed through. "What happened?"

The man's face was as white as new-fallen snow. Gareth's question seemed to settle him a little, however, and he said, "The prince dismounted, there was a scuffle, and a sudden press of men and horses. When everyone retreated, Prince Henry lay bleeding on the ground."

"Did you see who did it?" Gareth said.

The guard shook his head. "I didn't. Nobody did. We were all focused on the empress."

"How do you mean?" Gwen said. "Why the empress?"

"Earl Robert was waiting for Prince Henry on the steps to the keep," the guard said. "He signaled for the horns to blow, which they did, and then the empress made her grand entrance. By the time the noise stopped, the prince was—was—"

Gwen put a hand on his arm. "We understand. You've done well to stay at your post."

"Don't let anyone in or out," Gareth said. "I would have thought that order would already have been given."

"It-it-it was," the man said, still not recovered.

Gareth stepped closer. "You let us in."

"I recognized you."

"Did you let anyone out?" Gwen said.

The man shook his head.

Gareth nudged Gwen. "We need to keep moving. It's unlikely that the assassin would have tried to leave this way, not when there are other choices. We need to find where he did go."

"He could have gone through the tunnel, like you said before," Gwen said.

"That was my thought, too," Gareth said.

They hurried towards the northwest tower, though not without glancing towards the center of the courtyard, because they couldn't help it. Blood stained the ground and men milled around it, avoiding the spot but unable to stop looking at it.

"I don't understand it," Gareth said.

"What?"

"Nobody is paying us the slightest attention."

"Everyone is still in shock over what happened to Prince Henry," Gwen said.

"That's no excuse," Gareth said. "Where is Earl Robert or the empress? No one in authority is anywhere to be seen."

Gwen didn't have an answer for him. They clattered down the tower stairs to the guardroom; both guards were present and alert. "You heard?" Gareth said.

"Yes, sir," said the first guard, a tall, blonde man in his twenties with a thick beard. His face was very pale.

"Did anyone come through here?" Gareth said.

"No, sir!" The man stiffened to attention. "None except three of Earl Ranulf's men."

"What were they doing?" Gwen said.

"They said they'd seen the assassin escape and were chasing him," the guard said.

"But the assassin didn't come this way himself?" Gareth said.

"No sir, not through here. I assumed he meant that the assassin had escaped like that spy, Alard, by rope from over the battlement."

"Who's *he*?" Gwen moved to stand at Gareth's shoulder. "Which of Ranulf's men do you mean?"

"I—" The man looked from Gwen to Gareth, confused by their joint questioning. "It was Sir Amaury, with his arm in a sling. I don't know the names of the two men with him."

Gareth turned to Gwen. "We can leave the pursuit in this direction in Amaury's hands. With the friary and Philippe close by, he'll have the men he needs."

"I'm just happy that he was able to rise from his bed," Gwen said.

"Did they give you the name or a description of the one they were hunting?" Gareth said.

The soldier shook his head.

Gwen and Gareth returned to the bailey, wending their way through the crowd that remained. A few people talked among themselves, but most watched the entrance to the keep, hoping for news. Several men, one a priest, had gathered on the steps to hold a prayer vigil. Gareth and Gwen passed them by without a second glance and entered the anteroom to the great hall.

Once inside, Gwen hesitated. The door to the great hall was closed. Likely, Prince Henry had been laid on a table inside. Gareth kept going, but Gwen didn't follow. "I think we should go this way." Gwen changed direction, heading towards one of the side doors to the anteroom.

"Where are you going? Prince Rhun wanted me to offer my services to the earl." Gareth followed Gwen, but his tone told her that his patience was very thin.

"I think we should go first to Earl Robert's apartments," Gwen said.

"Earl Robert should be in the great hall ..." Gareth's voice trailed off as Gwen took the stairs up to the next level.

"Did Earl Robert strike you as a fool?" she said.

"Of course not," Gareth said.

"Or a man who held his nephew's life cheaply?" Gwen said.

"No—"

They had reached the corridor at the end of which lay the earl's rooms. When they'd first arrived at Newcastle and Gwen had explored the interior in a free moment, she'd noticed that maids always hovered around the farthest door. Today was no exception, except that instead of two in front of the door, there were three. The women hushed at Gwen and Gareth's approach.

"Don't you have something better to do?" Gareth said in French. "Why are you always here?"

Gwen put a hand on his arm. "They work for the earl, Gareth."

Gareth's brow furrowed, making Gwen smile despite the urgency of the moment. For all that he was used to having a wife who did men's work, Gareth still couldn't imagine other women doing the same. The maids smirked back at Gareth. "You shouldn't be here," said one of them, a slatternly-looking woman with a swirl of bright red hair.

"Earl Robert sent us to sit with Prince Henry until he could sort everything out," Gwen said.

The woman pursed her lips, but after a moment's pause, she nodded. "He's in a bad way." She opened the door to the room.

A boy not yet in his teens sat on a bench at the end of a four-poster bed hung with burgundy curtains. He was alone. And he was crying.

They entered the room and the maid/guard shut the door behind them. Prince Henry looked up at their entrance, but such was his defeat that he didn't protest at the appearance of complete strangers, just hung his head. "Bernard is dead. He died for me."

"I know." Gwen glided to Henry, sat beside him, and took his hand. "That was a risk he took, one that every man takes when he cares for the next King of England."

After a moment's hesitation, Henry took what Gwen was offering and put his face into her shoulder. He gave three or four heaving sobs before he sat up again, wiping his eyes. "My uncle will be ashamed of me if he sees me like this."

"There is no shame in grief," Gareth said to Henry and then switched to Welsh for Gwen's ears only. "How did you know?"

She lifted one shoulder. "It came to me as we crossed the bailey that Earl Robert might not have been as willing to risk his nephew's life as it first appeared. And if I was wrong, if the prince really was dead, we lost nothing in pursuing my hunch."

Prince Henry pushed away from Gwen and stood. He gripped his hair with both hands and then paced to the window and back. "I need to know what is happening out there."

"You need to stay here, where it's safe," Gwen said, back to speaking French, "else Bernard's sacrifice will be for nothing."

"That's what my uncle said," Henry said.

"While we wait for news, can you tell us what happened?" Gareth said, still in his position by the door. Gwen knew what he was thinking now: Those women might guard the prince, but he and Gwen had entered with no trouble at all. For all that Earl Robert had thought far enough ahead to arrange for a decoy for Prince Henry, it seemed he hadn't given as much thought to what came after.

Prince Henry lifted a hand and then dropped it in a gesture that looked very much like despair. He sat back down on the bench beside Gwen. "I rode here, well in the rear of the company. My primary guards protected Bernard; they always do. I'm not sure how many of them truly think that Bernard is the prince. Uncle Robert insisted on this arrangement and that I not give the game away by word or deed. Still, I had guards around me, too."

"Were you disguised for the whole journey or just as you approached the castle?" Gareth said.

"I've always been disguised," Henry said, and when Gwen and Gareth couldn't hide their puzzlement, he added, "even at Bristol, even when men came to greet me, it has always been Bernard that they see, not me."

Gwen found her jaw dropping at the audacity and complexity of the ruse, and her estimation of Earl Robert went up another three notches.

"I found it irritating at first," Henry said, continuing his story in the face of their stunned silence, "but when I realized how much more freedom it gave me, I embraced it. It was Bernard who was forced to attend the fine dinners and speak formally with visitors. I was usually with him, as one of his retainers and friends, but the lack of attention paid to me was refreshing after my father's house in France."

"Your father expects a great deal from you, doesn't he?" Gwen said.

"He expects me to inherit England, Normandy, and Anjou," Henry said matter-of-factly. "Nothing else matters."

King Owain's attitude wasn't any different; he possessed a similar pride and Gwen knew that Hywel, even as a second son, had felt that pressure his whole life.

"Did you see who killed Bernard?" Gareth said.

Gwen was glad that Gareth was the one to ask that of Henry. Sometimes a soft voice like hers was more likely than a gruff one to set off tears, and they needed Henry focused.

The boy swallowed. "I saw the man—or thought I saw him—but now I'm sure I was confused in all the chaos."

"We need to know the one you saw, even if you think you might have been mistaken." Gareth moved to crouch in front of Henry, ignoring the fact that there was something slightly unseemly about grilling a ten-year-old princeling for information about his friend's murder.

Henry still didn't want to say, but after hemming and hawing for another few heartbeats, he said, "It was that fellow who came with Ranulf to see Uncle Robert in Bristol last month. Amaury was his name."

"What?" Gwen spoke in Welsh, such was her shock. Gareth reached over to put a gentle hand on her leg.

"Amaury was among the men who greeted us when we entered the bailey just now. He grabbed the bridle of the horse next to Bernard's to hold him steady and then moved to help Bernard dismount. His left arm was in a sling, which made his motion awkward," Henry said. "Because of the sling, I continued to watch him, even after the trumpets rang and everyone turned to see my mother arrive on the steps of the keep.

"At that point, Bernard's horse blocked my view. By the time he shifted again, Amaury was gone and Bernard lay bleeding on the ground. I next saw Amaury running towards one of the towers, pointing and shouting at his men that he'd seen the assassin and they needed to come with him." Henry shook his head. "I can't say more than that."

"Could it be that—" Gwen looked at her husband, whose face had turned to stone.

"No," Gareth said. "It couldn't."

25

Gareth

Gareth held Henry by the shoulders. "You're sure? You're sure it was Amaury you saw?"

The boy nodded.

"Who else have you told?" Gareth said.

"Nobody! I couldn't tell anyone! Bernard went down and the guards brought me here. My mother screamed and screamed—" He put his hands to his ears as if he could still hear her.

Gareth, for his part, had a hard time imagining the empress screaming about anything except in anger.

"You need to go, Gareth," Gwen said, "just like before. I'll stay with Prince Henry until Earl Robert gets here."

"He's staying away so as not to attract anyone's attention to me," Henry said.

"That may be, but you are more than a prince today. You are the only witness to the murder." Gareth stood and took a step towards the door. "Your safety is still our first priority."

Prince Henry rose to his feet to follow him. "You may be right, but it is unseemly for a prince to cower in a room while others risk their lives for him."

"No!" Gareth and Gwen shouted in unison.

Gareth went down on one knee again before Henry. "We need to know that you, at least, remain safe. For you to appear now, alive, might not only put your life in danger but all our lives."

"How so?" said Henry, not ready to give in.

"Because the killer will know that he failed. He will be desperate to finish the job and won't care who is harmed in the process," Gareth said.

Prince Henry stuck out his chin, but then he sat down again with a sigh. "I accept what you say. Go."

Gareth glanced at Gwen, who gave him a quick smile. Ten-year-old boys seemed to be her forte, so he knew he could leave Henry to her. Gareth pulled open the door to find the three women still making a show of gossiping in the corridor. At the sight of them, he forced himself to accept what Prince Henry had told him: that Amaury had manipulated everyone, including him. Maybe all signs had pointed to Amaury all along and Gareth hadn't wanted to see it. He would have to examine the clues again later, when he had time, and discover where they'd all gone wrong. Where he'd gone wrong.

As he saw it now, Gareth had two choices: the first was to run after Amaury on the off-chance that he could overtake him. If Amaury fled Newcastle, he would ride to the court of King Stephen. A man didn't murder the son of an empress and expect to resume his normal life as if nothing had happened. Three emeralds would give him enough wealth to walk away from his old life.

Gareth's second choice—and the one he realized he had to choose—was to speak to Earl Robert and inspire him to organize a manhunt. Another few moments might make the difference between apprehending Amaury and not, but Gareth wouldn't consider the time wasted if he had the earl and all his resources at his disposal. If they were going to capture Amaury, they had an enormous amount of ground to cover in a short amount of time.

That didn't mean, however, that he shouldn't do what he could about Amaury right now. Gareth tugged the door closed and faced the women guards. "Prince Henry reports that it was Sir Amaury who killed Bernard. I will speak to the earl if one of you will run to the friary and find Prince Rhun or Philippe. Amaury could be long gone by now, but if we have a chance to stop him anywhere, it will be from there."

The three women gaped at him, and for a moment Gareth wondered if his French had been up to the task, but then one of the women, the same redhead who'd spoken earlier and seemed to be in charge, nodded. "I'll go."

They raced down the stairs and into the anteroom. While the woman disappeared through the main door to the bailey, Gareth came to a sudden stop, having nearly plowed through Evan, who stood swaying in front of him, his eyes crossing and re-crossing as he tried to focus them. Gareth grabbed his shoulders, just as he had Prince Henry's. "Where have you been?"

"I woke up underneath a bed." Evan waved a hand feebly towards an upper floor. "What's going on?"

"I don't have time to tell you." Gareth's eyes swept the anteroom, looking for anyone he could trust and coming up empty. He shoved Evan towards the doorway to the stairs. "Gwen is in Earl Robert's quarters. Go to her."

Evan gawked at Gareth. "She's where?"

Gareth tsked through his teeth at his friend's slow mind. Poppy juice, he guessed, and not his fault. He gripped both sides of Evan's head, making him focus on him. "This is important. Go to her. She will explain everything. I need you to protect her and the one she's with."

Gareth's urgency seemed to penetrate the fog in Evan's mind, because he nodded and, with a straighter back, turned on his heel and trotted up the stairs towards the earl's apartments. Gareth took in a deep breath, committing himself to his next course of action, come-what-may. He pushed open the door to the great hall.

While the uproar in the bailey had been ongoing, the great hall was unnaturally calm. Bernard lay in state on a table, a cloth covering him except for his head. Empress Maud was nowhere to be seen, but Earl Robert paced in front of the fire, barking commands and demanding answers while his retainers cowered around him. Gareth recognized none of the others on sight, but at Gareth's entrance, they all looked over to him.

"You can't be in here—" One of the men strode towards Gareth, motioning with his hands that Gareth should depart immediately.

"He's Prince Hywel's man," Earl Robert said. "Have him come to me."

The man seemed to hold no grudge towards Gareth, because his shooing hand gesture turned into a welcoming bow. "This way."

Gareth marched across the floor to join the circle of men around Earl Robert, though with a flick of one finger, all but two melted away. "What is it?" Earl Robert said.

"I have spoken with ... ah ... the boy in your quarters," Gareth said, not explaining more clearly since he didn't know how many of the earl's men knew about the deception.

The earl raised his eyebrows. "Did you?"

"He saw who murdered—" Gareth gestured to Bernard. "It was Amaury."

Another lord might have gasped, but Earl Robert gave away his surprise only by a tightening around the eyes. "I see." The other men had good control too.

"I spoke to the guards at the entrance to the tunnel. Amaury and two of his men left by that avenue immediately after—" Again Gareth's eyes skated to Bernard's body and back to Earl Robert, "—the event."

"The boy is sure?" Earl Robert said.

"Yes," Gareth said.

"All the boys who accompanied the prince, along with his adult retainers, are gathered in the next room," the earl said. "Nobody saw anything—or rather, everyone saw something and none of it the same."

"The boy recognized Amaury from his visit to Bristol a few months ago," Gareth said. "Today he noted Amaury's sling specifically."

"Christ on the cross." Earl Robert swung around and kicked at the logs stacked beside the fireplace. It was the first instance of emotion Gareth had seen in him.

"I left my wife in your quarters," Gareth said, "but I feel it is my duty to continue this investigation. Do I have your permission to pursue Sir Amaury as I see fit?"

"I am in your debt," Earl Robert said. "What is your first step?"

"To ride to the tunnel's exit in the abandoned chapel and try to find a trace of where Amaury went from there," Gareth said, and then he explained that he'd sent one of the women guards to the friary to warn Philippe and Prince Rhun of what Amaury had done.

"I will send men through the tunnel, to ensure that he isn't hiding inside it." And then Earl Robert was all action. He clapped his hands together, and his men converged on his position. With a few brief sentences, he sent them off to gather men and begin a manhunt throughout the countryside. By the time Gareth reached the door, half of the earl's men had already left the hall.

Once again, Gareth ran down the steps from the keep and across the bailey, making for one of the many horses picketed outside the stables. Gareth chose one and mounted before the stable lad could stop him. "But, sir!"

"I'll bring him back!" Gareth saluted the boy and urged the horse towards the gatehouse. He raised his voice. "Open the portcullis!"

But the order from Earl Robert had already gone out. Even before Gareth reached it, the gate was open. Gareth ducked underneath the metal spikes, turned the horse's head, and sent the animal heading north from the castle. As he flew through the village, people milled about the green, directionless. But at the sight of Gareth leaving and the newly opened gate, many moved towards the castle again. Gareth could have told them that they would see a gratifying amount of activity in a moment.

Once through the village, it was less than a quarter of a mile across a few fields to where the abandoned chapel nestled in its clearing among the trees. Gareth could see it before he reached it and slowed when he realized that no one was near or around it. He dismounted as he approached the ruins and led his horse to the altar with its stairs down to the crypt.

He paced around the altar. The grass that grew between the fallen stones and flagstones had been pressed flat, though Gareth couldn't distinguish any boot prints in particular. From the tracks, men had come through the tunnel and left the chapel, all following the same line: towards the friary.

Ten feet from the altar, a knife lay in the grass. Gareth looped the horse's reins around a half-fallen pillar and crouched to look at it. Blood stained the blade. If Amaury had been especially clever, the knife would prove to belong to someone else, perhaps Alard. Gareth could even imagine that Amaury had left the knife at the chapel to lead a pursuer astray. It was unlikely that he'd accidently dropped it having murdered Prince Henry with it a quarter of an hour earlier.

Gareth wrapped the knife in a cloth and stowed it in the saddle bags on the horse. The horse's owner had prepared for a journey, for the bags were already filled with food, a cloak, and blankets. Gareth took a drink from the water skin to find that it contained not water but a respectable wine. He gave a silent toast in thanks to the owner, who clearly liked his comforts.

Gareth eyed the steps going down into the crypt and decided he ought to check for Earl Robert's men before continuing on to the friary. He went down the steps and warily entered the crypt and the tunnel beyond. The two soldiers on duty rose to their feet at the sight of him, so he made sure to keep his hands up and unthreatening as he entered. "Did Sir Amaury come through here?"

"Yes, sir," the man said. "Not very long ago." He looked towards the tunnel. A faint echoing of footsteps came from it. "What's happened, sir? Sir Amaury said that the prince was dead."

"He is not dead," Gareth said.

The man's shoulders sagged in relief, and at that moment, five men from Newcastle popped out of the tunnel's entrance. The man in the lead lifted a hand. "Sir Gareth. What news?"

"Come with me." Leaving the guards at their post, Gareth led the way back through the crypt and up the stairs to the altar. Once outside, Gareth pulled the cloth-wrapped knife from his saddle bag and showed it to the soldier. "The murder weapon, I believe."

The man opened the cloth for a brief look and then closed it again. "Best if you keep it. We may not have the opportunity to return to the castle until nightfall."

"I'm for the friary," Gareth said. "Send one of your men back to the earl. If I'm right that Amaury went that way, Philippe might appreciate more men."

"Yes, sir," the man said. "The rest of us will follow you on foot."

Gareth urged his horse out of the chapel and onto the path the cart carrying Amaury had taken after he'd been shot. It seemed like a lifetime ago. The urgency of his task pushed Gareth on, and he left the earl's men far behind. While Gareth wanted to learn the answers to his myriad questions, as long as Amaury was at large, the prince's life remained in danger.

Amaury's treachery was far harder for Gareth to accept than Prince Cadwaladr's had been. Gareth had *wanted* Cadwaladr to be guilty because it fulfilled all his expectations, and he hated the man anyway. Gareth had started to count Amaury as a friend. Villains had escaped Gareth before—rarely, but it had happened—but he would feel personally affronted if he lost *this* one.

His horse jumped over a low stone wall, cantered through the friary's extensive gardens, and was approaching the cloister when four men spilled from the wooden gate in the hedge that separated the main friary buildings from the garden in this location. One of them waved his arms at Gareth and then grabbed the horse's bridle as Gareth reined in.

"Get down! Get down! You're a target up there."

Willing to listen, especially if it meant not getting killed, Gareth dropped off his horse and crouched behind the hedge with the monks, several barely into manhood. They clustered around him.

"What's happening?" Gareth said.

"It's hand-to-hand in the cloister!" said one monk, his hands tugging at his hood as if pulling it close around his ears would protect him from the violence. "Sir Philippe and Sir Amaury are in there with their men—"

"They're fighting each other?" Gareth looked towards the courtyard, and now that he knew what to listen for, he could hear the clash of sword against sword. "Stay here."

Gareth pulled out his sword, opened the gate, and went through the garden to the monastery square. Two monks crossed the cobbles, coming from the stables and supporting a third who was bleeding heavily from his side. They looked up at his approach, and the fear in their faces brought Gareth's heart into his mouth.

"Sir Gareth! Over here!" Dai appeared in front of Gareth and grabbed his free hand. "Come quickly! He's hurt!"

Next to the wall outside the cloister, Llelo crouched in front of Prince Rhun, who was holding his left bicep in his right hand. Blood seeped through his fingers.

"A scratch," said Prince Rhun as Gareth ran up. "It is no matter."

"What happened? Who did this?" Kneeling in front of Rhun, Gareth forced Rhun's hand aside to inspect the wound. He'd taken a sharp stab that went through the tissue all the way to the bone.

"Amaury," Rhun said. "I couldn't stop him."

"He's in there with Philippe!" Dai pointed towards the cloister.

Llelo pulled his shirt over his head and handed it to Gareth, who tore off a strip at the bottom with his teeth. "Quick thinking, Llelo."

"Is Prince Henry really dead?" Dai said.

Gareth glanced at Dai's white face out of the corner of his eye as he wrapped the cloth around Rhun's arm. "No." Rhun had lost more blood than was good for him, and his face was pale. "How did you know Amaury was the assassin?"

Rhun gestured towards the body of a woman lying on the ground near the stables. It was the servant/guard Gareth had sent to the friary. "She—her name was Clarice—told me what Amaury had done; I didn't believe her at first. Stupid of me. It was only after she confronted Amaury that I realized she was telling the truth. I was protecting her when he stabbed me, and then he ran her through." Rhun choked on the last words.

"I'm sorry," Gareth said.

Rhun's face twisted in pain. "It was just like you to send a woman."

"If I were Amaury, I would have been gone long before now." Gareth tied off the ends of the bandage, hoping that it would hold until he could get Rhun to the healer. "Why did he come back to the friary in the first place?"

"I imagine he thought he had the time," Rhun said, "and that nobody suspected him. By the time I spoke to him, he'd already sent most of Philippe's men to search the countryside for the phantom assassin. In addition, his wound had reopened, and he needed it bandaged. He was very calm at first, trying to persuade Clarice and me that all was well."

"If not for Clarice, everyone here would have believed Amaury's lies," Dai said.

"At least I prevented him from taking a horse," Rhun said.

The sound of clashing swords still came from the cloister. A man screamed in pain. Rhun pointed towards the door with his free hand.

Gareth didn't delay another moment. Picking up his sword from where he'd left it in order to attend to Rhun, he vaulted into the cloister and pulled up short in one of the archways, trying to look everywhere at once and, most importantly, to sort out the combatants. A half dozen men fought in and around the friary well, with four others wounded or dead on the ground.

"I cannot let you pass! You're a traitor!"

Gareth turned at Philippe's shout. Gareth had come in through the western door; Philippe and Amaury stood near the opposite exit that would take Amaury to the friary's eastern fields. Philippe held off Amaury with a sword, but even at this distance Gareth could see Philippe's wrist waver. Wounded shoulder or not, Amaury closed in on the old spy and knocked away his sword.

"One man's traitor is another man's patriot," Amaury answered, and Gareth heard glee in his voice.

"Amaury!" Trying to distract him from Philippe, Gareth raced down the covered walkway towards the pair.

Amaury swung around, spied Gareth coming towards him, and turned back to Philippe. Amaury then leapt towards the old spy and caught him around the shoulder with his wounded arm, which was already bleeding through his new bandage.

"So." Amaury pointed his sword at Gareth. "You know me now." With Philippe between them, all Amaury had to do was turn and run through the door behind him to reach freedom.

"Let him go, Amaury." Gareth advanced two more steps.

"You're too clever by half," Amaury said. Then, as Gareth took another step towards him, he flicked the point of his sword. "Tut! No closer or the old man dies."

"I'm dying anyway, Sir Gareth," Philippe said. "Better quickly here than slowly in my bed."

The sound of fighting still came from behind Gareth, but he didn't dare turn around to see how it was progressing or which side was winning, if he could even tell which side was which. Amaury's men and Philippe's looked just alike. "Your men fight for you, and yet you abandon them?"

"They were paid well and knew the risks." Amaury backed with Philippe closer to the doorway.

Philippe gritted his teeth. "I loved you like a son."

"And taught me everything I needed to know," Amaury said. "The weaker you became, the more you relied on me."

"Why would you do any of this?" Gareth said.

Amaury scoffed. "Why? Two years ago William of Ypres made me an offer I couldn't refuse."

"What about Ranulf?" Gareth would have asked anything if it meant he could to prevent Amaury from leaving, but this he actually wanted to know. He had been keeping track of the time that had passed. Earl Robert's men should have been here by now. "Did you lie about his loyalty, too, to protect him? He is your master, isn't he?"

If anything, Amaury's sneer deepened. "He thinks he is clever, playing Stephen and Maud off each other, switching sides so often even they don't know which of them he serves at any given time. I used him as I saw fit." Amaury lifted one shoulder. "He does serve the empress currently, not that it matters. He'll change sides again soon enough."

"But the crown—" Philippe tried to speak.

"This isn't about the crown, you imbecile. Let those fools tear the country apart between them. It matters not to me. This is about money, in my case, and power, in Ranulf's."

"Why did you help me when I came to Chester?" Gareth said.

"It suited me," Amaury said. "I knew Ranulf was negotiating with Cadwaladr. I thought it might be useful to have maintained good relations with King Owain through other means if things between those two went sour."

"Which they did," Gareth said.

Amaury's eyes narrowed at Gareth. "I would have thought your prince would be thanking me for what I've done, fostering chaos and killing Prince Henry, instead of hunting me down. Gwynedd can only benefit from war in England. As it is, you should know that I've had to take steps, for my own safety, to ensure that you won't harm me now."

"What steps?" Gareth wanted to close the distance between them, but the edge of Amaury's sword was a hair's-breadth from Philippe's neck.

Amaury smirked. "I knew as soon as Alard dropped that body at your feet that I needed a new plan. I knew you would follow this investigation wherever it led until you found the answers or died. Why couldn't you just go home? For Christ's sake, my man hurt your woman! No—" Amaury shook his head. "I needed leverage, just in case I found myself in this exact position. I always had the most to fear from you, as you are an honorable man." Amaury wasn't complimenting Gareth.

"Leverage?" Gareth took another step but froze as Amaury broke Philippe's skin with the edge of his sword. "What leverage?"

"If I don't send word to my man who guards Prince Hywel, by sundown he will be dead, and the girl with him. Their bodies will rot in their hiding place until the return of Arthur."

Gareth's hand clenched around the hilt of his sword. He wanted to ram the point right through Amaury's gullet. He'd *liked* the man. "Where are they?"

"Drop your sword and let me go," Amaury said, "after which I will tell you." When Gareth still hesitated, Amaury added, "Even if you refuse, even if you capture me and try to force the truth from me, I'll take their location to my grave."

"You wouldn't," Gareth said.

"I would out of spite."

Gareth had no choice. He bent his knees and slowly lowered his sword to the ground.

"No!" Philippe said.

Amaury's eyes lit, clearly delighted at the combination of Gareth's capitulation and Philippe's despair. Gareth hated to see that expression on Amaury's face, but Gareth's first duty was to his prince, not to justice.

"Your man could have killed Gwen—or Prior Rhys—when you sent men to take David's body. Why didn't he?" Gareth said.

"I don't hurt women. My man was overzealous. Besides, I couldn't have Gwen killed because you would have been like a rabid dog at a bone until you uncovered every secret in Newcastle. I couldn't risk it."

"Rosalind wasn't a woman?" Gareth said.

Amaury's lips twisted in distaste. "What is necessary isn't always what we might wish."

"Why didn't you just kill *me*, then? We've been alone a dozen times."

"By God, I wish I had." And with that, Amaury shoved Philippe towards Gareth and fled.

"Damn it." Gareth held Philippe, staggering under the sudden weight. Amaury had caught him off guard, but once Gareth recovered, he found that Philippe weighed hardly more than Gwen. "I misjudged. I didn't mean to make him angry. He didn't tell me where Prince Hywel and Mari are being kept."

"It isn't your fault, and you guessed right—about everything," Philippe said. "It's good to know the truth. I should have listened to you sooner."

As Gareth lowered him onto a bench against the wall, Philippe grasped Gareth's shoulder and shook him. "Leave me. He mustn't get away." While Philippe's voice was weak, it was also urgent.

Gareth couldn't agree more and wasn't going to deny a dying man his last wish. He picked up his sword and ran out the door after Amaury. Neither man had a horse, but Gareth had a strong will and a sound body, unlike Amaury, whose shoulder was bleeding heavily. Gareth raced into the friary's cemetery, dodging tombstones that had been placed haphazardly rather than in rows, almost slipping twice on the wet grass. He was saved the second time only by hanging onto a tombstone with a tall cross at the top. Amaury appeared to be aiming for a shed that sat on higher ground on the far side of the cemetery, beyond which lay a thick wood.

Gareth huffed up the hill and had just come around the shed when he pulled up. Hywel, Prior Rhys, and Alard stood in a half-circle on the other side of Amaury, whose back was to Gareth. Mari peered down at the scene from one of the lower branches of a nearby oak tree while her father stood sentry beneath it.

"Going somewhere, my friend?" Alard said.

Amaury flicked the tip of his sword at Alard and let out a laugh that was disconcerting, nearly maniacal. "I don't fear you." Amaury's laughter brought to Gareth's mind a vision of one of King Owain's companions whom they'd cornered in his treachery last winter. The man had killed himself rather than face the wrath of those he'd wronged. *That* wasn't going to happen again if Gareth had any say in the matter.

Only fifty feet separated Amaury from Gareth, and Gareth could see, even from the back, that Amaury's wound nagged him. He was hunching his left side, instinctively trying to protect himself against the pain. Gareth started forward at a run, his boots pounding on the turf. He was sure that Amaury could hear him, but the traitor didn't turn to look until Gareth was only a few paces away, at which point Gareth launched himself forward, catching Amaury around the shoulders and wrapping him up in a tight embrace.

Amaury screamed as they hit the soft grass of the churchyard. Gareth rolled off him and sat up, unhurt, but Amaury writhed in pain, holding his shoulder and unable to rise. The other men closed in. Amaury's sword had fallen from his hand at the impact, and Prior Rhys kicked it away. Amaury glared up at his captors, his face a rictus of hate and pain.

"Shall we try this again from the beginning?" Alard said.

26

Gwen

"**I** am honored to receive you." Earl Robert bowed low and held the pose longer than he might have if he hadn't wanted to convey his deepest respects.

The Welsh folk who faced him honored him in the same way. Gwen held her curtsey until she sensed Prince Hywel rise.

"We were pleased to be of service," Prince Rhun said.

From beside Gwen, Mari reached for her hand and squeezed it once as they followed Hywel and Rhun towards the high table to take their places on either side of the earl. Hywel sat on the earl's right, with Mari in the next seat down, while Rhun took the seat on Earl Robert's left. Alard and Ralph, though invited to the meal, still preferred the private to the public and had chosen to dine at the friary with their good friend Prior Rhys. That was one conversation Gwen would have very much liked to overhear.

Prince Henry, known as 'Richard', sat to Gwen's right, with Gareth on the other side of him. Everyone at Newcastle had been overjoyed to learn that Prince Henry was still alive, except the explanation the earl had given his people was that the prince had never left Bristol and the entire journey had been a ruse from beginning to end to draw out the assassin. 'Richard' remained one of the retinue and otherwise unremarkable.

"Are you well?" Gwen asked Richard/Prince Henry.

"More people have asked me that in the last few days than in my entire life. I am well." He looked at her with a fierce expression that belied his age. "I will not forget the service you and Sir Gareth rendered to the Crown of England. If you ever need anything from me, you have only to ask."

Gwen was happy to hear that—although if Henry did become king one day as his mother wished, that might be an oath he'd come to regret. Kings shouldn't make promises they couldn't keep.

"We could not have done otherwise," Gareth said.

"What I don't understand is how John and David could have betrayed the empress so profoundly after all their years of service," Prince Henry said, following the custom of referring to his mother—and himself—as if he wasn't himself and she wasn't his mother.

"I have spoken long with Amaury," Gareth said. "Once Philippe told his men that Alard was a traitor, they became pawns in Amaury's game. David and John never knew they were serving King Stephen instead of the empress."

"How could they not know?" For all that he'd been raised a prince, Henry was still only ten years old. Truth came in black and white to him.

"Because Philippe had begun to rely more and more on Amaury over the past few months," Gwen said. "When Amaury told David and John that the emeralds were payment for their long years of service to the empress, and they had only this one last task to do for her—to kill Alard—they believed him."

Prince Henry's brow furrowed as he thought. "Why give the emeralds to David and John at all? If they thought the order came from Philippe, they'd be doing no more than their duty to obey him. At the very least, Amaury could have paid them once Alard was dead."

"Ah, but then it would look as if the emeralds were payment for murder, not for long service," Gwen said.

"Amaury needed to keep them quiet and send them on their way once Alard was dead," Gareth said. "Reporting to Philippe would have been their natural instinct, and Amaury hoped they would be so focused on the emeralds, they would accept his instruction not to do that. They were to meet Amaury later at the farmhouse."

"At which point Amaury would have killed them and taken back the emeralds," Henry said. "Even I can see how Amaury thought this would work."

"Thanks to Alard, that part of the plan failed before it started," Gwen said.

"Amaury tried to recover the emeralds, to salvage what he could," Gareth said. "He arranged for his men to take David's remains from the chapel and had already removed the emerald from John's body by the time I examined it."

"But why kill Alard at all?" Henry said.

Gareth rested his elbows on the table and took a sip of wine. "This is where Amaury started to think too hard about what he was doing. He was afraid that Philippe, despite his infirmity, was growing suspicious of him. The messenger from William of Ypres had said Alard was the traitor, but Amaury was afraid that if Alard was alive to defend himself, Philippe would begin to doubt the authenticity of the messenger's claim."

Gareth shot Prince Henry a sardonic smile. "In addition, Amaury hoped that killing Alard would allow him closer access to Henry's retinue and perhaps even authority over his security at Newcastle. 'Prince Henry' would have been easy pickings for Amaury at that point."

"All the rest of what Amaury did that had us chasing our tails was his attempt to patch the holes that had been rent in his increasingly complicated plot," Gwen said.

"*Distract, delay, and divert* were his exact words," Gareth said, "even to the point of bribing that guard, Ieuan, at the camp to do whatever he could to obstruct me. It didn't matter to Amaury what that might be."

Mari leaned forward to speak across Gwen. "I am glad that you had the presence of mind to identify Amaury as the assassin, my lord."

"Thank you," Prince Henry said.

"What I don't understand," Mari said, "is why Bernard wasn't better protected."

Gwen's brow furrowed. "I assumed Earl Robert left Bernard open to attack because he was bait. That's not true?"

"Young lady, you have a quick tongue."

Gwen started. The earl, sitting beyond Mari and Hywel, had turned his steely blue eyes on her. She swallowed hard. "I apologize, my lord, for speaking out of turn. But Sir Amaury was playing a long game and didn't only fool you."

"That is no excuse in my case." Earl Robert stabbed a turnip with his knife and bit off the tip. "Bernard was my responsibility, and I failed to predict the possible danger that he might face in the bailey of my own castle. I didn't anticipate how the treachery of one man could be so hard to defend against."

"What I'd most like to know," Prince Henry said, "is *why* Amaury did it?"

"Every man has his price, and loyalty is more often about promises and payment than love," Earl Robert said. "Some men come cheaper than others, though for four emeralds, even small ones, Amaury didn't come cheap." He put down the knife and turned his full attention to their end of the table, his eyes this time on Prince Henry. "You should know that the empress has departed for Devizes with the traitor."

Gwen's heart hurt when Prince Henry's face crumpled at the news. "She never spoke to me, not even once."

"The empress is nearly as loving as my father," Mari said, in Welsh and under her breath.

Gwen shot her friend a wide-eyed look, afraid Earl Robert had heard her. "What will become of Amaury?" she said to change the subject.

"He will lose his head," Earl Robert said, having returned his attention to his food, "as an example to those who would betray the empress."

"What is to become of Prince Henry?" Henry said, sounding like the ten-year-old boy he was.

"As soon as it is feasible, I mean to send him back to his father in France," Earl Robert said. "He is too important to our cause to risk."

"You might send Alard and Ralph with him," Gwen said. "You know them now to be unwaveringly loyal."

"I intend exactly that." Earl Robert glanced down the table yet again, this time with a smile twitching at his mouth. "That may mean a slight delay, however, since Ralph's first responsibility will be to attend his daughter's wedding."

Mari and Hywel froze in identical postures of shock, food halfway to their lips. Slowly, Prince Hywel put down his knife, wiped the corners of his mouth with a cloth, and glanced at Mari. Gwen's heart leapt to see the smile they shared.

"Why didn't you tell me?" Gwen elbowed her friend in the ribs.

Mari just smiled and looked down at her lap.

Prince Hywel cleared his throat. "I must confer first with my father before anything can be decided." Then he grinned and his eyes lit, turning them to blue sapphires. Gwen hadn't seen such happiness in him in a long time. "But Earl Robert is right. I have spoken to Mari and she has agreed, despite the numerous flaws in my character, to become my wife."

27

St. Kentigern's Monastery, St. Asaph

Hywel

Hywel stepped out from behind the pillar, stopping Prior Rhys in his tracks. The prior hesitated before raising his lantern. "Are you here to kill me, Prince Hywel?"

"Have you done something worth killing over?" Hywel said, and then amended, "Recently, I mean?"

"I didn't expect you to be the one to come." Rhys gestured with one hand, indicating that Hywel should walk with him. They left the cloister and headed along the pathway that led through the monastery gardens. "Or rather, I was expecting someone else."

"Gareth," Hywel said.

Prior Rhys canted his head, not giving anything away, but agreeing nonetheless.

"Before our last parting, you answered his questions to his satisfaction," Hywel said.

"But not to yours?" Rhys said, with a sideways glance at Hywel.

"He has his questions; I have mine."

Rhys stopped and turned. "Don't you have some place to be? You've been married all of two days. Don't tell me your wife won't notice your absence from her bed."

Hywel pulled up with him. "She is sleeping. Rhuddlan Castle is not far away. I will return to her before the sun rises."

Rhys peered at Hywel. "This is customary for you, isn't it? How long have you passed off your nocturnal activities as liaisons rather than give voice to what you're really doing?"

Hywel tsked through his teeth. "A while."

"You cultivate a guise of willful promiscuity to hide ... what ... secret meetings with your spies?" At the expression on Hywel's face, Prior Rhys went on, "Don't get me wrong. I'm sure you've had your share of women, but—"

"Gareth warned me about you," Hywel said.

"What did he say?"

"That if I came to see you, I might end up giving more than I got."

Rhys laughed, and this time it was genuine. "I like that boy."

"So we now have spent valuable time talking about me instead of about you," Hywel said. "I have questions, as I said."

"So ask them."

Now that it came to it, Hywel wasn't sure where to begin. He had important questions, ones that Rhys wasn't going to want to answer. Perhaps it was better to start with an easy one: "Just to be clear—who was the archer that shot Amaury?"

"Ah. Everyone seemed to have forgotten about him. I hoped you had too. I should have known better."

"Well?" Hywel said when Rhys didn't continue immediately. He could waste a little time wooing the prior, but the man was right that he had Mari to get home to.

"The hours lay heavy in my hands after I was injured and gave me too much time to think," Prior Rhys said. "I began to wonder, merely by the process of elimination, if Amaury could be at the heart of the crimes we witnessed. But of course, I was injured enough that I had little ability to find proof of treachery on my own."

"I wish you'd spoken to me or Gareth," Hywel said.

"You were suspicious of me, as you may recall, because of what I'd hidden about myself," said Rhys. "To accuse another, a friend, might make me appear disingenuous. In addition, you weren't telling me everything either. I didn't know you had an emerald until after the incident at the abandoned chapel."

Hywel bowed slightly at the waist. "That is true. My apologies."

Prior Rhys looked down at his hands.

When he didn't continue speaking, Hywel prodded him for a second time. "The archer?"

Prior Rhys nodded. "I saw him when we entered Newcastle that first day, that very first moment, in fact. He was standing by the gatehouse, speaking with one of the guards. I have a good memory for faces, but I didn't need it in this case, since I'd used him a time or two."

"He was an assassin," Hywel said.

Prior Rhys lifted one shoulder in a half-shrug. "Think of him as the best shot in your arsenal. You use him if you can."

Hywel folded his arms across his chest, ready to hazard a guess. "You got to him, didn't you? You ordered him to miss Ralph!"

Prior Rhys laughed. "Not quite. He told me that Philippe, via our friend Amaury, had tasked him with bringing down Alard—not to kill him, mind you, but to injure him just enough that he could be captured. A nice leg wound would have done very well. I merely suggested that he was on the side of the devil if he followed that order and that he might find life more hospitable in the court of King Owain in the land of his birth. I was very persuasive."

Hywel was glad it was dark because his jaw had dropped at Prior Rhys's audacity. Hywel would do well to take lessons on intrigue from this man.

Prior Rhys went on: "Before Amaury led you through the tunnel, he ordered my archer to the woods outside the abandoned chapel, in the hopes that Alard would put in an appearance. The site was remote enough, and exposed enough, to be the perfect place for an ambush."

"Had you suggested that he shoot Amaury instead?" Hywel was incredulous, near laughter at the outrageousness of it.

"Certainly not! That was on his own initiative. Still—may the Lord forgive me—once it was done, I was not sorry," said Rhys. "While I had no evidence against Amaury beyond instinct, I was curious to see if the action stopped when he did."

"But it didn't," Hywel said.

"It was too little, too late," said Rhys, "though I didn't realize it at the time. I absolved Amaury of any wrongdoing, other than overzealousness in the pursuit of a man his master had declared a traitor and lying about his loyalties to Gareth. You and Mari almost lost your lives because of my failure."

"Too bad for the archer that he ended up dead," Hywel said.

Prior Rhys bit his lip, suppressing a smile. "Oh ... he's not dead."

Hywel's eyes narrowed. "What about the dead archer Gareth found?"

"Oddly, Philippe was half-right about that man not being the archer. The dead man Gareth found was some poor soldier, one of Philippe's men, whom the real archer brought along as a spotter. He killed him to throw you off his scent."

Hywel growled deep in his throat as understanding rose in him. "Your archer is the man we picked up on our way home as we entered Wales. You vouched for him, and I let him join our company."

"Cadoc is a very good shot," said Rhys.

"You should have told me more of this at the time," Hywel said.

"Old habits die hard, keeping secrets being one of the last to go. I had revealed myself to you as a horseman by then, but I didn't want you asking questions of me, not before it was safe."

"You didn't want Gareth asking questions, you mean," Hywel said.

"You do realize what you have in him, and Gwen too, don't you?" said Rhys, as usual diverting Hywel from something he didn't want to answer with a question of his own.

"Believe me, I do." Hywel gave a mocking laugh. "You'd be surprised what they know and what they have been willing to forgive."

Prior Rhys studied Hywel. "You are speaking from experience."

Hywel wasn't going to respond to that. It was his turn to ask the questions. "Why did you leave the empress's service? And don't tell me it was because your commission sickened you. It has to be more than that."

Rhys looked away. His eyes followed the line of the orchard wall, just visible in the moonlight, and he began walking again. Hywel came with him, and when they reached a bench set against the wall of the orchard, Rhys lowered himself onto it. It faced south, and on days when the sun peeked through the cloud cover would provide the gardeners a warm place to sit. "I spoke the truth."

"But not all of it." Hywel sat beside the prior and leaned back against the wall.

"Why do you want to know?" said Rhys.

"You know why. Because without it, I am missing a piece of the puzzle."

"And that's important to you?"

"The past informs the present," Hywel said. "If I know *this*, then it might help me someday with *that*."

"I don't know why I'm even talking to you. I shouldn't be telling you any of this, but I know that you are good at keeping secrets." Prior Rhys eyed Hywel again. Even in the moonlight, Hywel had the sense that the prior could see right through him. "This tale isn't really about me at all but about Ralph."

"Ah." Hywel smiled, satisfaction coursing through him. He had been right to come.

"Yes." Prior Rhys glanced at Hywel again in that way he had, assessing. "Your new father-in-law has more secrets than I do. What he told Mari about leaving her to spy for the empress in King Stephen's court was true as far as it goes."

"But again, not the whole truth," Hywel said.

"Ralph didn't have a choice but to leave," said Rhys. "It would have been unsafe for him to stay. Myself, I'm surprised the empress hasn't had him murdered long since."

Hywel sat up straighter. "Go on."

"It was I who helped Ralph fake his own death and then ensured my own. Mari hasn't realized yet that she knew me as a child. When she sat with me at Newcastle, after Amaury sent his mercenary to incapacitate me, I was sure she would recognize me, but she never did." Rhys clasped his hands together. "It was a long time ago."

The questions spilled over in Hywel's mind so fast, he was at a loss to articulate even one. Finally he managed, *"Why?"*

"Old King Henry didn't die from eating too many lampreys," said Rhys. "It was poison."

The word *poison* echoed in Hywel's ears. "Ralph murdered him?"

"For many years I assumed so, though now I'm not so sure. If it wasn't him, he knows who did."

"Philippe," Hywel said on impulse, pulling the name out of nothing but a hundred impressions and questions he hadn't yet thought to ask.

"Very good," said Rhys. "If not Ralph, that would be my guess too. Philippe and Ralph moved in the same circles, far above mine. And as you know, Philippe replaced Ralph as spymaster when he left."

"If it was Philippe, his secret will never be safe as long as you and Ralph live," Hywel said. "As you wondered, why are any of you still living?"

"Initially, we were allowed to live as long as we were useful, and now we are old and discredited," said Rhys. "Philippe and Ralph would never betray each other; they were friends once, and among spies, friends are few and far between."

"That still doesn't—"

"You have to understand what the atmosphere is like at the empress's court, my prince. At times, it is poisonous. She plays men off one another, encouraging them to vie for her favor." At Hywel's expression, Rhys hastened to add, "Not that kind—I'm talking about land, power, money. She wields men like weapons, even her own against her own."

Hywel straightened his legs in front of him. "Knowing that, why didn't Ralph defect to King Stephen in truth as well as name?"

Prior Rhys canted his head as he looked at Hywel. "You really don't understand the Norman mind if you have to ask that."

"Enlighten me." Hywel felt like he was ten again and being instructed by Gwen's father in a particularly difficult Latin conjugation.

"To those who follow her, the empress is the rightful heir to the English throne. Stephen is a usurper. No matter how much they might fear her, even despair of her as a queen who cannot bend even for a moment for the good of her people, to follow Stephen would be to turn away from God."

"Do you feel that way?" Hywel said.

Rhys smiled. "I am Welsh and far more practical than Ralph. Still, what did I do? I chose to leave England and my chosen profession entirely rather than serve another earthly master."

"I find it incredible that all of you are still keeping these secrets after all these years, even Ranulf, about whom far too little has been said so far."

Prior Rhys coughed a laugh. "Ranulf keeps many secrets."

That brought Hywel's eyes to Rhys's face. "His loyalty is in question, isn't it? Gareth brought that information from Amaury, but the man is an excellent liar, and I didn't know whether or not to believe him."

"I have a feeling that when my brethren write the history of King Stephen's reign, it will never be entirely clear as to which side, other than his own, Ranulf was ever on during this war," said Rhys.

Hywel stared down at his hands. From the very beginning, the scope of this investigation had been beyond anything he'd experienced before. "So Maud had her father murdered."

Prior Rhys jerked his head to look at Hywel. "What? No. Did I say that?"

"Didn't you?" Hywel said.

"I apologize for giving you that impression," said Rhys, "but that isn't it at all. Maud loved her father. Philippe and Ralph served Geoffrey of Anjou, Maud's husband, before they came to England to serve her."

The last piece of the puzzle fell into place, and it was one that Hywel had no difficulty reconciling with what he knew, even if it was entirely unexpected. "Geoffrey had King Henry killed because he didn't support Geoffrey's territorial ambitions in France."

"King Henry did not, but Geoffrey knew that his wife would if she were on the throne, straddling the English Channel between England and Normandy." Prior Rhys nodded. "Gareth—and you—were deceived from the beginning in this."

"How so?"

"The four horsemen weren't Maud's men, not at the start. We were Geoffrey's."

28

Gwen

Gareth and Gwen sat cross-legged on their bed facing each other. They were finally in their own home, for the first time in a month, having made the journey from Aber Castle that very day. The last miles home, Gwen could barely keep her eyes open. Now, though all she wanted to do was sleep, Gareth had spent the last quarter of an hour telling her about his plans for the next few days, as full summer had finally come. Every day would see them working from dawn to dusk on their land. Finally Gwen leaned in and put a finger to his lips.

Gareth stopped talking. "What is it?"

"I have something to tell you."

"Is it about Mari and Hywel?" Gareth said. "Before they rode to Rhuddlan Castle, Hywel swore to me that he loved Mari and would do everything in his power to make her happy."

"I know he will," Gwen said. "This isn't about Mari and Hywel. This is about us."

"Is the upcoming journey to Ceredigion worrying you?" Gareth said. "I don't want to be parted from you either, but perhaps if you kept Mari company, it would make it easier to be separated from me? You can be sure that Hywel will want to settle his affairs in Ceredigion quickly, either to prepare for Mari's arrival, or to hurry home to her before the harvest."

"Gareth—"

"I had a thought, also, that you might enjoy having Llelo and Dai stay with you for the summer if their uncle grants them leave," he said. "I know you've grown fond of them—"

"We're having a baby."

Gareth's last words had overlapped hers, so Gwen wasn't sure at first that he'd caught what she said. Then he gave such a whoop that she feared he might wake everyone in the village.

"You are with child? You're certain?"

"I desperately wanted to tell you sooner, but with everything that happened at Newcastle, and the wedding immediately after, I thought it might be better to wait until it was just the two of us, and I was sure. It's been weeks since I began to hope, and now I believe."

First Gareth laughed, and then he threw his arms around Gwen and rolled with her to the blankets, ending up with her resting on top of him. She lay with her cheek on his chest, reveling in the thudding of his heart.

"You're happy about it, then?" she said.

Gwen felt the laughter bubbling up in his chest before she heard it. "Happy? Gwen—" Gareth hugged her tighter. "I'm terrified, of course, but how could I not be happy?"

Gwen sighed and snuggled against him. He released her only long enough to draw a blanket over both of them.

"It's Prince Hywel who won't be happy," Gareth said.

"Why is that?"

Gareth raised his head and she lifted hers, so they could see into each other's eyes. "I won't go so far as to forbid you to be involved in any more of Prince Hywel's investigations, but I must tell Hywel that he's not to call upon his best spy for a good long while."

Gwen patted her husband's chest reassuringly but didn't reply. She tucked the blanket under her chin, thinking but not saying, since it seemed wise to humor her husband in this instance: *We'll see.*

The End

Historical Note

The Fourth Horseman is set in the time of what has come to be known as *The Anarchy*, the period in England's history where the succession to the throne was in question, fought over by Stephen of Blois, grandson of William the Conqueror, and Maud, daughter of King Henry I of England. As relayed in the opening excerpt from *The Anglo-Saxon Chronicle*, civil war reigned for nineteen years.

The dispute over the succession came about after King Henry's only legitimate son died when 'the White Ship' went down in the English Channel in 1120, leaving Maud as his only other heir. Because of the prejudice against crowning a woman, King Henry subsequently arranged for his barons to swear an oath to support Maud's claim to the throne upon his death, but as the years went by, discontentment with that oath developed and grew. Eventually, Maud and her husband, Geoffrey of Anjou, grew concerned enough about the dissent to urge King Henry to bestow Normandy (a region of France) upon Maud in advance of his death. He refused.

King Henry died on 1 December 1135, allegedly from eating 'a surfeit of lampreys'—that is, he ate too many fish— while he, Maud, and Stephen were all in France. It is important to remember that the rulers of England at this time, including these three, were Norman French, not 'English,' and were as much interested in maintaining their hold on their lands in France as they were in ruling England. Maud had married Geoffrey, Count of Anjou, and was pregnant with her third child. Stephen was visiting his estates in Boulogne, acquired when he married his wife, Matilda. His elder brother, Theobold, technically the next male in line for the English throne, had never set foot in England. He ruled Blois, a region in the south of France.

Stephen had spent many years in King Henry's court, however, and had developed a following among the Anglo-Norman barons. When he learned of Henry's death, he high-tailed it across the English Channel and was was hailed king by the citizens of London. Stephen was crowned by another of his brothers, Henry, who had become powerful in the English Church as the Bishop of Winchester and was the second richest man in England, after King Henry himself.

Meanwhile, Maud and Geoffrey maintained a hold on Normandy, eventually controlling the entire region. After several years of inciting rebellion against King Stephen and wooing allies in England, Maud crossed the English Channel with an invasion force in 1139, beginning the active phase of the civil war.

By 1144, when *The Fourth Horseman* takes place, England had experienced five long years of war. It wasn't until 1153 that the issue of the succession was finally settled and a treaty signed. Empress Maud renounced her right to the throne in favor of her son, Henry, whom Stephen agreed to name as his heir. Oddly, like King Henry, whom he'd succeeded, King Stephen died unexpectedly of a 'stomach disorder' in October of 1154, only a year after the treaty was signed.

Acknowledgments

First and foremost, I'd like to thank my lovely readers for encouraging me to continue the *Gareth and Gwen Medieval Mysteries*. I have always been passionate about these books, and it's wonderful to be able to share my stories with readers who love them too.

Thank you to my family who has been nothing but encouraging of my writing, despite the fact that I spend half my life in medieval Wales. Thank you particularly to my mother, to whom this book is dedicated, for her long-standing love of mysteries and her unending support of my writing. Thank you also to my beta readers: Darlene, Anna, Jolie, Melissa, Cassandra, Eleanor, Brynne, Carew, and Dan. I couldn't do this without you.

About the Author

With two historian parents, Sarah couldn't help but develop an interest in the past. She went on to get more than enough education herself (in anthropology) and began writing fiction when the stories in her head overflowed and demanded she let them out. While her ancestry is Welsh, she only visited Wales for the first time while in college. She has been in love with the country, language, and people ever since. She even convinced her husband to give all four of their children Welsh names.

She makes her home in Oregon.

www.sarahwoodbury.com

Made in the USA
San Bernardino, CA
11 June 2013